Far and Away

FERN MICHAELS

Far and Away

KENSINGTON PUBLISHING CORP.
www.kensingtonbooks.com

KENSINGTON BOOKS are published by

Kensington Publishing Corp.
119 West 40th Street
New York, NY 10018

ISBN-13: 978-1-64385-364-2

Printed in the United States of America

Contents

Dear Readers,

At long last you hold in your hands the final book in the Godmothers series.

First, a big thank you for picking up not only this book but also for supporting this series over the course of *seven* books! I've had so much fun writing these characters since they first appeared in *The Scoop*. These girls (and their guys, their kids and their four-legged friends) hold a special place in my heart, and based on the letters and e-mails I've received over the years, they mean a lot to you as well. Beside inspiring a lot of laughter, Toots, Ida, Mavis and Sophie help remind us that life doesn't necessarily slow down as you get older—and the one constant in their lives is the friendship that holds them together.

This story first appeared as three separate e-novellas: *Hideaway*, *Spirited Away* and *Getaway*. But a lot (and I mean A LOT!) of you wrote and asked when it would be available in print. So here it is, as requested, as a single print book for the very first time. *Far and Away* is special to me for a couple of reasons. With this book I decided to go back in time and show how the Godmothers first met in junior high school, laying the groundwork for decades of future friendship. But I also consider this the last book in the series, with the perfect grand finale for their stories. That said, as satisfying as it was to provide the Godmothers with their happy ending, they do have a history of reinvention . . . so who knows where they might show up again in the future?

For now, please enjoy *Far and Away* and I hope you agree that I gave Toots, Sophie, Mavis and Ida the send-off they deserve.

Happy reading!

Fern

HIDEAWAY

Prologue

Dabney House

Florence Dabney waited at the top of the staircase while Theodore said goodbye to their guests. They had celebrated their one-year wedding anniversary tonight, and she couldn't wait for the evening to end. Just couldn't wait to be alone with her husband.

Her low-waisted, bright scarlet dress, with a full, just-below-the-knee hemline and bodice typical of the times, fell around her, yet when she tried to grasp the silky material, her hand appeared as though it was passing through her dress. Again, she tried to touch her dress, yet she still could not feel the material in her hand. She remembered dressing earlier tonight as she prepared for their evening dinner party. Ruth, her personal maid, had made sure that the way her dress fell around her hid the slight burgeoning of her waistline. She recalled Matilda Watson's remark last week, pointing out that Florence was no longer as thin as Cora Russell, and that maybe she should not overindulge in Cook's sweets. Florence had smiled, knowing full well that there was a perfectly reasonable explanation for her thickening midsection.

Tonight, she would tell Theodore all about that reason. Though she was unsure of exactly what his response would be to her important news, she took heart. Ever since their nuptials, he'd talked of nothing else but having an heir. Possibly, he would visit her rooms *later tonight—after he learned she was with child, carrying his much-desired heir.*

Though Florence had dreaded that part of their marriage once she and Theodore were betrothed, she knew it was required and gave Theodore his needed relief. As a child, when her mother entertained guests, she'd very often overheard whispered discussions about what took place on one's wedding night. Truthfully, being raised as she had been, until her own wedding night, she'd been completely unaware of what happened between a husband and a wife. Though it had not been as pleasurable as the hushed whispers had suggested, making her wonder what all the fuss was about, other than experiencing a moment of intense pain, she had found the experience not entirely unacceptable.

Again, she reached for the luxurious silk, and, for the second time, she was unable to feel the soft texture of the fine material that had been shipped all the way from Spain. For a moment, she felt a slight tremor of fright, but then disregarded it. There was nothing for her to fear. Her evening had been pleasant if somewhat long. The Hamiltons had been very impressed with Cook's baked quail and peas. Conversation about the arrival of goods for use in a new method of using waste products to fertilize the fields had dominated the evening. Theodore was quite excited about the new shipment arriving and could hardly talk of anything else. Actually, she thought it was distasteful dinner conversation, but it was not her place to voice an opinion.

Downstairs, she could hear Theodore bid a final goodnight to the Hamiltons. As she waited for him, she smiled in anticipation, suddenly even more excited. A child would make Theodore happy. As of late, their marriage had not been quite as pleasant as it had been those first few months, since dear Theodore had so many responsibilities running the plantation he'd inherited from his father on the day of their wedding in June of 1921. Florence adored her position as the lady of the manor and took her duties as a wife quite seriously.

Taking a deep breath, she suddenly felt chilled, and the air around her had become icy, unlike anything she'd ever known. It was so cold, and as she exhaled, she saw wafts of air come from her mouth. Again, she felt frightened and desperately wished that Theodore would finish up with whatever was taking him so long and come upstairs. She peered down the stairs in search of him, but the scene before her was not what she expected to see.

The staircase, which should have displayed a brilliant polish on the gleaming oak surface, seemed aged and in need of repair, dilapidated. The rich tapestries that had been hanging on the walls were no longer there. The sconces, lit when she'd come upstairs, were not only snuffed out but were no longer even visible. Florence moved her hand toward her chest. It felt strange. She looked at her hand as she placed it across her heart and saw it as an eerie luminescence, more like a misty fog than her own flesh-colored appendage. As she pushed her hand harder against her chest, waiting to feel the reassuring beat of her heart, she became still when she felt absolutely nothing other than her hand slowly gliding through her dress and right through her flesh.

Dear Lord, she must be dreaming. Taking a deep breath, she was sure this must be a result of her condition. She was having a nightmare and would wake up in the morning, at which time she would tell Theodore all about this, and the two of them would have a good laugh discussing the utter silliness of her dream.

But no, this was different. She felt as though she was wide-awake. "Theo," she called out. Again, she felt cold, and again, she saw wisps of a white, smokelike substance coming from her mouth. "Theo, please, where are you? I am quite frightened."

Suddenly, another frigid blast of cold air swirled around her. She observed the phenomenon as though in shock. The cold gust swirled around her, then stopped as quickly as it started. "Theodore?"

And, suddenly, Theodore was there, right in front of her. Then a cruel, cackling laughter emanated from the man. But it wasn't her Theo standing there; he wasn't the man with whom she had dined earlier. No, this was some evil form of Theo. His finely tailored clothes hung in shreds, and his eyes glowed, as though a candle were lit behind them. "If this is a dream, please wake up," she said aloud. "I don't like this."

She reached out for the image of Theo before her. Her hands went right through him. She yanked them away, so frightened now that she backed away from the evil image and tried grabbing the banister for support. As she tried to steady herself again, her hand seemed to melt right through the wood. And before she knew what was happening, she felt a heavy hand at the small of her back, a hand with great power.

Theodore's hand? Except it wasn't as comforting as she remembered. No, this was forceful. Before she could turn around and ask him to please remove his hand, she felt him shove her forward, toward the staircase. "Theodore!" Those were the last words Florence Dabney uttered before everything went totally blank.

Chapter One

Sophie jerked upright in the bed, stunned. Her heart drummed against her chest, sweat dampened her forehead, and the back of her neck was slick with perspiration. Unsure whether she had just experienced a vision by way of a dream, she reached for the lamp on the bedside table. Turning it on, she could see that she was safe in the master bedroom, with Goebel snoring contentedly beside her. They'd celebrated their first wedding anniversary that evening. Poor Goebel! He rarely drank, and had imbibed one too many celebratory glasses of champagne. Not wanting to wake him, she grabbed her robe from the bedpost and tiptoed out of the room, not bothering to turn out the light. She knew that Goebel wouldn't hear her. His soft snores were comforting as Sophie crept out of their room and headed downstairs.

She didn't even want to begin to analyze her dream, or rather her vision, until she'd had a cigarette. As usual, Goebel had been after her to quit, and, as usual, she said she would think about it. Downstairs in their newly renovated kitchen, Sophie found her cigarettes and lighter on the counter by the back door. Just like at Toots's house, she thought. Except she didn't have a coffee can full of sand in which to stub out her cigarettes. She'd actually bought one of those ashtrays used in public places, the kind where you dropped the cigarette in a small hole and it went out as soon as it began to suffer from oxygen deprivation.

Sophie stepped outside on the screened-in veranda, into air al-

8 • *Fern Michaels*

most oppressively thick with humidity. Goebel's bubble-gum tree filled the air with its sweet scent. Birds chirped and the occasional croak of a frog could be heard, all the ordinary night noises that were normally soothing. But after what she had just experienced, Sophie found them annoying. She stepped outside, where she had a lounge chair and table for this very purpose. She lit her cigarette and took several drags, letting the nicotine's calming effect settle her nerves. She thought about the dream or vision she'd had.

The woman in her dream had been dressed in clothes from the early 1920s, before the flappers but after the drab style of the World War I era. And she had been excited, then all at once frightened; Sophie felt the woman's fear again. She closed her eyes and focused, something that was becoming easier with time. Last year, Sophie had developed a new psychic skill, *clairsentience.* By touch she was able to see through the eyes of another, to feel what they were feeling in real time. She returned her focus to the woman in the dream. Her dress was scarlet, made of the finest silk. Sophie saw a bolt of cloth on a ship, which startled her. "That wasn't a dream," she said out loud.

Knowing this, she lay back against the recliner's plump cushions, closing her eyes and trying earnestly to decipher the images imprinted on her mind. Taking several deep breaths, Sophie could feel herself relax, the way she did right before she fell into a trance. Unlike a trance, however, she was very much aware of the woman, her fears, and her physical pain.

She'd been celebrating; Sophie knew this as she felt the woman's anticipation. Focusing on the emotions coursing through the woman, Sophie again felt the woman's fright when it rekindled the same fear in Sophie that had awoken her from a sound sleep. The first trickle of apprehension coursed through her, *the woman,* as Sophie's external self would refer to her.

A tinge of alarm was replaced by an icy-cold fear that permeated the woman as she called out a name. Sophie homed in on the words that only she could hear.

"Theodore?"

Anxious, Sophie concentrated on the name, hoping that her perceptiveness would lead her to find the meaning behind the woman's fear as she spoke the man's name. Again, centering every ounce of her psychic abilities on the emotions felt by this woman, she experienced a stabbing fear so great, she felt panicky. Acknowledging her gift, yet sometimes unsure of her own power, Sophie felt the force of the woman's complete and utter fear spread through her nervous system like an electrical jolt.

Leaning forward in the chaise lounge, Sophie catapulted from her visions of another's past and became instantly aware of her present surroundings. She was sitting in the backyard, her pack of cigarettes lying on the small table beside her. Her hands shook as she reached for the lighter and smokes. This dream, this vision, this *clairsentience*, if that's what had just happened, was unlike anything she'd ever experienced. Last year, she'd discovered this ability when two children had gone missing. She'd been able to touch their possessions, feel their emotions in real time, seeing through their eyes as they'd been led down into a dank basement in Charleston. By the grace of God, the police found them before they were shipped off to a known pedophile.

But this experience was different. She knew she was seeing through the woman's eyes, and the woman had lived in the early 1920s. Sophie could almost feel the lightness of her undergarments, something very different from the corsets of the previous decade. Most likely she was wearing a chemise or a camisole and bloomers. Her low-waisted gown with the just-below-the-knee hemline and the bodice typical of the time was made of the finest silk embellished with rhinestones that sparkled when the right lighting hit them. She was waiting at the top of the staircase for her husband. All of this Sophie knew.

That's it, Sophie thought. *Theodore was the woman's husband!*

Sophie took some deep breaths, hoping to steady her erratic heartbeat. Confused and trying to make sense of what she'd seen as she reached for yet another cigarette, she almost jumped out of her skin as she heard the back door slam.

Placing a shaking hand on her chest, she shouted, "Damn you, Goebel, you just about scared the life right out of me."

Goebel, wearing a navy robe and carrying two mugs of steaming coffee, sat down at the foot of the chaise. "When I woke up, you were gone. Figured I'd find you out here huffing." He held the coffee cup out for her.

She sipped at the hot brew, then placed the cup on the table. "*Huffing*? Goebel, you're going to have to check your choice of words in the future. Do you really know what huffing is?" Sophie didn't want to talk about her dream, her vision, just yet. Still the world's leading expert at changing the subject when it suited her, most often to distract her from her own thoughts, she raised an eyebrow, demanding an answer. "Well, do you?" she asked again. She pulled her legs up to her chest and drank her coffee, patiently waiting for her husband of one year and one day, almost, to answer.

Goebel sighed, patted her on her knee, and took a sip of his coffee. "Why do I think you're about to tell me?" he asked, his voice laced with humor.

"I can't believe you, a former New York police officer, don't know what huffing is."

"Okay, Soph, you got me on that one. Of course I know what it is. It's called all kinds of names. *Bagging, dusting, sniffing*. All ways to partake of a chemically soaked rag or a can of something, like cooking spray or Freon, and I'm sure there are more than even I know, but yes, to answer your question, I know what huffing is. Next time I refer to your cigarette habit, I'll make sure not to use the word *huffing*. So now that that important information is out of the way, I would love to know why you, my intelligent and sexy wife, are lounging in the backyard in the wee hours of the morning?"

Sophie couldn't help it; she laughed. God, she loved this man. He knew her too well, but in her case, it was a good thing. "I wanted to huff."

They both laughed at her words.

"Seriously," Goebel coaxed. "Are you feeling okay?"

Sophie knew he wasn't asking if she was physically well. He wanted to know her mental state, if her psyche was in a good place. Not wanting to discuss her vision just yet but knowing she would tell him soon enough anyway, she asked, "Another cup of coffee?" That would give her a few much-needed minutes to try to figure out how exactly to explain what she'd seen to Goebel.

He reached for her cup. "Two minutes." Light on his feet since he'd lost over a hundred pounds with their friend Mavis's encouragement and rigid diet, he hurried inside, leaving her alone with her crazy thoughts.

It wasn't that she didn't *want* to tell Goebel what had actually brought her outside in the wee hours of the morning. The problem was that she didn't really know how to describe this very new experience. What she'd seen had been from the 1920s, close to a century ago. But that wasn't what was really bothering her. No, her main concern was that something was nagging at her subconscious, something Sophie needed to know, something that *the woman* wanted her to know.

For no reason that she could come up with, the words *the attic* came to mind. Sophie recalled several large trunks she'd seen when Goebel and she had first moved in to the old plantation house outside of Charleston, months earlier. At the time she didn't give them too much thought. Old houses always had items left behind from previous owners. She'd planned on going through them, but the timing never seemed to be right. She always seemed to have more important tasks to attend to. Now, though, she knew that there was something she had to investigate and that whatever she was supposed to find would be in one or more of those trunks. She would immediately put the task on her to-do list.

Goebel let the back door slam behind him, startling her. She sat cross-legged and put her smokes beside her, giving him room for the tray he carried. "You've either done something you don't want me to find out about, or you're trying to butter me up. Which is it?" Sophie asked, as Goebel refilled her mug.

He snickered. "Neither. Now, quit stalling and tell me why you're out here at this ungodly hour." He'd put prepackaged blueberry muffins on two plates, along with the butter dish. He sliced a muffin in half, slathering it with butter. "Is that real?" Sophie asked, eyeing the butter.

Goebel continued to swipe the butter on the muffin. "No, it's not. If you don't stop stalling, I might be forced to rub this fake butter all over you. Then of course we would be forced to shower together to clean ourselves, or I could just lick—"

"I get your drift, Mr. Blevins."

"And?"

"I know you'll accuse me of stalling, but I'm being serious. When you bought this house, did you research its history? Did you get the names of any previous families who'd lived here? Did Toots share anything with you?"

Goebel had formally proposed to her the night he took her to see this house, telling her it was theirs to do with as they pleased. He'd actually carried her across the threshold. She smiled at the memory.

"As you know, Toots had the place for a few years. Before she bought it, it was owned by the great-great nephew of the original plantation owners. I think it was built sometime in the first half of the nineteenth century, maybe in the eighteen thirties. I think that the great-great-nephew inherited it sometime in the nineteen seventies or eighties, maybe a hundred and fifty or so years after it was built. Why all the sudden interest? I thought you hated history."

"Do you know the great-great nephew's name?"

"It's somewhere in all the papers I have. Is it important? If so, I'll go look now."

Sophie took a pull of her lukewarm coffee. "It's important, yes, but you don't need to look now. This is so strange, I'm not sure how to put it into words."

"You're never at a loss for words, Soph," Goebel encouraged.

As the sun started its ascent, the sky became a hazy bluish gray, replete with oranges and pinks. The birds were chirping loudly, and, from somewhere in the distance, Sophie could hear a car door slam. Most likely that little place across the road, where a young couple lived. She'd yet to meet them but had seen them coming and going. Probably yuppies, she thought, with jobs downtown in Charleston.

"You're distracted, Soph. Go on, try to focus and tell me why you came outside so early."

"I thought I was dreaming when I first woke. I was sweating, my heart felt like it was going to explode. I was nervous and shaky, thinking I'd had a nightmare. I felt a woman's fear and pain, saw her as she tumbled down a set of stairs, but it wasn't like I was seeing this as it happened now. This wasn't in real time like those kids who went missing last year. This was in the nineteen twenties. The woman—that's what I've been calling her in my mind—wore a low-waisted dress with a hemline and bodice typical of the early nineteen twenties. She had on a chemise or camisole and bloomers, no corset. That's what is so weird. I *felt* the lightness of her undergarments. Very different from what I would have felt had she been wearing a corset.

"As you can see"—she touched her nightgown—"there is nothing at all restraining here." She wore a loose, light green, cotton gown with a pocket. Sophie was big on pockets. "This is perfectly comfortable, with no pressure on me at all. And that was the same way that woman's undergarments felt."

"I can see that, but you know I like you better without it," he added, with a twinkle in his eye. "Now, go on and finish your story. I'm not going anywhere."

Sophie reached for his hand, giving him a quick, reassuring squeeze. "I'll hunt you down if you do."

"Never. I love you too much."

"Ditto, sweet man. Keep talking to me that way, and I'll never get the words out."

"And you're stalling," Goebel said, leaning forward to place a light kiss on her nose.

"As I was telling you, I could feel what the woman felt, see through her eyes, but nothing more. I can't identify her, I haven't held any items belonging to her, or at least any that I know of. But as she went tumbling down the stairs, she called out the name *Theodore*. That's an old name, not that common now. I feel as though there is something I'm missing, like this woman, whoever she is, wants me to know . . . that's just it, I don't know what it is she wants me to know. When you went inside a few minutes ago, the words *the attic* came to me. I think this woman wants me to look in those trunks. Sounds crazy, but it is what it is. Tell me, Mr. Detective, does this make any sense at all?"

"It's not too far off from the messages you get during a séance. Maybe you should have the girls over tonight, hold a séance, see if this woman, whoever she is, will try to make contact with you. It's worked in the past, so I don't see why it wouldn't work now."

Sophie pondered the idea. In the past, séances had always been held at Toots's place. Since she and Goebel had moved into the house, she'd kept one small room, located at the top of the stairs and around the corner, for that express purpose. Nothing had been touched. The walls were still covered in wallpaper, a faded pattern that neither she nor Toots had been able to identify. It didn't matter to her, but there was something about that particular room that said leave it alone. In her mind, it had already become her séance room, though she had yet to hold a single séance there. She and Goebel had had several psychic investigating jobs, but they all took place in other people's old homes and buildings. Old haunting grounds, she liked to think of them.

"Yes, I think you're right. I'll call Toots and see if I can drag her away from Jonathan and Amy for a few hours." Toots's daughter Abby and her husband Chris were now the proud parents of one-year-old twins. Toots rarely let a day go by without seeing her grandson and granddaughter. Of course, Sophie, Mavis, and Ida all used any and every excuse under the sun to see the precious pair as well. After all, they were all Abby's godmothers and had been friends for decades. The twins had brought even more joy and light into all of their lives. Poor kids were going to be so spoiled by the time they reached school age that poor Abby would have to homeschool the pair of them. Sophie thought this a good idea, and would mention it to Abby the next time she saw her. She couldn't bear the thought of those two spending hours and hours away at school.

Sophie downed the last of her coffee, grabbed the tray, and tossed her smokes and lighter into her pocket. "Come inside, Goebel. You have papers to search through, and I have to make a phone call."

Goebel shook his head, a goofy grin on his face. Hot damn, he'd never been this happy ever. And it just kept getting better and better.

Chapter Two

Sophie, now showered and dressed, busied herself making another pot of coffee while Goebel searched the records for the house. "What's taking you so long?" she called out as she filled two clean mugs with coffee. None of that two-hundred-dollar-per-pound stuff from the Philippines that Toots had bought. Nope, she and Goebel liked the good old three-dollar Folgers brand.

Goebel was so different from that idiot first husband of hers, Walter. Marriage the second time around for her had been nothing like her first. Almost daily, she discovered things about Goebel, good things, things that showed his strength of character, things that made her love him just a little bit more with each passing day. Walter, the old bastard whom she hoped was roasting in the fires of alcoholic hell, had been an abuser, a drunk, and, once he'd lost his job at the bank, a lazy son of a bitch.

Goebel was a man. A real man. He cared for her, always put her needs before his, and never, since the first night they'd spent together as husband and wife, had he gone to sleep without telling her how much he loved her. Tears pooled in her eyes, and she dabbed at them with a tea towel. If he saw her bawling, he'd tease her to no end, especially if she told him why. Good old, pure happy tears. Nothing more.

"Be there in a minute," Goebel called from the other room.

"Gotcha," she answered.

She looked at the clock on the stove. It was already six thirty.

She'd better call Toots now or she'd miss her. Taking the portable phone and her coffee out to the veranda, she punched in the number she knew by heart. She and Toots called each other every day. No matter what.

"Hello."

"Bernice, it's me. Put Toots on the phone. It's very important," Sophie said in her most professional voice. She crossed her fingers.

"Oh, hold on," Bernice said in her usual dragged-out tone. Bernice was still alive and kicking two years after major heart surgery. In fact, Sophie thought, the old coot was better than ever. She'd been screwing Robert, the new neighbor, for the past year. Good for her, she thought, but no way in hell was Sophie going to tell this to Bernice. She loved the older woman, but she loved aggravating her even more.

"Sophie. What's up?" Toots asked.

"Glad I caught you. I figured you would be at Chris and Abby's with the kids."

"No, not now. I promised Abby I would stop coming over before nine in the morning. She said she and Chris need family time alone with the twins. Of course, I agreed with her, but I truly don't because I am their grandmother, and the last time I heard, that was considered family, too. But, you know Abby, headstrong as ever. More so since she's become a mother. She watches those two little ones like a hawk." Toots stopped to catch a breath.

"I agree with you one hundred percent, but that isn't what I called to talk about. Do you think Mavis and Ida, and yourself, of course, could come over tonight, say around nine o'clock, when it's dark? I want to have a séance."

"Oh shit, Sophie, for the love of God, are you really serious? At nine o'clock? Why so late?"

"Oh my gosh! You are really turning into an old woman! Why, nine o'clock is the beginning of the evening for Goebel and me. Hell, we're up all hours doing all kinds of fun and nasty stuff." Sophie laughed and heard Toots follow suit.

"Phil and I have been spending our evenings preparing for his book-launch party. All the big guns will be there. He's nervous. Told me that open-heart surgery was far less nerve-racking. His book is good, Soph. Really, really good. I think he's every bit as good as Robin Cook. He's onto something with these medical thrillers."

How well Sophie knew. His success in the book world would far surpass his career as a cardiac surgeon, at least on the financial side. The importance scale, not so much. She'd told this to Toots before, and Sophie knew that Toots had never told Phil of her prediction.

"And I can't wait to read it once it's published, you know that. However, I've had an ... let's say another unusual experience. I'm not sure if this is another episode of *clairsentience,* but it's alarming me enough that I feel I must do something. Goebel suggested a séance and I think that he's exactly right. I'm going to have it in the room, you know the one, with the strange-looking wallpaper?"

"Yes, and I also know there is something extra creepy about that room. I felt it the last time I was over. I don't know why I didn't mention it to you," Toots said.

Sophie knew what she meant, but to her it wasn't a feeling of creepiness. No, not creepiness but something altogether different, and that's another thing that really puzzled her. She could not pinpoint what it was that bothered her about the room. She knew, without a doubt, that whatever it happened to be was connected to her vision this morning. How she knew it and why she was just now acknowledging it was a total mystery. And those were things that she needed to find out.

"Can you make it? Phil is welcome and, of course, Ida and Daniel, too." Daniel was Bernice's long-lost son, who'd returned to Charleston last year as a well-to-do practicing attorney. He and Ida had been an item ever since. "And Mavis and Wade. I always feel better when I know they're willing to attend. They kind of see dead people like I do, so it's nice that we have that in common." Mavis and Wade were business partners and lovers who now jointly owned and operated a funeral parlor with plans to franchise.

"Yes, they're both here. Well, Mavis is at Wade's. Robert has practically moved in with Bernice since she bought that new condo, so they're usually there for a while during the day doing their afternoon delight. Of course, Robert still lives with Wade, but more often than not, when Robert and Bernice are preparing for their afternoon of delight, that's about the time Wade and Mavis return to his house after a long day of dealing with death. Bernice and Robert usually stop over so Wade and Mavis can indulge themselves."

"Toots, I do not give a good rat's ass about the sex lives of Bernice or Mavis. Actually, I think it's a good thing, but please don't tell either of them I said that, or I will personally slice your tits off. Now, the reason I called. Can all of you come over tonight?"

She could hear Toots's intake of breath over the phone. "I think we can manage. I'll tell the others that it's a matter of life and death."

"Don't lie, for crying out loud!"

"So, it's not?" Toots asked.

Sophie thought about it for a few seconds. *It could be.* "Yes, you can go ahead and tell them that, but don't scare any of them. They already think I'm off my rocker."

"You are, and we all know it and love you in spite of the fact," Toots teased.

"So I can count on the gang to be here around nine o'clock?" Sophie asked.

"With bells on," Toots said before hanging up.

With that behind her, Sophie headed upstairs; she wanted to do a quick search in the attic. She needed to have a look inside those trunks to see what, if anything, captured her attention, called out to her.

The steps leading to the attic were located on the third floor. Sophie opened the door to the small, narrow staircase. After brushing several spiderwebs off the stair rails, Sophie felt her way to the center of the attic, where she located the single low-wattage lightbulb in a fixture hanging from the ceiling. She pulled a leather string, and the immediate area filled with a bit of light but not enough to allow her to roam about freely. "Why in the heck didn't I think to bring a flashlight?" she asked herself, disgusted with her lack of forethought. She stood in the center of the space, turning until she spied the trunks stacked in the corner. From where she stood, there appeared to be at least four of them, but there could be more behind them. Carefully, she walked across the area, then paused when she felt a board beneath her start to break. Someone had started renovations up here, Sophie could see, but whoever it was had never completed them. The electrical was rudimentary at best, the floors too weak to risk walking across. Taking a mental inventory, she knew she wouldn't venture up here again until some basic safety measures were put in place. The trunks would have to wait for now. Later, she thought as she made her way down the narrow staircase. Goebel could add this to his ever-growing list of projects.

When she reached the set of stairs on the second-floor landing, Sophie felt a blast of air so cold she actually shivered. She raised her head to see if one of the new air-conditioning vents was above her.

But there was nothing.

Wanting to spend some time by herself in the room, she'd insisted they leave it alone. Since she wanted the room for her séances, she felt compelled to enter it now in order to get the feel of whatever it was she was supposed to be feeling. Or seeing.

But again, nothing. Chilled, and unsure why, Sophie remained in the room, and the temperature soon returned to normal. She planned to use the old dining-room table, which could seat as many as twelve, for her séances. Toots had found the table on one of her many antiquing excursions, buying it and telling Sophie it was perfect as it was solid oak and round. Since wood was sometimes a conduit to the spirit world, plus the fact that the table was old, as in hundreds of years old, Sophie had gratefully accepted Toots's gift.

She walked over to the table and reached down to touch the

wood. It was warm. She traced the nicks and gouges, knowing there was a story for each mark. Walking around the table, she let her fingers continue to trail across the wood while she focused on the vision that had come to her in her dream, and what it meant. She left her mind open, a clean slate, in order to receive a message from the woman who'd earlier taken possession of it. Sophie had thoughts that were so dark, and filled with such intense feelings of doom, that she knew that if she pursued them, they would lead her down a path where evil unlike any she'd ever known would suck the life right out of her.

No, don't think that way! We were not talking about demonic possession here. Unsettled that her thoughts were leading her down this path, a path she knew not to enter, she quickly left the room in search of Goebel.

"There you are," he said from the bottom of the staircase, smiling up at her. "I've been searching all over for you."

She returned a wan smile. "Big house to search," she said as she went downstairs, stopping when she was halfway down. Another burst of cold air rushed at her with such force, she thought it might knock her down. Again, she looked above her. This time she saw a giant opening where the air-conditioning vent had yet to be covered.

"I'm still searching for a cover for that. I don't want to use just any old plate, you know. I'm looking for something old, something that will allow the air to come through, yet when people see it, they won't know what it is," Goebel said.

Relieved, Sophie continued the journey to the bottom of the staircase.

"I'm sure between you and Toots, you'll find what you're looking for. And speaking of finding things, did you find anything in your search?"

"That's why I came looking for you. The great-great nephew"— Goebel skimmed through the papers he held in his hand—"went by the name of Ted, though, of course, his given name was Theodore. Theodore Dabney."

Theodore! That was the name the woman shouted out as she fell down the stairs!

"What?" Goebel asked.

"In the dream I had, or rather the vision, that's the name the woman called out when she fell. *Theodore*." Once again, a frigid blast of icy air occupied the space surrounding her. "Can you feel that?" she asked in a whisper.

Goebel shook his head. "Feel what?"

As quickly as the gush of coldness had overtaken the space around her, it was gone. Confused, Sophie said, "The cold air. You couldn't feel it?"

Goebel placed the papers he held on the bottom step before wrapping his arms around Sophie. "You're shivering," he said, shocked.

"I've never felt so cold," was all she could manage to say, as Goebel guided her through the many rooms downstairs leading to the back door.

Stepping outside, Sophie saw that the sun was now up, and its warmth permeated her. She folded her hands across her chest and rubbed her upper arms. "I . . . I've felt cool air before. During a séance, you know how the temperature always seems to lower a few degrees?" Sophie paused, waiting for Goebel to acknowledge her words.

"Yes, I've felt it myself on more than one occasion."

Sophie walked over to the chaise lounge and sat down. She motioned for Goebel to sit beside her. "This was very different. It was almost like stepping inside one of those giant freezers restaurants use. Instant, bone-killing cold." She wrapped her arms around herself. "The kind of cold that hurts. Have you ever felt that kind of cold?"

Goebel took a deep breath. "I'm not sure that I have, actually. Have I frozen my ass off? You're damned right I have. New York winters can be treacherous. The cold winds that come off the ocean can be killers. But what you felt in there"—he nodded toward the house—"I can't say that I know the kind of cold you're referring to." He paused as if in deep thought, then asked, "Are you frightened?"

Sophie thought for a minute before answering. "No. I'm not. Maybe I should be. I'm more . . . perplexed, I guess. This damned dream, vision, whatever the hell it is, means something. I don't know what it is, but the cold and that room upstairs, it all fits. It's up to me to figure out how all the pieces fit, and if they even go together. Does that make any sense to you at all?" She didn't even want to think about what she had felt in the attic. Voicing her thoughts would only make them more real, which she knew was just exactly what this . . . this malevolent, preternatural being, whatever it was, thrived on. She cleared all further thoughts from her mind.

"Sure. Happened to me a lot when I was a cop. Gut instinct, that feeling that something is staring you directly in the face, and, for the life of you, you can't seem to figure out what the hell it is. In my case, it was usually the most obvious. Simple, right there in front of you. For me, it was simply a matter of allowing myself to relax, rid my mind of all the unnecessary details. A mental walk is what I always thought of it as. Most of the time, it worked. Possibly this is what you need to do, Soph? Forget about it for a while."

Of course, as usual, Goebel was right. What he said made perfect sense. But still, the feelings were there, and she just didn't know how to sort them out, how to put them into the proper perspective. What was bothering her mostly was the fact that she couldn't figure out why she was unable to pinpoint the exact reason she felt this way. Sophie was used to having answers, and more often than not, they came to her swiftly, decisively. Not this time. If anything, she was more confused than ever. "Let's do something," Sophie said. "Anything that takes me out of this house for a while."

Goebel laughed. "Well, I was thinking we could go upstairs and fool around, but it requires both of us to go inside, and since that's out of the question now, why don't we go for a walk? It's a beautiful day."

"Great idea. Let me grab my smokes, and I'll be right back."

Sophie raced inside to the kitchen, where she found her cigarettes on the floor, the package crushed, as though someone had stomped on them. *Goebel, you shit. I told you I am not ready to quit smoking!* she thought to herself. *You should be ashamed. But I have more.*

Before bending down to pick up the crushed pack of cigarettes and toss it into the garbage can, she walked over to the freezer and removed a fresh pack. Something she'd learned from Toots. Kept them fresh.

Before she could turn around and pick up the cigarette pack from the floor, Sophie heard Goebel say, "Stay where you are, Sophie. Don't move." His tone of voice stopped her dead in her tracks.

She closed the freezer door, turning to face him. He held his finger to his lips, indicating that she should remain quiet. She nodded, remaining glued to the spot.

Accelerating like he had an internal engine, Goebel's instincts had kicked in the second he saw the crumbled pack of cigarettes on the floor. He raced through the house, stopping before entering each room, his cop instincts on full alert as he scanned the rooms for anything or anyone that wasn't supposed to be there. When he reached the foyer, he quickly removed his 9mm Glock from the top of the antique armoire. *Maybe not the safest place*, he thought as he swiftly checked the clip. Seeing that it was fully loaded with seventeen shots, plus one extra if seventeen weren't enough, he rapidly made his way up the stairs, holding the gun out in front of him in a two-handed grip as he'd been trained to do all those years ago in the police academy. At the top of the stairs, he felt a stir in the air, something or someone whose scent was left behind, an unfamiliar smell that shouldn't be there. Carefully, he entered the master bedroom, checking the closets, the master bath, and, lastly, beneath the bed. When he was satisfied that the room was safe he gave a mental "all clear" and headed to the next room, another bedroom still in the midst of being redecorated. Swatches of material lay on the bed. He scanned the room, corner to corner, top to bottom, then again looked under the bed. Nothing. *Clear here, too*, he thought as he darted out of the room and entered the broad expanse of the hall that wrapped around, leading to the three other bedrooms and a bath. Efficiently, methodically, he cleared all the rooms, then relaxed his grip on his weapon. "Sophie!" he called out as he made his way back to the kitchen.

"Goebel!" Sophie eyed the gun, now held tightly against his right leg, as if he were trying to hide it from her. "What in the hell is *that*?" she asked, as her eyes went from the gun to his face.

He hadn't told her he kept a gun in the house, and now Goebel knew he should have. He didn't want there to be any lies between them. "I should have told you, Soph. I'm sorry."

Sophie remained in front of the freezer. "You didn't stomp on that pack of smokes, did you?" was all she could say.

"No," he replied.

"So?"

"I thought there was an intruder. The cop in me kicked in, Soph. This"—he held the gun in front of him, released the clip containing the bullets and stuffed it in his pocket—"I should have told you I was keeping a gun in the house. I don't know why I didn't. I'm sorry for not telling you."

Sophie shook her head, jammed the pack of cold cigarettes in her pocket, then went to where Goebel stood. She wrapped her arms around his waist and laid her head against his chest. "Oh, Goebel, I don't care about the gun. I suspect that all retired cops have a gun lying around somewhere, hopefully in a safe place."

He crammed the gun in his other pocket, then placed his hands on her shoulders. "This isn't what I expected," he said as he kissed the top of her head.

Sophie leaned back so she could look at him. "There isn't anyone here besides us, right?" she asked.

"No, at least if they were, they're gone now. Though I did smell something unfamiliar. We were always trained to use all of our senses, and smell being one of them, I picked up a scent of something . . . floral, I guess. Not your perfume, I would recognize that anywhere. It smelled like old flowers, and a bit musty."

Sophie stepped out of his embrace. "Let's go for that walk, and we can talk then," she said and practically ran out the back door, with Goebel close on her heels.

Once they were off their property, walking alongside one another, Sophie finally lit the cigarette she'd tried to light half an hour ago. "So, what say you? You're too quiet." She took a long pull from her cigarette, then turned her head to the side so as not to blow the smoke in Goebel's face.

"I don't like the idea of someone sneaking into our house, that's all," Goebel replied.

"I'm pretty sure there wasn't anyone in the house, other than us."

Sprawling oak trees canopied them as they continued their walk down the side road. Goebel reached for her hand. "What do you mean?"

Sophie gave a half laugh. "What do you think I mean?"

He squeezed her hand. "I would guess you're thinking something, some otherworldly being, is residing in our home, and I would also say that you're going to tell me the floral scent I smelled was evidence of their—her, I suppose—recent visit."

"Damn, Goebel, you keep this shit up, and you'll have me one-upped. Pretty close to what I was thinking. You're not going all psychic and weird on me now, are you?"

He chuckled. "No need to worry about that. One of you is more than enough for me."

Sophie playfully elbowed him. "I'd better be."

"You are, and you know it. Now, can we get serious for a minute?" Goebel stopped, pulling her close to him by her hand, which he was still holding.

"Okay. I'm serious. What?"

"You tell me. The crushed smokes in the kitchen. You don't think we had an intruder, do you?"

Sophie linked her arm through his, gently urging him to continue walking with her. Walking and talking was a good thing, she thought, as she contemplated her answer. She needed to do this more often, the way she had in California. She and Toots had spent many evenings walking along the beach in Malibu. Walking always seemed to clear her mind. Whether it was simply the physicality of the act or just taking her mind away from her troubles because she forced them away, she didn't know. Didn't matter because whatever the reason, the desired effect was as calming as a soft caress.

"No, I don't believe our 'intruder' is of this world. At one time, yes. A very long time ago. What I'm not sure about is why smash a pack of cigarettes?"

"Maybe our otherworldly intruder died of lung cancer, and they're trying to give you a message."

"No, it's not that. Don't ask me how I can be so sure of that yet have no clue about all the other happenings, but I know we didn't have a break-in this morning. We weren't even outside that long." Sophie dropped her cigarette on the ground, crushed it out with her foot, then put the butt inside the cellophane part of the pack. She might be a smoker, but she wasn't a nasty one. Well, except to Ida. The thought of blowing smoke in Ida's face made her smile.

"What's so funny?" Goebel asked, seeing the smile on her face.

"I was thinking of Ida and how much she hates smoking."

"Well, I, for one, agree with her," Goebel said.

"Yep, you do tend to remind me every chance you get," Sophie said, her tone light, teasing.

They'd reached the end of the road when Sophie saw how far they'd walked. "You want to continue on to Toots's place? Maybe Jamie dropped off some baked goodies this morning."

Jamie was constantly trying out her newest recipes on Toots, knowing how Sophie's dearest friend and partner in crime had an unquenchable sweet tooth. It was highly probable that today, a Sunday, she'd made a batch of something absolutely delectable.

"Whatever you want, Sophie. I just want to be with you, and it doesn't matter where we're going."

She stopped and turned to him. "You really are a prize, you know that? I cannot believe some woman didn't snatch you up and have a houseful of kids, a house with the white picket fence, a station wagon, and two weeks spent camping in the summers." She often wondered what her life would have been like had she and Walter, the ass, had children, and even now, as old as she was, she still sometimes wondered what it would be like if she and Goebel had met when they were young enough to have a family of their own. Sometimes, these thoughts made her sad, knowing motherhood was one of the greatest joys ever, as she'd seen this firsthand, watching Abby grow from a sweet baby to a headstrong, independent woman. She knew this kind of thinking was pointless, so she took a deep breath and shot her husband her best knock-'em-dead killer smile.

"I'm glad you think of me as a prize, Sophie. I think I was single all those years because you were out there, just waiting for me to find you. I have no regrets at all. None whatsoever. Does that answer your question?"

Damn! Tears filled her eyes. She was turning into nothing but a wimpy caterwauler. "Yes, it does. I still can't believe we've been married a whole year. That anniversary party Toots threw for us last night was a blast, don't you think?" Sophie had begged Toots not to go to any trouble, but, as usual, Toots hadn't listened to a single word she had said. Toots had hired a local band to play in the gardens at her house, had McCrady's, Sophie and Goebel's new favorite restaurant, cater the event. Champagne flowed freely throughout the evening; they had danced, laughed, and even cried a little bit when they talked about the past, but they were good tears. Goebel had overindulged in the champagne, but she didn't care. He was fun and goofy, and he'd made them laugh. Phil had been the perfect host, right there with Toots at his side. Sophie didn't know why they hadn't tied the knot themselves, but she suspected that Toots's eight marriages, each ending in widowhood and, incidentally, making her a very, very, very wealthy woman, were keeping her from taking a ninth leap. Whatever; Sophie wanted Toots, her best friend in the entire world, to be as happy as she was. Yes, they were all aging, but thanks to Ida's blockbuster concoction from her Seasons cosmetic line, they could all easily take ten to fifteen years off their age, though Ida was the only one who still lied about aging. Mavis was as gorgeous and sweet as ever. Surely, she and Wade would marry one day, Sophie thought. Maybe she and Toots could have a double wedding. Sophie would mention this to them the next time they were alone and the topic of marriage came up.

"Nothing Toots undertakes is half-assed. Look at the Canine Café. She has people and their pets lined up at the door daily, according to Phil. She has the magic touch. And, more important, she's good people, too," Goebel added.

Goebel's total acceptance of her old friends and all their foibles meant a lot to Sophie because Toots was family. Ida and Mavis, too. All of them were lucky to have found men who were totally accepting of the entire group of women and, now, the other guys.

And, of course, Abby, the link that had kept them together all these years. Seeking to calm herself with happy memories, Sophie recalled the first time she had met Toots.

Chapter Three

September 1955
New Jersey

Teresa Loudenberry hated the navy wool skirt and vest she was forced to wear. Hated the heavily starched white blouse, and what was even worse, the stupid white anklets and saddle shoes that made up the uniform for her first day of seventh grade at Bishop Verot Catholic School, her first day of junior high. She'd dreaded the day all summer.

Right now she totally despised her parents for insisting that she attend this stupid school. She didn't know a single person there since she'd spent her first six years in public school. Her father had insisted this was best for her, telling her he wanted to protect her from being influenced by the hooligans she'd hung with for most of her life. She didn't get it. Teresa had hung around with the same group since third grade, and all of a sudden her father was referring to them as hooligans. And all because the guys had the beginnings of peach fuzz that they called mustaches, and slicked their hair back using Brylcreem. Her parents were so square, it was embarrassing. Of course, she would never voice those thoughts because doing so would ensure she'd be grounded for a month. For a year. Until she was older than her grandmother.

"Teresa, hurry up. You don't want to miss breakfast on your first day of school," her mother called from the kitchen.

Oh yes I do, she thought as she eyed herself in the mirror one last time. "Coming, Mother," she dutifully replied, knowing that saying what she thought would certainly land her in hot water. She'd grown two inches over the summer, which made her taller than most of the boys her age. Her legs were way too long, and when you added in her red hair, she was sure to be doomed before she set foot in the sacred halls of Bishop Verot Catholic School. On the bright side, so far anyway, it was coed. At least her father hadn't insisted she attend Our Sacred Angels of Mercy, an all-girls school. At least she'd be around boys.

"Teresa!" her mother called again.

"Sorry, Mom," she answered. She grabbed her book satchel, then hurried to the kitchen.

As usual, her mother and father were sitting at the table, her mother sipping a small glass of orange juice and her father reading the morning paper and downing cups of coffee as fast as her mother could pour them. Teresa liked coffee, even though her parents didn't allow her to drink it. She'd spent a few nickels at the fountain down at Woolworth's sampling the stuff.

Taking his eyes away from his paper, her father said, "You look very . . . academic."

She wanted to roll her eyes but managed to refrain from doing so. "Thanks, Dad," was all she could come up with.

"I love your hair when it's curled. Aren't you glad we took the time to curl your hair last night?" Mrs. Loudenberry asked as she got up and pulled a chair out for her daughter.

"Yes, Mother. I love it. I can't wait to do it again." This time, however, she did roll her eyes. "I hate it, if you really want the truth." *There*, she thought as she saw the look of horror on her mother's face.

"Why, Teresa Amelia Loudenberry, I should wash your mouth out with Lava soap. We do not say *hate* in this household."

She refrained from rolling her eyes again. "Sorry, Mom. I'd just rather go . . . natural. I don't want to do this every night. My scalp hurts."

"Oh, honey, I'm sorry. I must have tied the rags too tight.

Now"—her mother's perkiness instantly returned—"what will you have to drink this morning?"

Teresa figured it wouldn't hurt to say what she really wanted, so she replied, "Coffee. Lots of sugar and cream."

Her father lowered his paper and peered over the top to glance at her. "Since when did you start drinking coffee?"

Knowing she was caught and not wanting to start the day off with any more lies than she had to, she said, "I tried it at Woolworth's. Once," she added, crossing her fingers under the kitchen table.

Her father grinned, then went back to reading his paper. "Ella, pour Teresa a cup of coffee if she wants it. Today is a special day for her."

"Sam! Surely you're not serious? Why, I read in *Ladies' Home Journal* that coffee stunts a child's growth!"

Teresa didn't have to see her father's face to know he was laughing when he spoke. "Go on, give her a cup. I'm guessing a bit of growth stunting doesn't matter much to her. Right, Toots?"

She hated it when her father called her Toots, though since he was just teasing, and he had said she could have coffee, she bit her tongue. "Right, Pops." She'd gotten her height from her father, who at six-foot-four and 190 pounds cut quite the figure. God help her if she ever grew that tall. At twelve, she already stood a bit over five-seven. If coffee was supposed to stunt growth, it hadn't worked for her.

"Well, I suppose one cup won't hurt her as long as she uses plenty of milk and sugar." Her mother removed a cup and saucer from the cabinet and poured from the new percolator she'd recently purchased from the S&H Green Stamps catalogue.

"Thank you, Mom. I do like lots of sugar and milk."

Her mother filled the cup with a few tablespoons of coffee, then added milk and several spoons of sugar. Teresa took a sip, her eyes lighting up. "This is much better than the stuff they serve at Woolworth's." Quickly, she gulped down the rest of her coffee before her parents caught on to what she'd said. "I really have to go now. I . . . don't want to be late on my first day of seventh grade." Actually, she did, but she didn't want to hang around in the kitchen either.

"You haven't eaten one bite, Teresa. You can't go to school hungry. What if your stomach growls? You'll have the nuns thinking we don't feed you enough."

Her mother's goal in life was to feed her as much as she could. She did have a point, though. "I'll just take this toast." She grabbed a piece of toast from the plate in the center of the table. "I can eat on my way to school."

Her father shook the paper twice, then folded it exactly as he'd found it, laying it next to his plate. "I can drive you if you want," he said.

"No! I mean . . . I think there are a few girls who are meeting around the corner. We're, uh, going to walk together."

"That's wonderful, don't you think, Sam? Already our sweet Teresa is making new friends."

Yeah, she thought to herself, and wondered just exactly how many Hail Marys she'd have to say to receive forgiveness. At the rate she was telling lies, she'd have to spend the entire year in the confessional.

Sophia De Luca removed a cigarette from the cup of her bra and placed it between her lips. She could only imagine how horrified her mom would be if she saw her with a weed dangling out of her mouth as she walked down Conway Street. She giggled as she lit up. She'd been sneaking her dad's Camels since she was ten, and her mother had yet to find out.

She'd prayed all night this day would never come, but despite her best efforts, it had, and here she was with dark circles beneath her eyes, and as usual she was running late. She didn't care, really, but she knew the prissy old nuns would chew her out in front of everyone if she came to class with a tardy slip in hand—not that she really cared, but it was the first day of school. Junior high, no less.

She'd begged her mom not to send her back to Bishop Verot.

She'd spent every stinking day of her life, well almost, in that dirty dump of a school. She'd argued again and again with her parents, telling them it was time they allowed her to make her own decisions where her education was concerned, but, of course, they refused to listen to her, saying she was only twelve, a very mature twelve, her mother had added with a smile. But whatever Sophia thought, they had said that until she was of legal age or married and out of the house, they would continue to make all decisions for her. And then her father had threatened to whip her good if she brought the topic up again. Knowing that he meant every word he said, she'd swallowed the comeback and accepted Bishop Verot as her fate.

"Screw 'em," she said loudly as she walked down Conway Street. Sophia had been making this trek since third grade, when she was finally allowed to walk to school with the other kids on the block.

"Hey, De Suck Face," Billy Watson called out to her as she walked past his apartment complex.

"Hey yourself, shit eater," Sophia tossed back. It was a well-known fact among all the students at Bishop Verot that Billy Watson ate a pile of dog shit in fifth grade, all on a dare that the jerk didn't have enough sense to know wasn't really a dare at all.

"Ah, go suck yourself," he yelled back.

Sophia stopped and waited for Billy Watson to catch up with her. They'd been classmates since before conception, according to her mother. Her mom often told the story of how she met Mrs. Watson the day they both found out they were expecting. Sophia hated the story and wished her mother would get a case of amnesia where her beginnings were concerned, but that wish hadn't come true either. None of her wishes ever did.

Surely she could make one wish come true today. She wished that Billy Watson would scream like a girl. When he was less than three feet behind her she decided to do something about it and tossed her cigarette butt at him, hitting him squarely in the face. He wiped at his face as though he were being attacked by a swarm of bees. "You tramp! You just wait! I'm gonna tell on you for smoking," he screamed at her as she raced ahead of him, laughing until it made her side hurt. Sophia didn't stop running until she reached the yard of the school where she was destined to spend the next six years of her life, starting today. The thought made her stomach twist in knots, but she knew she had to go to school. She wanted to be a nurse, and without a high school education, there was no way she would get into a reputable nursing school. She didn't have a lot of friends and didn't give a crud. Everyone thought she was as mean as her old man since she'd told the nuns at school that it was okay for a man to hit a woman because her father knocked her mom around all the time. That'd been in third grade. Most of the kids in her neighborhood were forbidden to play with her when word of her tale spread. She didn't have time for friends anyway. When she wasn't studying, she stayed close to her mother when her father was home because she knew he wouldn't be as likely to use her mom as a punching bag when she was around.

Sophia knew she was older than her years, but she didn't mind. She listened to the other girls on the block talk about what was playing at the movies, boys, and the latest fashion fads, and none of it held her interest in the slightest; all of their talk seemed so dumb to her. Her mother was always after her to go outside, play with the kids in the neighborhood, and sometimes she did it just to make her mother happy, but she really wasn't accepted in the neighborhood as one of the popular girls because her parents weren't accepted either. It'd taken her a while to figure that out, but when she had, she made sure everyone knew she chose not to have them as *her* friends, making it appear as though she'd shunned them when, in reality, it was the other way around.

Arriving at school on time in spite of her late start, Sophia saw the tallest girl she'd ever seen waiting by the entrance with a few others who didn't realize this was the back entrance of the church and not the school. They'd miss the first bell, and all of them would be embarrassed. Trying to make up for her earlier mean-ness to Billy Watson, Sophia inserted herself in the middle of the group. "This is the church. You hang around here any longer you'll all be late. Follow me," she said before turning around and heading to the front of the church, where the entrance to the school was located. She hoped they followed her; otherwise, she would be making an idiot out of herself again. She dared a look over her shoulder. The only one in the group to follow her was the tall girl with the dark red hair. Sophia stopped so the girl could catch up with her.

"Thanks," the red-haired girl said as she walked alongside her. "I'm Teresa Loudenberry."

Sophia looked up at the girl beside her. She had an honest face, and Sophia liked her straightaway. "I'm Sophia De Luca. Hang with me, and I'll show you the ropes around this place. I've been going here since conception."

She saw she'd made the girl blush. "It's a long story. I might tell you all about it at lunch. Deal?" Sophia asked before they entered the door that would take them to their classrooms.

Teresa held her hand out. "Deal." They shook hands, both wearing grins as wide as the moon.

Chapter Four

Sophie and Goebel spent the better part of the morning with Toots at her house, then the afternoon working in the flower garden they had started as soon as they had moved in last year. Sophie hadn't wanted to go inside after the episode with the cigarettes, so she'd spent the afternoon and evening at Goebel's side, both working contentedly in the flower garden.

A rainbow of color had taken the place of the overgrown, weedy lawn they'd had at the beginning. Dark green shrubbery formed a curtain around the front lawn. The oak trees were fertilized, revitalized, and now appeared strong and healthy. Sophie had fallen in love with hydrangeas on one of their many trips to the nursery, and the path leading from the back veranda to the edge of their property blossomed with ivory, periwinkle, lavender, pink, and yellow hydrangeas, a pastiche of colors flanking the stone path, their scent overpowering and intoxicating. Sophie never tired of stepping outside to view Goebel's work. He'd become as passionate about gardening as she was about speaking to those who had crossed over. They often teased each other that the combination of their passions equaled a funeral parlor. Flowers and death. Someone else would have been mortified at the comparison, but Sophie knew death wasn't as frightening as many were led to believe. It was the character of one's departed soul, sometimes good and sometimes evil, that she thought of as frightening. She and Goebel had discussed this at great length, both admitting that they weren't ready to kick the bucket just yet, but when they did, they promised each other they'd let the other know when they were around. She told Goebel he would smell the strong, heady scent of hydrangeas since she loved them so much, and he said she would see a hydrangea growing in a place where it shouldn't. They had discussed so much in their short marriage, Sophie truly felt that Goebel was her soul mate. Bittersweet memories of her parents' cruel and loveless marriage assured her that she would never allow a man to control her life again. When she'd married Walter she'd made the same mistake her mother had, but not the second time. No, this time around her choice was as close to perfection as it would ever be.

It was almost ten o'clock that night, after Sophia and Goebel had spent a long afternoon in the garden and eaten dinner, before the rest of the Godmothers, along with their various significant others, arrived.

"Now that we're all here, let's get started," Sophie said, leading the group upstairs to the room they had yet to remodel and probably never would.

"The table fits perfectly, just as I thought," Toots commented upon seeing the wooden table she'd purchased for this exact purpose. She held Frankie, her adorable dachshund, in her arms. He growled when he realized he was not going to be the center of attention. Toots gently rubbed the space between his ears. He immediately quieted.

"And tonight we're going to find out if this . . . wood has all the magic Sophia claims it has," Ida said, her voice shrill, an indication of her nervousness. Then she gave Toots a dirty look when she saw Frankie.

"I promise not to disappoint you either. Though I do want you to keep in mind that *this wood*"—Sophie nodded at the long table in the center of the small room—"isn't the kind of *wood* that has the sort of magic you're referring to." Sophie grinned, not caring that she had embarrassed Ida in front of Daniel. After a year together, he should know Ida's uppermost thoughts always included a reference to sex, whether consciously or not.

"Now, don't you two get started. This is Daniel's first séance, and we definitely do not want him to think that this isn't serious business, now do we?" Mavis, ever the peacemaker, asked. She'd brought Coco, her Chihuahua, who was absolutely convinced that she—the dog, not Mavis—was royalty. "Can we keep Coco and Frankie in the kitchen?"

"Of course you can. I've already fixed a spot for them," Sophie said, then returned her attention to Ida.

"Rest assured I have told Daniel of your successes, Sophia," Ida said in her best know-it-all voice. "And thank you, Mavis." Ida smiled at Mavis.

"You're most welcome, dear," Mavis said sweetly.

"Yes, and I must say, I'm impressed," Daniel said. "I've never been too much of a believer in all this hocus-pocus, personally, but both Ida and Mother insist you're the real thing. I know Charleston is a hotbed for anything paranormal. Last week, Ida and I went on a ghost walking tour. I have to admit, it was a bit unsettling."

"Then you'd best be prepared tonight because I can promise you, after an evening with Sophie and her séances, you will be more than a bit unsettled," Toots informed Daniel. "She's the real deal. Nothing phony or fake about her. Right, Goebel?"

Goebel nodded, then spoke as he finished arranging the chairs around the table. "Absolutely. If you're okay with having the daylights scared out of you, stay. If not, it might be best to leave now before any ghostly apparitions make themselves known."

Daniel gave a nervous laugh. "I'll stick around. Since I've moved back to Charleston full-time, it's probably fitting that I have at least one ghost experience, so I'll have something to converse about with new clients—just in case the topic happens to come up in conversation."

Ida shot him a dirty look. "You discuss ghosts with your clients? Why am I just now hearing this?"

All eyes focused on Daniel and Ida. It looked as though they were about to have their first argument, or at least the first to be witnessed.

"No, dear lady, I do not discuss ghosts with my clients. As I said, if the subject happens to come up—in the future—then I will have a true, bona fide experience to share."

For once, Ida kept quiet.

"I say it's time we get started. It's getting late, and I promised Wade I would call him before I went to sleep tonight," Mavis said. "He wants to stay close to Robert since he's been acting . . . odd."

"Shit, Mavis, Robert *is* odd. He likes Bernice. There is absolutely nothing wrong with that man, other than he's so smitten with Bernice that's all he thinks about. Phil agrees, don't you?" Toots asked.

"I couldn't say for sure and be one hundred percent sure without examining him, but I haven't seen any signs of real dementia, as Wade seems to think. I think the old guy is in love. And love will make a man do all sorts of crazy things, right, Toots?" Phil said to her.

Toots chuckled. "Depends on what you call crazy. So what kind of crazy things are we talking about here?"

"I think I'd best keep my mouth shut before I end up sticking my foot in it and swallowing it," Phil diplomatically replied. "Sophie wants to get down to business, so we can talk about this later. When we're alone."

"Okay, enough bullshit. Ida, take the pooches downstairs. I agree that it's time we get down to serious business. Let's everyone find a seat," Sophie said. As soon as Ida returned from the kitchen downstairs, they all gathered around the table.

"First, thanks for doing this for me. I know it's late, but it is what it is, and I wouldn't have asked any of you to come over this late"—she eyed Toots—"even though it's early for me. I had a very disturbing dream last night, or what I thought was a dream, and now I know it wasn't. That's why I wanted to perform the séance tonight. I wanted to do this while the memory is still fresh and vivid in my mind. Now, since Daniel hasn't attended one of my séances before, I'll tell him what we do, then we can turn out the lights, and, Mavis, if you would do the honors of lighting the candles when we're ready, it will be close to how we did things in California." It had been several months since Sophie had performed a séance with the girls, and this would be the first in her new home. Before speaking further, she gave a silent prayer for the spirit to be filled with love, and that those in the room with her would not walk away with fears and doubts.

"Of course I will," Mavis said. "I enjoy helping the process. I just wish Wade were here. He would love this sort of thing."

"Next time bring him, and the hell with Robert and Bernice's wackiness. I know Bernice secretly wants a dachshund. She can't seem to keep her hands off Frankie, at least when she thinks I'm not looking," Toots said.

"Toots? Are we finished?" Sophie asked in a low voice, the voice that they knew meant business, and that business was making contact with the spirit world.

"Sorry," Toots said, then reached for Phil's hand beneath the table, where she gave him a reassuring squeeze that he instantly returned.

The wooden table was round, yet Sophie sat with her back to the single window, facing the door. Toots took the seat to her right, and Phil sat next to Toots. On Sophie's left was Goebel, then Ida, who seemed a bit eager to grab Goebel's hand, but Sophie knew full well that while Goebel tolerated Ida's foolishness, he only had eyes for his wife. After she finished lighting the candles, Mavis took her seat next to Daniel, reached for his hand, then took Phil's hand when he offered it to her.

"Daniel, just listen and follow my instructions. First, in order for one to make a connection to the other side, we must clear our minds of all things negative. Fill our minds with good thoughts, pleasant images. A beach, a stream alongside a mountain, flowers gently blowing in the wind, the sound of a soft rain as it falls from the sky." Sophie paused so the group could clear their minds. After a few seconds had passed, she spoke again, only this time her voice was softer, yet deeper. "First, let us say a prayer for those who have departed and want to reach out to us now. May we touch their souls with love and light, so they may find eternal peace unto the end of time. Let's join hands."

Sophie wasn't following the exact protocol she'd used in the past because she knew it wasn't needed. No rocks or glass would fly across the table by way of answers, nor would they see any free writing done by this spirit. Sophie knew what to expect and found her heart racing. Taking a deep, calming breath, Sophie inhaled and exhaled several times before her heart rate returned to a normal beat. She could hear the others following her breathing patterns. Good, she thought. The more relaxed they were, the more likely the spirit would make itself known to them.

Sophie continued to speak out, yet it wasn't to anyone in the room, or at least any living someone in the room now. "You came to me in a dream, a vision. I felt your constraints, I felt your excitement." Sophie paused, allowing all of them time to get used to something different. Except for Daniel, as this was a first for him, it would be what he would continue to expect if he were asked to attend any future séances.

"You are from another time, long ago. Hundreds of years ago." Sophie slowly released each word as though each were sacred. "I mean you no harm," she added. This was Sophie's rule, that she let those from the other side know that she would not harm their spirit; nor would she allow a spirit to harm any who attended.

They all were totally silent, the room dim except for the four candles Mavis placed on the table, one at each corner representing the four points of the compass. Sophie didn't always use this particular arrangement, but it had proved to be just one more way to ensure that a spirit found her. Again, she did not know why, just that it did.

"Let's all clear our minds, open them to our spirit, let her know she is welcome and that we mean her no harm." Sophie took deep breaths, in and out, slowly. The others followed. "Yes, blow all the negative thoughts away from your mind, free them, let them go. Only positive, loving thoughts now," she said, almost in a whisper. "I want to understand you, and help you," Sophie continued, encouraging the spirit with her soft, mesmerizing words.

Normally, Sophie was able to make contact with the other side fairly quickly. Tonight, her method wasn't working as fast. "Please show yourself, let me help you. We all want to help you. These are friends, family."

Often, if a spirit felt there were too many people in the space it normally occupied, it stayed away. Sophie wanted to make sure her spirit knew she was safe to show herself in this room as this is where she felt most comfortable. Sophie guessed that the room held a special meaning for her.

"Let's concentrate. Remove all the negativity from our minds," Sophie repeated softly. She started doing the deep-breathing exercises again, keeping her eyes closed, trying her best to call up the image of the woman in her vision. She opened her eyes, fully expecting to see the woman, but again, all she saw were her dear friends gathered around the table doing their best to concentrate on also clearing their minds so that she could figure out what this meant. "You all are doing great," she added in a soft voice.

Encouragement never hurt, she thought as she closed her eyes again. There was more deep breathing, in and out, trying to clear away the bad energy. Sophie was about to open her eyes when she heard what sounded like a soft, tinkling sound, a bell. Toots squeezed her hand, Sophie gave a squeeze back. "We're here to help you, whoever you are. We are your friends," Sophie repeated. This spirit was not going to show itself easily.

"I know that you were hurt, I felt your pain when you fell." Sophie thought these might be the words this particular spirit needed to hear. "Is this what you want me to acknowledge? Your pain?"

One of the candles in the south position flickered for a few seconds, then went out. Smoke from the wick spiraled above the candle. All eyes were focused on this. The smoke formed a small whirlwind and flew across the room so fast, everyone at the table felt a small gush of air! "Are you here now? Did you just blow out the candle?"

Another candle was extinguished, and the smoke from that candle withered away into the air as it would have had someone pinched its wick. "See?" Ida whispered to Daniel.

"Shhh, be quiet, Ida," Sophie admonished.

"Are you here in the room with us now? If you are, let us know by extinguishing another candle." All eyes focused on the two remaining candles on the table. The red, orange, and gold flames barely moved.

For the next minute or so, no one took their eyes away from the two remaining candles.

"I don't think our spirit is ready to make contact yet. I feel as though she is . . . afraid." Sophie mumbled the last word.

They returned their attention to Sophie when she spoke. "Something terrible must have happened to her."

Chapter Five

The pain seared throughout her body, and she felt as though her entire being were on fire. Then, as fast as the pain came, it was gone, replaced by a warm, pleasant feeling as though she were being held by a ray of the brightest sun. She looked around her and saw herself splayed out at the bottom of the steps. Her right leg was twisted at an unnatural angle from the knee down. Her left leg appeared uninjured, though both arms were broken in half between the elbow and the wrist. Her head tilted upward, her eyes frozen, and she stared up at the ceiling.

Unable to comprehend why she felt just fine, yet able to see herself, unmoving, in a heap at the bottom of the staircase, Florence looked around her, and again, she felt different, changed somehow, as though she was in another world. Yet how could that be, she thought as she walked around the crumpled woman who appeared to be herself. Again, it must be another dream.

She walked back upstairs to wait for Theodore. Not understanding what was taking him so long, she decided to go ahead and prepare for bed.

"Ruth," she called out as soon as she entered her suite of rooms. Shaking her head, then closing and opening her eyes, surely, she thought, she was quite out of her mind.

These were not her rooms, yet they were!

She stared at the room, her room, or what she thought to be her room, and what she observed did not make sense to her at all.

She'd had no wine with dinner, nothing to cause her to feel so out of sorts. She tried closing her eyes for a few moments, then opened them yet again.

Her cherry four-poster bed was no longer in the room. In its place was a small bed, without ornaments of any kind, its coverings extremely plain. Fearful of her thoughts and where they would lead, she forced herself to focus further on the room and its contents. This room was not her *room. She stepped fully into the large area, searching for anything familiar, but she saw that nothing was as she'd left it earlier in the evening.*

On the bed was a contraption holding different types of fabrics, yet still, nothing in the room seemed familiar. Surely, she must be in the midst of a nightmare. With one hand, she reached for the other. When she tried to pinch her wrist, her fingers slipped right through her skin! Again, she tried to pinch herself, and her fingers were unable to grab anything!

Dear God, *she thought,* have I been poisoned? *Surely there was some explanation for this, even though she could not begin to imagine what it could possibly be. She walked around the perimeter of her room, a room she thought had once belonged to her. But nothing was as it should be. Before she lost complete control of herself, she hurried out of the room and down the hall to the small room she planned to use as a nursery. She forced herself to think she was in the midst of a dream, and in doing so, she found she was anxious to see what awaited her.*

She hesitated before entering the nursery, again reminding herself this had to be a dream, though actually it was more like a nightmare that had come to life. There were no other words to describe what she was experiencing. Had she somehow unknowingly consumed liquor? She hadn't had any alcoholic beverages for weeks, unless she'd mistakenly drunk out of Theodore's glass; but, no, that was ridiculous. She would never be that careless, especially in her condition. No, there had to be another explanation.

Forcefully pushing the door aside, Florence entered the nursery, or what she planned to be the nursery. She had ordered a very spe-

cial wallpaper for this room just last week. The pattern would be perfect for a baby's room, boy or girl. Puffy clouds, pale blue skies, and adorable little lambs leaping over a fence in a lovely green pasture. It was sure to be calming. Clearing her mind in order to focus on her current situation, she took in her surroundings. Odd, as this room appeared as it had the last time she'd been in here. The walls were bare, as they were being prepared for hanging the wallpaper that was scheduled to arrive next month. The single window remained unadorned, waiting for her to choose a fabric to coordinate with the wallpaper.

She stood by the window, expecting to see nothing but darkness, as it was quite late. Instead, she saw that it was daylight, early afternoon if the sun's position was correct.

This can't be!

Cook had served dinner just as the sun was setting; she remembered this because Theodore had commented how warm it was today as he'd ridden throughout the plantation, remarking how much he had looked forward to the cool evening.

Sick with panic, she paced the small room, careful not to look out the window. This was simply a nightmare from which she would soon awaken. Of course it was, it had to be. There was no other possible explanation. Or was there?

Suddenly, she felt that she had to leave the room and return to her place at the top of the stairs. If he thought she had retired for the night, Theodore might go to bed without giving her a chance to tell him the wonderful news.

Hurrying back to wait at the top of the staircase, Florence stood where she had only moments ago. She peered over the banister, hoping to see Theodore, or at the very least see her home as it was moments ago.

Taking in the scene below, she saw her home stripped of its furnishings, decorations, even the lamps nowhere to be seen. Everything was gone, except for the staircase and banister, and it looked much older, as though it hadn't been well cared for.

No!

She closed her eyes and would keep them tightly shut until morning. Ruth would awaken her with a soft tap on her door, then enter with a pot of hot tea and a plate of piping-hot biscuits fresh from the oven, liberally slathered with butter and fresh peach jam made with peaches from their own trees, just as she had every single day since Florence had become Mrs. Theodore Dabney.

Praying she would soon wake up to her familiar surroundings, Florence remained at the top of the staircase. When several minutes passed, she opened her eyes.

Again, she was greeted by unfamiliarity, and a complete and utter silence. This was not a dream; it couldn't be, because she felt herself to be wide-awake. Her senses were never this heightened during a dream, whether it was pleasant or not. Inhaling, she detected a scent uncommon to her home. Normally, one could smell lemon oil throughout the house, but there was not a trace of the aromatic oil in the air. She focused on trying to identify the odor, but it was so unusual, she could not. Possibly Theodore's clothing, she thought, though she did not recall smelling it when he came home this afternoon. It didn't matter, she told herself.

What mattered most, she thought, was that she was not losing her mind! This . . . episode she was having would surely cause Theodore to question her sanity! How could she expect him to accept this when she herself could not?

Walking to the edge of the staircase, she looked down the spiral stairs, and, again, she saw herself crumpled at the foot of the stairs.

Like a broken china doll, *Florence thought, and she suddenly knew her life as she'd known it would never, ever be the same again.*

"Sophie?" Goebel said in a loud whisper. "Are you all right?"

Releasing his hand, she placed a finger against her lips and nodded. "The woman . . . she knows she is . . . *changed.*" Sophie didn't know why she'd used that word, but knew it was how the woman felt. She tried as hard as she could to focus on the woman's thoughts, anything to get more of a feel for who she was, and why was she trying to contact Sophie, but the spirit seemed to back off whenever she was close to connecting. It was difficult to figure out the mind of someone who might or might not have existed.

"Let's focus on the young woman . . . *spirit*," Sophie corrected herself, then thought that if they all concentrated, their combined energies would enable this *spirit* woman to trust them.

Again, they held hands, though this time they placed them openly on top of the table, where they could be viewed.

"Let's focus on the spirit," she instructed those gathered around the table. "We don't know who you are, or why you're here," Sophie coaxed in a soft voice. "We want to help you reach the other side." Though she didn't know why this spirit woman had yet to make the journey across to the other side, she knew that she hadn't done so, and that was enough reason for Sophie to continue to try to reach out to her.

Everyone remained silent, hoping for a sign that they were connecting to the spirit world. The two candles glowed, their flames steady, unmoving.

Again, Sophie took a breath, deciding this time she would try another route, one she didn't use too often. But at this point, anything was worth a shot. "You know you're dead, right?"

The flames on the candles flickered wildly, then returned to normal as fast as they'd flickered. "Are you making the flames dance?" Sophie asked. Never had it taken so much effort to make contact. When nothing happened, Sophie blew out the candles.

"Why did you do that?" Toots asked. "We didn't connect with anyone."

Sophie got out of her chair and walked across the room, where she located the light switch and turned it on. A golden light radiated throughout the small room. "This isn't the time. I'm trying too hard, and she isn't ready. Something is holding her back."

Ida cleared her throat. "And I promised Daniel you would make him change his mind."

Sophie sat back down. "I appreciate the vote of confidence, but

I offer no guarantees. We can try again tomorrow. That is if you all want to."

"I'm game," Toots said.

"I suppose I could, too. I may invite Wade, if that's all right with you," Mavis added.

"Sure, Wade is welcome, but whatever you do, don't invite Robert. He'd scare the dead with his talk."

They all laughed. Robert was none too outspoken about his feelings concerning the afterlife. His words, *dead is dead*, said it all. He was not a believer in Sophie's ability to speak with the dearly departed, though he refused to say this to her. Personally, she knew he was frightened by the unknown, and that was okay. Not everyone had to agree with her on this particular subject.

"I don't think we need to concern ourselves with Robert. He and Bernice are too busy with their recipes—they're organizing them now. I heard him mention something about a cookbook the other day," Mavis informed them.

"Maybe Phil could send a publisher his way," Daniel said.

"Once my book is published, and if Robert is serious about publishing a cookbook, I'll be happy to help in any way I can," Phil replied.

Goebel cleared his throat. "I say we all go downstairs and have something to drink and check on those two rascals. This talk of death and recipes has made me thirsty." He lifted his eyebrows up and down, Groucho Marx style.

"I'm with Goebel," Daniel said, then practically leapt out of his chair for the door, Phil close behind him.

"Chicken shit," Sophie said.

"Why do you always have to cuss? I swear, Sophia, you've got the filthiest mouth," Ida said, following Daniel to the door.

"I like the shock effect; and you should know that, after more than fifty years. And you, my friend, have the filthiest mind, though I'm sure Daniel knows this. Firsthand." She laughed, but her heart wasn't really in the lighthearted, if somewhat ill-timed grumbling.

Ida had the good grace to keep whatever comeback she had to herself.

"Goebel made strawberry lemonade yesterday. It's fantastic laced with a shot of vodka," Sophie tossed out, as they all trailed behind her down the stairs.

"You're becoming quite the little housewife," Toots jokingly said to Goebel. "Sounds good to me, but I can only have a little. Phil is afraid I'll become a drunkard."

"I doubt that. Remember, I used to be married to one. When you start sucking down the mouthwash and cough syrup, then Phil will have something to worry about. Until then, I think you're safe to have a drink once in a blue moon. Now, I, for one, am going to smoke before I do anything else. You with me?" Sophie asked Toots as soon as everyone was scattered around the veranda.

"Nasty old women," Ida said.

Both Sophie and Toots gave her the bird.

Once they were away from the others, and had taken a few puffs from their smokes, Toots spoke, her tone serious. "So, why weren't you able to contact this . . . woman tonight?"

"She is afraid," Sophie said, a gust of white smoke coming out of her mouth with each word.

"Are you sure?" Toots asked.

Sophie gave a harsh laugh. "I'm never sure, Toots. We're talking about dead people, ghosts, spirits, the afterlife, whatever term you want to use. I can't ever be one hundred percent sure about any of it."

Toots took a drag from her cigarette, then said, "Are you losing your touch?"

No, Sophie thought to herself, she wasn't losing her touch. If anything, it was more honed than ever because she knew a portal had been opened, one that should've remained closed forever. And now it was up to her to seal it away again, before those she loved came to harm.

Chapter Six

"I think you hurt Toots's feelings, Abs," Chris said as he wiped creamed spinach from Amy's face.

Abby airplane-fed Jonathan another spoonful of carrots. "No, I didn't. Mom understands. She may not like it, though she would've told me if I hurt her feelings." Jonathan tongued–chewed his favorite baby food, his little mouth remaining open like a little chick.

Once the twins started eating baby food, Abby and Chris re-arranged the kitchen to accommodate two high chairs, their small kitchen table, plus the bench she'd bought around the time she found out she was pregnant. Amy held on to the edge of the bench when she toddled around the kitchen. Jonathan had yet to walk, but he crawled much faster than Amy could walk.

"Da! Da!" Amy cooed.

"Give me a second, little lady," Chris said as he opened an-other jar of creamed spinach. "You're sure it's okay to give her this much spinach?" he asked Abby.

"If Popeye can eat it all the time, then I think it's okay," Abby joked. "Seriously, the pediatrician said it was fine, give them all the veggies they want. This stuff"—she nodded at the array of baby-food jars on the table—"is about to end. They're old enough to eat people food now."

Chris laughed. "They have the teeth for it, that's for sure."

Chester, who watched lazily while he reclined in his giant

dog bed, barked. Abby and Chris laughed. Chester would not be left out.

Life had been one giant party since having the twins. Rarely did a day go by that Abby or Chris didn't observe one milestone or another. Last week, Jonathan had tried to say Chester. It came out "Hetter" instead, but they both knew what he was trying to say as his pudgy little arms were wrapped around the German shepherd as he spoke.

"Six teeth to be exact, right, Mr. Clay?" Abby teased Jonathan. "We're not talking about steaks here. Just fresh fruit and soft veggies." She wiped his mouth with her thumb.

They continued to feed the babies and talk. It was a rare moment to have the other's undivided attention. "Did you tell Toots I was going out of town to that legal-aid conference? You know that she and the three G's will move in so they can help you while I'm gone." Chris volunteered his legal services one day a week at Charleston's legal aid offices. Conference attendance was required if he wanted to continue, and they both agreed he should give back. It was the right thing to do.

Abby laughed. "That's what I'm afraid of."

"Their intentions are good, you know that," Chris said.

"And I appreciate them. More than they know; I just don't want to tell them that for fear of what might happen. Heck, knowing them, they'll set up tents on the front lawn." Abby kissed her son's chubby cheek, then lifted him out of his high chair. "Between these two, their daddy, and the dogs, I'm busy, but I'm smart enough to know when to accept their help, too. Mom offered to sit with them one afternoon a week so I can pitch in where I'm needed with the animals." Abby and Chris had turned the plantation's former slave quarters into a facility for animals. As a nonprofit organization, Dogs Displaced by Disaster was already making a name for itself. After the fires in Colorado, and her mother's opening the Canine Café, organizations from around the world were standing in line to volunteer their services and assist them. Abby had been so busy with the two babies she hadn't devoted as much time to the animals as she had originally planned. Now that Amy and Jonathan were somewhat mobile, an afternoon a week spent with their grandmother would be a welcome respite for both Abby and the kids.

"I like the idea," Chris said, then he removed Amy from her high chair. "Someone needs a bath," he said when he saw the dark green spinach in Amy's blond hair. "Her hair needs to be washed, too."

"And you're telling this to me, *why?*" Abby asked, heading upstairs, with Jonathan secured to her hip.

"Because Dad doesn't like to wash hair," Chris said, coming up behind her and resisting the urge to give her a pinch. "No, let me rephrase that. Dad is afraid he will get shampoo in his daughter's big blue eyes."

"Good one, Pops, but I'm no fool," Abby said upon entering the nursery. "I know how my little girl squirms when her head is wet."

Both Abby and Chris automatically placed a baby on his or her changing table, removing their carrot- and spinach-covered clothes. "What good are these things?" Chris asked as he tossed Amy's bib into the clothes hamper next to the table.

"I think you're supposed to wipe their mouths with them. Whatever their intended purpose, these two have most definitely defied it."

"Here, you take this young lady while I run their bath." Chris handed Amy to Abby, who once again had Jonathan tucked against her hip. "Think you can handle two at a time?" Chris teased as he passed the baby to her.

"Hey, watch your mouth! I can handle two babies—you and Chester. And Mom. Sophie, too." Abby glanced uneasily over her shoulder, though what she expected to find, she had no clue. Must be mentioning Sophie's name. She'd had an unusual experience at Sophie's house the other day. She wanted to tell Chris but feared she would come off as overprotective and downright weird if she brought the incident up. Maybe later.

"Okay, okay, I get the message. I'm gonna run the water while I'm ahead," Chris tossed over his shoulder. Abby watched him, still amazed that this beautiful man was actually her husband. Handsome as ever, his faded jeans tight in all the right places, the black T-shirt he wore outlining his muscular chest. Barefoot, hair tousled in a sexy, messed-up way, he was completely opposite of the entertainment attorney she'd known in Los Angeles who wore tailored suits and handmade Italian leather shoes. She felt a jolt of desire as she watched him walk down the hallway. She smiled when he stopped and did a quick butt wiggle before entering the bathroom.

"I saw that!"

"Good," he called out. "It was meant for you."

"Amy and Jonathan saw it, too," she shouted as she made her way down the hall. Inside the bathroom Chris was stooped over the tub. "You're lucky I've got two squirmy babies in my arms; otherwise, I think I just might kick that butt I'm staring at."

"I dare you," Chris said as he adjusted the water temperature, filling the large Jacuzzi tub with a couple inches of water before placing the collapsible baby baths in the tub. Ida had purchased these for her, and Abby thought they were an odd gift. Boon Naked they were called. Now that the twins were old enough to use the tub instead of the kitchen sink, they had become her most-used baby-shower item.

"Okay, here is number one." Abby held Amy out so Chris could put her in the secure bath ring. "And coming in close behind is number two," she said, as he took Jonathan from her.

As soon as they were settled in the bath, Abby sat on the side of the tub and watched her most precious cargo. Chester had followed them upstairs, and now he was sitting just outside the door while they bathed the twins.

They kicked their feet in the air, sending water everywhere, another added assurance that Chester would stay put. The big shepherd didn't like water. Amy was not the biggest fan of water either.

Jonathan, on the other hand, was the next Michael Phelps. He adored the water, kicking and splashing his tiny hands and feet around as if he were training for the perfect breaststroke. "Let's give him swimming lessons as soon as he walks. Something tells me this little man is gonna do big things in the water." The words were no more out of her mouth than Jonathan decided to pee.

"Oh!" Abby said when she felt the warm urine hit her leg.

Chris doubled over laughing. "Now that's my son."

Abby laughed, too. "If I didn't know better, I would think you two planned this."

"How do you know that we didn't?" Chris asked.

She rolled her eyes. "I'll be the first one to agree with you—this kid is smarter than average. And yes, I know all mothers say this about their children, but in his case, it's actually true. However, I don't think he's quite as clever as his father seems to think. Not yet anyway. Right, Amy?" When she heard her name, Amy grinned and made all kinds of happy sounds, then kicked at the water, sending it splashing all over Chris's shirt.

Abby and Chris looked at each other, then burst out in peals of laughter.

"I'm not so sure about these two," Chris said. "I think they both know just exactly what they're doing to Mom and Dad."

"Yep, I think they do. Now, you two little tricksters," Abby said as she leaned over to drain the bathwater. "We're gonna do this all over again. Can't have my kids smelling like pee."

"You are the best mom," Chris said, amazed at her constant patience with the two.

"I know that," she replied matter-of-factly.

"Now, let's finish bathing them so I can change. I don't want to smell like pee either."

For the next ten minutes Abby lathered up the two soft, squirmy babies with baby soap and made a game of rinsing them off, so much so that both were laughing out loud. Then, while they were still laughing, she made faces at them while Chris gently wet their carrot-

and spinach-covered heads. "Keep it up, Dad, you're doing just fine," Abby said, then continued to make funny faces at the pair so they wouldn't focus on their wet heads.

Five minutes later, Abby took Amy, and Chris took Jonathan back to the nursery, where they powdered and diapered them before slipping their pajamas on. Chester followed them around like a shadow. Abby wasn't sure if it was out of jealously or protection. She suspected it was a bit of both.

Once they were ready for bed, they went to the master bedroom, where Grandmother Toots had insisted she use the antique rocking chair that Abby herself was rocked in. Her mother had searched the entire East Coast and found another matching rocker, telling Abby that she would thank her later. Abby had, and still continued to do so. After changing into a clean pair of yoga pants and a T-shirt, she rocked Amy, while Chris took Jonathan. In a matter of minutes, the two one-year-olds were sound asleep. Abby didn't put them in bed right away as she enjoyed just looking at them, when they were quiet and all hers. She knew, because her mother told her this almost on a daily basis, that they would be grown and on their own before she knew it and to cherish every minute that she could. Abby had no problem following her mother's advice. It was pure joy to watch them.

"You look like you're a million miles away," Chris said, keeping his voice very quiet so as not to startle the twins.

"I was just thinking about when they leave home, moments like this will never happen again. I want to enjoy them as much as possible and not waste a single minute."

"I think you're doing just that."

Abby smiled, leaning her head back against the chair. "I am."

They sat in silence for a few minutes, each lost in their own thoughts.

"I was at Sophie and Goebel's the other day," Abby said out of the blue. "The day you were at Daniel's office. She wanted to see the twins, and I needed to get out of the house, so we went over for a while."

She wasn't sure how to go about telling Chris what had happened, but it was about Sophie, so really, she thought, Chris would understand. "When we were there, Sophie was showing me around, all the remodeling stuff. They're really turning that place into a showpiece."

"I already know all about this, Abs. What gives?"

"It's nothing really. I feel stupid even mentioning it, but it was Sophie's house. Anyway, she was showing me the *séance* room. Mom gave her that antique table, and I think she just wanted to show it to me. I was holding Amy, and Sophie carried Jonathan." Abby waved her free hand in the air. "It's probably nothing, but the twins seemed to . . . I don't know. They acted strange, like they were seeing something that wasn't really there. I watched them, their eyes as they appeared to follow something around in the room. I didn't see anything, and Sophie says she didn't either, but then she rushed me out of the room so fast, I felt like she didn't want me in there. Is that crazy or what?"

"No, not coming from Sophie. There's more, isn't there?"

She nodded. "As soon as we were at the top of the staircase, I felt an incredible blast of cold. I'm talking icy, North-Pole cold."

"You *were* at Sophie's. Anything paranormal going on there, or has she mentioned this to you?"

"No, but that's not what is bothering me. The twins started screaming, not crying, but screaming. There were no tears. They acted like they were . . . frightened. I swear, it sounds beyond crazy, but I know they were terrified." Abby shivered at the memory, hating that her children had felt true terror, and at such a young age. It had been bothering her ever since, and she just had to tell someone.

"What did Sophie say or do when they started screaming?"

"That's just it. As you know full well, normally nothing fazes Sophie, but that wasn't the case. She grabbed me by the arm and pulled me down the stairs so fast I almost tripped and fell. I was kind of pissed that she would do that, with both of us carrying the kids."

"Did you say anything to her about it?" Chris asked, concern etching his face.

"No. She didn't give me a chance. She practically tossed us out the door. I didn't even get a chance to say hi to Goebel."

"Have you discussed this with your mother?" Chris asked her.

"No. I haven't really had the opportunity to. She's always surrounded by people. I wanted to tell her privately. Maybe there is something going on at that house that Sophie doesn't want me to know. Or Mom. Which brings up the question, why? We all know Sophie has no secrets. She's always pretty open about her psychic stuff. I don't understand why she would clam up and not tell me if something weird was going on in her house. It's not like her, and that's what bothers me the most." Abby ran a hand over Amy's soft blond curls, so much like her own.

"Let's put them in their cribs," Chris suggested.

Careful so as not to wake the babies, Abby tiptoed out of the master bedroom to the nursery, where they put the twins in separate cribs. She pulled a light blanket over each child, traced a finger lovingly across their puffy cheeks, and dotted their heads with light kisses before stepping out of the room.

Downstairs, she filled two glasses with ice while Chris removed the tea from the refrigerator. Once they were settled at the small table, still scattered with empty baby-food jars, Chris spoke. "Do you think we need to speak to Sophie? Or at least ask Toots if she's aware of anything going on that we need to know about?"

Abby took a sip of her tea before answering. "I'm not sure. I would hate to go behind Sophie's back, because I wouldn't want to hurt her feelings. But on the other hand, if there is some paranormal activity going on, I would think Mom would know. She and Sophie live, eat, and breathe the stuff."

"Call your mother. Who knows? Sophie could've been in the

midst of some wild discovery and simply wanted you and the kids out of the house."

Abby had her doubts. Her reporter instincts were kicking in, big-time. Whatever was going on at Sophie's house, she would find out.

Come hell or high water, she thought as she drained the last of her tea.

Chapter Seven

Sophie opened her eyes, surprised to find sunlight filtering through the slats from the plantation shutters. She glanced at the clock beside the bed. Nine thirty. "Shit." She tossed the duvet aside and raked a hand through her tangled hair. Her head throbbed when she moved. She'd had one too many glasses of Goebel's spiked strawberry lemonade last night. Looking down at herself, she saw that she was wearing nothing but her bra and underwear, which meant that Goebel must've undressed her and put her to bed.

Taking a deep breath, careful not to move her head too fast, she went to the master bath, where she stripped off what little she wore before turning the shower on, then eased herself under the warm spray. Careful not to jolt her pounding head, she raised her shoulders and let the water release the tension in them. Tilting her head back, she reached for the shampoo on the corner shelf. Being careful not to move too much, she washed her hair and vigorously tried to scrub last night away.

Stepping out of the shower, she wrapped a giant bath towel around herself and a smaller one around her head. She brushed her teeth twice, gargled with mouthwash, then spritzed herself with her favorite body spray, one with a light freesia scent. Wanting to do something yet nothing, Sophie mostly didn't want to face her thoughts, her failure last night. She grabbed a pair of jeans and a red blouse out of the closet and tossed them on the bed while she removed a matching bra and panty set from the bureau. Dressing quickly, she returned to the bathroom, where she combed out her hair and secured the mass on top of her head with a clip. The scent of coffee wafting from the kitchen forced her to speed up, then slow down again as her head began to throb once more.

She went downstairs as fast as she could without jarring her head too much. Goebel was at the stove, stirring something that smelled utterly delicious. "I figured you'd sleep in," he said as she came up behind him and wrapped her arms around his waist.

"You figured right. Damn, how much of that strawberry lemonade did I drink?" She let go of him and poured herself a cup of coffee.

"Apparently more than you should. You and Toots were both snookered. Mavis had to drive Toots home; she could hardly walk." Goebel grinned. "I think I may have forgotten to tell you the lemonade was already spiked. You two gals just kept adding that vodka. I should've said something, but you were both too gone to care by the time I thought about telling you."

Sophie refilled her cup. "You just wanted to get me drunk so you could take advantage of me. I saw I only had my undies on."

"The thought crossed my mind, I won't deny it, but you were too wiped out to join in. Besides, someone snored all night. It was a turnoff."

Sophie felt herself blush. "Did I really?"

"So loud I came downstairs and slept on the sofa," Goebel said as he removed the skillet from the stove.

"I would offer to say I'm sorry, but if you knew that stuff was spiked, and let me add to it, then a night on the couch is justified. Now, Mr. Blevins, sir, I am going to smoke, then you can tell me what it is in that skillet that smells so good."

Taking her cigarettes from the counter, she stepped outside and lit up, still being careful not to move too quickly. Her headache wasn't going to go away easily. After a few puffs, she crushed out the cigarette, then returned to the kitchen, where Goebel had a plate of food waiting for her. He refilled their coffee mugs before fixing a plate for himself.

"What's this?" Sophie asked. She forked into the yellow fluffiness. "Yum, whatever it is."

"That's my New York omelet. Smoked sausage, onions, green peppers, potatoes, and lots of cheddar cheese. I used to make that for myself almost every day. It helped to contribute to all the fat I was carrying around."

Bemused, Sophie looked at him. "And you're feeding this to me, why?" She winked, taking another bite from her omelet.

"Once in a while doesn't hurt. Mavis taught me that. After last night, I figured we could both splurge a bit."

"Why do you say that?" Her senses were suddenly on high alert.

Goebel took a bite and chewed his food thoroughly before answering her. Another habit ingrained in him by Mavis. Chew each and every bite at least twenty times. If she were here now, Sophie would cram the rest of her omelet down Mavis's throat.

He took a sip of coffee. "You were off your game, and you were smashed. I'm figuring you got smashed because you weren't able to connect with this spirit."

Sophie thought about what he said. It made perfect sense but was so far off the mark it was pathetic. "I'm usually able to make contact quickly, but this psychic business isn't scientific. There are no guarantees. I'm just sorry that Daniel didn't get a good scare." She took another bite of her omelet. Her headache was all but gone, for which she was thankful. Not wanting to lie to Goebel because he was her husband, and because she figured they owed each other total honesty, she spoke up without giving away too much. "That's not exactly what went on last night, and at this point, I won't risk trying to pinpoint a particular event that caused me to be off my game, but I think there's a lot more going on. Here. In this house." Sophie watched Goebel chew his food but knew from his expression that he was contemplating her words. He wasn't a man given to rash thoughts, especially anything on a personal level. Professionally, he was a very quick study when it came to making decisions. She let him think. "I'm going to have another smoke. I'll put a fresh pot of coffee on when I'm finished." She took her plate, rinsed it, then placed it on the bottom rack of the dishwasher before stepping out.

Once outside, she lit up, walking down the stone path and inhaling the morning scent of all the hydrangeas. Quiet, just what she needed this morning. Living most of her adult life in New York City, she'd never had much of an interest in growing things or in nature. She had never really cared about it one way or another. But now that she found herself surrounded by the giant oaks, enchanted by the rainbow of flowers scattered throughout the mini-gardens, and captivated by the feel of the soft grass that tickled her bare feet, Sophie craved what she now had and sometimes wondered how she had survived without it.

Calming her racing mind, she stopped to smell the lavender hydrangea bush. *Sweet and intoxicating*, she thought as she stubbed her cigarette out in the empty pack. Figuring Goebel would come looking for her, she hurried down the stone path, blades of freshly mown grass clinging to the bottom of feet dampened by the stones. She wiped her feet on the sweetgrass floor mat she'd purchased from a young woman on one of her many trips to the City Market, her new favorite place in the historical city she was coming to love—as much as one could love a city.

"I thought you'd run off," Goebel called when he heard the back door open.

Sophie returned to the kitchen and wrapped her arms around her husband, placing a quick kiss on his freshly shaved cheek. She inhaled, loving his clean, manly scent. "You smell good. I had to check the hydrangeas, make sure they still smelled good, too. Now, sit and let me make another pot of coffee, or I will kick your ass." Sophie rinsed the pot out, filled the coffee machine with fresh water, scooped Folgers coffee into the basket, then leaned against the counter, facing Goebel, who sat on one of the bar stools around the kitchen island.

"You scare me, you know that? But having said that, I know

what you're doing, Mrs. Blevins. Might as well spit it out and get it over with."

Damn, he did know her, she thought as she watched him.

"What is it you think I need to 'spit out'?" She took the carafe of coffee to the island and refilled both their cups. "I'm not hiding anything," Sophie added.

"I know you're not, but I know you're stewing about something. You always get this certain look in your eyes when you're deep in thought."

"What kind of look?" she asked, trying to lighten the mood before it became somber. She didn't want to explain her suspicions to Goebel just yet.

"Get a mirror and see for yourself."

Sophie didn't have a comeback this time. "Last thing I want to do. I saw myself in the mirror this morning."

"Okay, you don't want to talk about whatever it is that's drawn that curtain across your eyes, so let's talk about something else. Remember those papers I found the other day?" Goebel paused, waiting for her to comment.

"I do. Why? Did you find something else?" she asked, forcing herself to truly listen.

"I did a bit of snooping around on the Internet, made a few phone calls. I wanted to see if I could locate this Ted Dabney, the last ancestor who lived here."

Sophie's heart raced. "And?"

"I found him. I called and left word for him to call me. Seems he's some kind of investment banker, travels the world. I told the woman I spoke with that I needed to get in touch with him, and to make sure she told him it was urgent." Goebel watched her.

"This is good. But why? What do you hope to find out?"

"More of the history on this place, if anything happened here that we should know about. Stuff like that. Plus I want to know about that room upstairs. Your séance room, the bad vibes you're getting."

"Are you telling me you think there's something wrong in that room just because I wasn't able to make contact with that spirit, ghost, whatever it is, last night? Because if that's the case, you're traveling down the wrong path. Goebel, promise me you won't mess with anything in that room. I need it to remain as it is. I know I can make contact with this spirit, but it's not like all the other times. There is more to this woman; she desperately wants to tell me her story, but something is holding her back. I know it. Let me handle this." There, she'd said it. Kind of, sort of. She didn't even want to say the words out loud, fearing the consequences.

"I'm not going to do anything to the room, Soph. We agreed to leave it alone for as long as you want. I don't care if it stays that way forever. I saw you race out of there the other day. I saw you at the top of the stairs. You were frightened, and you don't get frightened easily. I thought it might be a good idea to see if there was an accident in the house. You know how the old plantation homes are. There's always a story to tell, some haunting or dark tale."

"So you're going to just ask this Ted Dabney if anything weird happened here?" Sophie asked.

"I might phrase it a bit differently, but yes, that's what I hope to find out. It was his family home, and he sold it to Toots. I don't think he got rid of it because he needed the money. From what I gather, his portfolio is quite hefty. So that leads me to wonder why he would sell his family home. Why not keep it in the family? Renovate it, let the historical society give tours or something. I thought you'd be pleased to hear this," Goebel said, his tone serious, all business now.

Damn, she thought, she'd upset him, and that was the last thing she wanted to do. "I'm glad you're doing this. If we're going to spend the rest of our lives in this house, then I want to know about the history as much as you do. I just don't want you to make more than you should out of my not being able to connect to the spirit world. And I'm not so sure I would tell this Dabney guy that you're married to me. At least, don't mention my name. As much as I've enjoyed the fame, and helping people, I don't want a bunch of weirdos including me and our home on a ghost tour."

"I promise to keep your name out of the conversation if he calls. He might not, so don't worry about something that hasn't even happened."

He was right, she thought, but there was more. And just saying the words put anyone who entered the house at risk. Which reminded her of her plans for later that evening. "I want to call off the séance tonight. I don't think I've recovered enough physically to do it again so soon. I want to meditate awhile before trying again. Like I said, this spirit is confused, and she doesn't know . . . doesn't know she's dead, at least that is what I believe at this point. She is frightened, and this is new to her, no matter if she's dead or alive in this . . . vision I'm having."

"Sophie, if I didn't know you, I would think you were out of your mind, but I do know you, and I trust your judgment. If you imagine this is what's happening, then I agree. I don't think you're telling me the whole story, and you have your reasons. I can live with that. For now. We can call off the séance, it's fine with me, but I don't want to see you worry yourself sick over this. Maybe we can go to Abby's today, see those two little stinkers. I didn't get to see them when they stopped by the other day."

"No!" Sophie screamed. Calming herself, she lowered her voice. "I mean we can't, because Toots said Abby asked her to stop coming over daily. Said something about family time and all. I don't want to interfere. I know they have to have their space, that's all. We can call her later," Sophie said, hoping to end the discussion. She did not even want to talk about the twins in this house. There was too much at risk.

"Whatever you say, but I would bet Abby and Chris would welcome a break. We could sit with the babes for a bit; maybe they'll want to go to dinner tonight. You should at least ask Abby. Did she tell Toots that applied to her godmothers too? You aren't over there every day."

For once, Sophie wished Goebel would forget about her issues. "Let's go sit in the garden. I need to smell some fresh air and soak up a bit of sun. We spend too much time indoors."

"For you, I will do anything, Soph. But we are going to finish this conversation later. Okay?"

"Whatever you want, Goebel. Whatever you want," Sophie agreed.

At that point, she would've agreed to anything just to change the subject. Until she knew exactly what was going on in this house, no one, and especially the twins, were coming within an inch of it. No, those babies weren't equipped to fight what she knew would be the fight of their lives.

She would fight this or die trying.

Chapter Eight

Toots felt absolutely awful, like she'd chewed cotton and gargled with rocks. She practically had to peel her tongue from the roof of her mouth. Swallowing, trying to moisten her mouth, she rolled over in bed and saw that she'd slept much later than normal. And that was when she remembered last night.

"Oh, damn," she mumbled, glad that Phil wasn't lying beside her to witness her hungover state, glad he'd told her before she'd gotten sloshed that he was going to spend the night at his place in Charleston.

Slowly, she pushed herself into a sitting position and leaned back against the bed's headboard. Seated on the pillow next to her was Frankie. He guarded her like she was the queen of England. She patted his nose. "Give me a few minutes, okay? I think I had too much to drink last night."

He barked three times in response. Toots thought of this as his reprimand bark. "I know, I know, it's not a good thing."

Her head felt as if an orchestra was playing inside, and there was an extra set of drums playing exclusively for her appreciation. She remembered the séance, then going downstairs. She and Sophie had drunk way too much strawberry lemonade laced with vodka, and she didn't remember much after that. Somehow—she had no idea how—she'd managed to make it home with Frankie and crawl into her bed. But that was it. She lowered her eyes to her chest. She still wore the silk blouse she'd had on last night.

She wiggled her toes. At least she'd thought to remove her shoes. She moved her legs against the sheets. Yep, she'd taken her slacks off, too.

Shifting her legs over the edge of the mattress, she eased her way off the bed, careful to walk very, very slowly. The hammering inside her head forced her to stop midway across the room. She waited for a few seconds, hoping to calm the band in her head, but she could tell that this was not going to be one of those hangovers cured by a couple of aspirin and a strong cup of coffee. A soak in the tub was in order. She thought about going outside to smoke first, but it quickly passed. Just thinking about smoking gagged her.

Inside the bathroom, she filled her garden tub with hot water and a sprinkling of her favorite gardenia bath salts. Stripping off her panties and blouse, she lowered herself into the scented water, careful not to make any sudden movements. As soon as she relaxed, her cell phone began to ring. Never knowing who or what it could be, she stepped out of the tub, not bothering to dry off. She must've left the phone in here last night. Toots picked up the phone from the top of the counter and said "Hello" in a none-too-friendly tone of voice.

"Mom, you okay?" Abby said.

Toots breathed a sigh of relief. "Yes and no." She took the phone with her and eased herself back into the warm water. She just might spend the day here, she thought to herself.

"What's that mean?"

"It means I'm okay, but I feel like shit. We were at Sophie and Goebel's last night. To put it simply, I have a bitch of a hangover."

Toots heard Abby giggling. "I hope you didn't drive."

She hoped so, too, but wouldn't voice her thoughts to Abby. "Of course not," she said, trying her best to sound indignant, though it set off the drums once again.

"Just saying—"

"How are my two favorite grandkids this morning?" Toots interrupted, wanting to change the subject.

"They are happy and well fed. I made them eggs this morning, and they loved them," Abby said.

"Not too much, Abby. Remember their cholesterol."

"They're babies, Mom. They need protein. And you're one to talk about good eating habits? Give me a break."

"True, but don't start them out with bad habits. Remember, I started drinking coffee when I was twelve, and look at me now."

"And you're just fine, Mom," Abby said. "I didn't call to discuss bad eating habits."

Toots perked up, instantly alert. "Is everything all right?" Hearing the alarm in her voice, Frankie hurried down the ramp they'd had made for him after his back surgery. His toenails clicked against the oak floors as he scampered to the bathroom. Toots blew him a kiss.

She heard Abby's intake of breath. "I'm not sure. I mean, we're all okay, but there is something I've been meaning to discuss with you, but the timing is always off."

"I'm all ears now if this is a good time," Toots said, amazed that her headache had receded to a dull throb.

"I guess. I wanted to talk face-to-face, but I don't think that's gonna happen anytime soon. Here's the thing. Is there anything weird going on at Sophie's? Something she doesn't want me to know about?"

Toots shifted the phone to her other ear. "Not that I'm aware of. I mean, yes she believes there is some kind of . . . *woman spirit* hanging around her place, but I'm sure she isn't trying to keep this a secret. We were there last night, she had a séance, trying to make contact. Why, is there something going on that I don't know about?"

"You just answered my question. At least I think you did. Tell me about this *woman spirit*. What's her story?"

"Nothing really. Sophie says there is a ghost in her house that hasn't crossed over to the other side. Apparently she believes this ghost is asking for her help, but the ghost isn't taking it just yet." Toots found it very easy to discuss ghosts and anything paranormal these days. Ten years ago, she would've been scared out of her mind. Having a best friend who is a psychic really changed her attitude.

"You're sure that's it?" Abby asked. "She's not hiding anything from you?"

Toots swirled the water around with her foot. "Nothing I'm aware of. Of course, if she was hiding something, I wouldn't know, would I? But truly, I don't think she is. She wasn't able to make contact with this ghost last night. I'm guessing she's upset about that, but it would only be a guess. I haven't spoken to her since last night, and we were both a bit inebriated."

Abby laughed, but Toots could tell her heart wasn't in it. "There's more, isn't there?" she asked her daughter.

"Yes and no. Here's the gist. I was there the other day with the twins. We stopped by. Sophie wanted to show me the table you gave her, the one in the séance room."

"Yes, she really liked that table," Toots commented.

"We weren't there but a few minutes, and I swear, the twins started acting odd. They acted like they were looking at something that only they could see. Their little heads were moving from side to side, like they were watching a game of tennis. I asked Soph if there was anything going on in the room, and she told me there wasn't. Then, when she saw how the kids were behaving, she hurried me out of the room. When we were at the top of the landing heading downstairs, Amy and Jonathan started screaming. I mean really screaming. No tears, it wasn't a normal cry like they needed to be changed or were hungry. They were frightened of something they saw. I know they were. Then Sophie grabbed my hand, and I swear she almost caused me to fall down the darned stairs. I was holding Amy, she had Jonathan. She practically tossed us out the door. I didn't even get a chance to say hi to Goebel. It was like she couldn't wait to get me out of her house. It made me feel weird since Sophie's usually pretty up-front about everything she sees."

Toots flicked the drain with her foot, stood up, and grabbed a bath towel off the rack. "Hold on, Abby." She wrapped herself in the towel, then went back to her bedroom, with Frankie at her heels. "Okay. I was in the tub and had to get out. You're right. This isn't like Sophie."

"She hasn't mentioned anything at all, not even a hint about this to you? I thought she'd run over and tell you right away. You know how she is."

Toots contemplated her daughter's words. Yes, she knew Sophie, and this was very much unlike her. "Do you want me to talk to her? Because I can. I'm sure she didn't mean to . . . to chase you off. Maybe she and Goebel had plans, and she didn't want to be rude. No, forget I said that. Sophie thrives on being rude. Doesn't matter who it is, either."

"I'm not sure if either of us should say anything. Maybe Sophie was just having a bad day. Maybe I popped in at a bad time. It wasn't like I had an invitation."

"You don't need one with Sophie or Goebel," Toots observed.

"That's what I've always been led to believe."

Toots peered out the window, deciding she'd make a trip to Sophie's as soon as she dressed. If something was going on, she wanted to know what it was. "I'm going over there."

"Mom, promise me you won't . . . just feel her out first. I may be overreacting. It's just that I've never seen the kids scream like that. Pure, bloodcurdling screams. They were afraid, I'm telling you."

"A mother knows her own children, that's true. I believe you, Abby. Now, let me go, so I can get over there. If something sneaky is going on, I intend to find out."

"Okay, I'll wait to hear from you," Abby said, then clicked off.

As soon as Toots hung up, she hurriedly dressed in a pair of khakis and a navy blouse. Sliding her feet into a pair of denim Toms shoes, Toots ran a brush through her hair before racing downstairs.

In the kitchen, she filled Frankie's bowl with kibble, which she knew he wouldn't eat because he was spoiled by Mavis's chicken, but in case he decided he wanted it, it was there. She freshened his water dish with bottled water, then poured herself a large to-go cup of coffee, grabbed her smokes, and hurried to the garage. Toots slid into the Lincoln, cranked over the engine, then backed out of the garage. She hadn't seen a soul around the house, and wondered where Bernice was and what she was up to. The coffee was made, so she was around somewhere. Probably off delivering a new recipe to Robert. The two were glued together at the hip but in a good way.

She wheeled out of the gates, then headed toward Sophie's. Though she didn't remember much from last night, she did remember the séance and its lack of results. Toots hadn't put her heart in the evening's event because her mind had been elsewhere. George Spector, a major newspaper mogul, had made an offer on the *Informer*, the L.A.–based tabloid she owned. It was a decent offer, and he'd even said Abby could return as editor-in-chief anytime. Sure that Abby and Chris wouldn't be packing up and moving back to the West Coast anytime soon, Toots was seriously considering the offer. She hadn't told Abby or Phil yet. She hadn't made any promises one way or the other. Of course she would discuss this with Chris and Abby before making a major decision, but not now. *Later*, she thought as she pulled into Sophie's drive. Right now, she was on a mission to find out what in the hell was going on with Sophie.

She turned off the ignition and remained in the car for a few minutes, giving herself time to gather her thoughts and decide what she would say to Sophie. She didn't want her to feel as though she were being blindsided, but as a mother and a grandmother, there was no way in hell Toots was going to dismiss Abby's story without at least trying to find out whatever it was that Sophie apparently didn't want her to find out. With that thought in mind, she opened the car door, not even bothering to remove the keys from the ignition. The odds of anyone's stealing her old Lincoln Town Car were slim to none, especially in this neck of the woods.

She hurried to the front door, knocked lightly, then pushed the door open. "Sophie? Goebel? It's me. If you're naked or doing anything you don't want me to see, now would be the time to bring it to a halt." Toots couldn't help but laugh. She doubted they were in a compromising situation, but she had to give them fair warning.

"In here," Goebel called. "I was just making another pot of coffee. Sophie's outside smoking her weed. Want me to get her?"

Toots surveyed the scene in the kitchen. The room was nice and tidy. Sophie and Goebel had really modernized the kitchen without taking away the uniqueness of the past. The sink was solid brass, as it was before, only now polished like a shiny penny. Dents in all the appropriate places made the sink look as genuine as it must have been in its day. The cabinets were original and had been restored to their natural oak luster. Goebel had ordered customized knobs to match the brass sink. Herbs in brass pots were scattered along the windowsill. Sophie had followed Toots's pattern for the kitchen curtains, only hers were forest green and white checkered, rather than the red and white that Toots had in her own kitchen. Matching seat cushions covered the old pine chairs that Goebel had found at an estate sale and refinished himself. The place looked like an honest-to-goodness home, and for that Toots was thrilled, as she knew that neither Sophie nor Goebel had ever really lived in an actual house. Both of them had grown up in apartments. She was glad she'd hung on to the old place as long as she had.

"No, I smoked on the ride over. I will take a cup of coffee, though," Toots said as she removed a cup from the cupboard above the coffeemaker. "You two still brewing that cheap old Folgers stuff?" she asked as she filled her cup.

Goebel snickered. "We are. You're welcome to bring that expensive stuff of yours over anytime, Toots."

"Yeah, you can, you cheap old woman," Sophie called out as she entered the kitchen through the back door.

"Cheap old woman, my ass!" Toots parroted.

"I know you hoard that coffee, I've seen you hide it from Bernice," Sophie said.

"And Bernice couldn't care less, too," Toots added, wondering why in the hell they were discussing coffee. She cleared her throat. It was time to get down to business.

Sophie poured a cup of coffee for Goebel and one for herself. She nodded toward the table. "So, what brings you over here on a morning when by all rights you should have the hangover from hell? It can't be for more of that spiked strawberry lemonade we had last night." Sophie pulled out a chair and sat down. Goebel eased into the chair next to her.

Toots found a spot across from the couple. She wanted to see Sophie's expression. She could read the woman like a book. If there was something going on in this house, and Sophie was lying about it, Toots would know just by the expression on her face. They'd been friends since they were twelve years old. It was a rare moment, when something really important was at stake, that either of them could get away with telling a lie, or even a half-truth.

"No, I didn't come over here for that shit. I was so drunk, I don't remember leaving here last night. Did you do that on purpose?" She took a sip of her cream-filled, sugar-laced coffee.

Sophie laughed. "I don't recall forcing you to drink the stuff." Sophie turned to her husband, questioning, "Did I?"

"Did you what?" he asked.

"Force her?"

He chuckled. "Not that I saw. I think you both had way too much to drink. I have to take the blame, too. I saw you adding vodka and didn't have the heart to tell you the stuff was already loaded with enough liquor to knock out an elephant."

"Then it is your fault that I felt as if I gnawed cotton balls all night, and it is also your fault that an orchestra decided to set up shop in my head this morning, too. For that alone, I ought to smack you upside the head with one of those shiny pots." She motioned to the rack above the kitchen's island. "But I won't since I'm not one for violence." Toots smiled and took another sip of her coffee.

They all laughed. "I'll make sure to inform both of you the next time I decide to spike the punch," Goebel promised.

"Sure you will," Toots said dryly.

"Okay, now that we have all of the bullshit out of the way, tell me why you're really here. You're not here for the coffee, that much I know. You cringe every time you take a sip." Sophie said all of this while staring Toots directly in the eye.

Toots looked down at her slacks, swiped at an imaginary thread, then returned her gaze to Sophie.

"Is it that obvious?" Toots asked.

"Yep. It is."

"You can see right through me, huh?"

"Not in the literal sense, but I do know you're here for something that seems urgent to you."

That's putting it mildly, Toots thought.

It was now or never. "Abby called me this morning." She let her words hang in the air, waiting, hoping that Sophie would take the bait. A few seconds passed. Toots realized she was going to have to tell her exactly what Abby had relayed to her as Sophie continued to stare at her, her dark brown eyes two deep pools of mystery.

"You talk to Abby every day. Why are you telling me something I already know?"

She wasn't making this easy, but it had to be said. "Abby thinks there is something going on in this house. She said you practically tossed her out the other day when she stopped over with the twins. She told me that Jonathan and Amy were frightened, scared out of their wits, and they were screaming, yet they didn't shed a tear. I'm hoping you have an explanation for this." There! She'd said it. Now all she had to do was wait for Sophie's version of events, not that she didn't believe Abby. No, that wasn't the case at all. Toots knew she would get the truth from Sophie even if it wasn't what either of them wanted to hear.

Sophie's expression changed from one of neutrality to dread. Toots recognized the look, one she'd seen more than once on her friend's face. The atmosphere in the kitchen went from jovial to ominous in less than a second. Goebel's features hardened, his dark eyes suddenly sharp, assessing. This alone told Toots there was something major going on.

"So, what do you have to tell me?" Toots asked.

Sophie drew in a deep breath, exhaled, then nodded. "Yes, there is something going on, you're right about that. Or Abby is. We can't pull anything over her eyes anymore, especially since she's become a mother. Not that I'm trying to deceive her, it's just . . . there is something here in this house. I am not exactly sure how to phrase my suspicions."

Toots perked up. "I can't believe that you of all people are at a loss for words."

"It does happen, though only on very rare occasions," Goebel added.

"Yes, it's rare for me, we all agree on that." Sophie nodded, then looked at Toots. "I am almost afraid to voice what I'm experiencing. Not that I don't want to tell you, but I'm fearful that if I put what I suspect into words, this will somehow validate my suspicions even more."

Toots drew her brows together. "Call me slow, but I don't understand."

"You're not slow, Toots. You know better. Well, at least not all the time," Sophie added, her full lips tilted upward in a slight grin. "No, forget I said that. Seriously, this is something that I have to deal with my own way and in my own time. I'm not avoiding telling you, really. You'll just have to take my word and trust me on this."

More than frustrated, Toots spoke up, "I do trust you, but I need answers, Soph. My grandkids felt frightened in this house. I have to know why. If you can't tell me, then I will . . . I'll hire someone to come and find out. Do a cleansing on this place, whatever the hell it needs."

The three remained silent, all of them lost in their own thoughts for the moment. Words weren't necessary as they all knew something had to be done, and it had to be done now. As soon as possible. Though Goebel and Toots weren't one hundred percent sure exactly what had scared the twins so badly, they knew that Sophie did and that time was running out.

Something must be done before two innocent babies were put in harm's way again.

SPIRITED AWAY

Chapter One

"You're serious?" Toots asked. "You won't tell me?"

Sophie drained the last of her coffee, then walked over to the sink. She rinsed out her cup, placing it in the dishwasher. "It's not that I don't want to tell you, Toots. I can't. I don't feel right about this, and you know what happens when I have one of my feelings and I don't listen."

True, Toots thought. Her friend Sophie's intuition, gut instinct, psychic abilities, whatever she currently sensed, must be acknowledged and taken very seriously. Sophie was always spot-on, and as much as she didn't want to acquiesce, she didn't really have a choice. Frustrated, Toots glanced at Sophie, then rested her gaze on Sophie's husband, Goebel. "Has she told you about any of this?"

"No, and I am as curious as you are. I know it has something to do with this house; though what, I can't say. I can tell you this. I did contact the great-great nephew of the original owner; he's some hotshot financial guru. He's out of the country right now, but I e-mailed him in hopes that he will have some background on this old place. It was in his family for more years than I can count. Maybe he knows about something that might've happened in this house." He looked at Sophie. "Something she knows and doesn't feel it's safe for the rest of us to know." Goebel was only guessing, but he knew his wife. She rarely kept things to herself when it came to her psychic abilities. She wanted to help others, to share her experiences, to offer comfort to those who sought out her services. Sophie was a giver, despite the hard-ass exterior she displayed to the world. "I'm surprised you don't know anything about the property. You owned it yourself for years. As much as you enjoy decorating, learning the histories of all the antiques you've bought, I would have thought you of all people would know if something . . . *bad* happened in this house."

Goebel was right, Toots thought. And normally she would, but she'd purchased this house when she and her friends were in California and had been so occupied with running the *Informer* and trying to keep her daughter, Abby, from discovering that she was the new owner of the newspaper, that she hadn't thought too much about the history of the old house when she'd purchased it. Now, she wished she had taken the time to hire a professional to research that history, though she knew this wasn't as hard as she was making it. The historical society would know, and she was a member. Indeed, her own home was on the national historical register, too. She was sure all she needed to do was make a few phone calls and she could find out anything she wanted about the house's past. Though she wasn't sure if she should. If Sophie refused to divulge her fears, then Toots might want to listen to her and stay out of it.

"What?" Sophie asked Toots. "I know you and that evil mind of yours. Go on, spit it out."

Taking another deep breath, Toots nodded. She would not deceive Sophie, not now. For once, she was truly going to listen to her and stay out of things until she was told otherwise. "I never bothered researching the history when I bought the place. I was thinking I could call the historical society, and they might know what, if anything, *untoward* happened in this house. But then I changed my mind. That's all."

"You're sure?" Sophie asked.

Toots had to resist the urge to cross her fingers, but she remembered her twin grandchildren and kept both hands splayed out on the table in front of her just in case she was tempted. "One hundred percent."

Sophie gave her the eagle eye.

"I swear I won't call anyone or do anything that would put Jonathan or Amy, or any of us, in harm's way. I'll leave the ghost stuff to the pros."

"Well, then it's settled. You won't do anything until I say it's clear. Tell Abby . . . tell her—shit, I hate to lie to her, but right now I think it's for her and the twins' protection. Tell her we found a . . . a carbon monoxide leak in the house. Yes! I'll tell her that's why I acted so strange—I'd breathed in too much carbon monoxide, and it affected my thinking. I can say I just found out the day she brought the twins over. It will at least keep her away, plus it will give me time to, uh, work on the problem." Sophie didn't dare voice what she knew. Not yet.

"I don't like lying to Abby," Toots stated.

"Oh for Pete's sakes! You lied to her for years about owning the *Informer*! Why in the world would you even question telling an itty-bitty lie that's for her safety and the safety of her children?"

Goebel laughed. "She does have a point, Toots."

"I know."

"So, are you going to tell her, or do you want me to tell her?" Sophie demanded. "We need to do this as soon as possible so we can put her worries aside and get on with . . . with whatever it is I need to do."

Toots pondered the question. It was probably best if she let Sophie handle things. "You tell her. Go to her house today. Explain that you were . . . embarrassed or something. Tell her you felt like an idiot for not having the old place checked for carbon monoxide leaks before moving in. Make it sound sincere and grovel a bit. Abby always gives in when groveling is involved. At least that's what Chris has told me. I've never seen it from her personally, but as her husband, he knows a side of her that we don't. I hope that he does not see it too often."

"I can't see Chris groveling for any reason, but if you think this will get me off the hook, then I'm willing to do whatever is necessary to keep her and those babies out of this house."

"And what about the rest of us?" Toots asked. "Should we stay away, too?"

"Yes, I think it's best that you and the gang stay put until I think it's safe. Tell the others the same story. I was always told when you have to lie, to keep it simple, so tell them I was stupid and simply neglected to have the place checked out. Ida won't have any trouble believing you. She lives for any opportunity to throw me under the bus. This will make her day. Now, I have to go to Abby's, and you, my dearest and oldest friend, have to make damned sure no one comes over here. Can you do that?"

Toots shot her an icy look, but nodded. "Yes, yes, I can keep everyone at bay, though I would really like to tell them you have syphilis of the face, but they won't believe me."

They all laughed, but beneath their laughter were ominous and foreboding undertones. They went their separate ways with thoughts that were too dark to share.

Chapter Two

Teresa waited for Sophia at the entrance to the lunchroom as promised. Since it was her first day at a new school, and Sophia was the only one to show her any kindness earlier in the day, she figured it was worth waiting. Yeasty bread scented the air, reminding her of the lone piece of toast she'd had for breakfast. Her stomach grumbled, and she looked around to make sure no one heard. She would just die. The students would think she came from a poor family and didn't get enough to eat. But, really, she thought to herself, why did she even care?

"Hey, Red, I was hopin' to find you here," Sophia called out in a voice so loud that the entire cafeteria went silent for a split second.

"Yeah, I waited," was all she could come up with.

"Then let's go see what crap the nuns cooked up today. For the record, the food ain't all that bad here. Beats the hell out of the shit they serve in the public schools. Or at least that's what I heard."

Teresa wanted to ask her where and from whom she'd heard this but decided it didn't matter. What mattered was they were about to be fed.

"You got a lunch ticket, I presume?" Sophie asked as they entered the cafeteria.

"Uh, sure. My mom prepaid for the entire year." God, she sounded stupid! She was sure it was not cool to pay for a year's lunch in advance.

"That's good. Bring your lunch when you don't like what's on the menu, then you can sell your lunch ticket to the highest bidder for cigarette money." Sophie stopped and looked over her shoulder. In a none-too-quiet voice she asked, "You do smoke, right?"

Feeling her face turn as red as the Jell-O being served, she gave a quick nod and prayed Sophia would forget this one-sided conversation.

They each took a pale green plastic tray from a large stack at the beginning of the lunch line. Forks, knives, and spoons were in metal bins next to the napkins. Teresa carefully chose a clean set of flatware and took two napkins even though there was a handwritten sign taped to the napkin holder that read Take Only One! She was messy and didn't care. Tomorrow, she would grab a few napkins from the house before she left.

"You breakin' rules already, I like that," Sophia said. "I do what I want, when I want. Screw 'em." Sophia laughed.

Teresa wanted to disappear, but no one else seemed to care that Sophia talked like a sailor, so she would go along with the others. Maybe Catholic school wasn't going to be that bad after all.

"Sophia, you will report to my office the moment the lunch bell rings." A tall woman dressed in a full nun's habit smacked Sophia on the knuckles with a wooden ruler as she held out her lunch card to be punched.

"For what?" Sophia challenged, and again, Teresa wanted to die right there on the spot. Maybe she would choke to death on the red Jell-O that'd just been placed on her tray.

The nun, whose name Teresa had yet to learn, took Sophia by the arm. "I can see you haven't changed much, young lady. That foul mouth of yours will land you in detention all year if you're not careful. We do not say 'screw 'em' in this school. Do you understand, Miss De Luca?"

"Okay, but what should I say instead of 'screw 'em,' Sister Mary Rose? Fu—"

"Don't you dare!" Teresa said before she could stop herself.

Sophia turned to look at her. She grinned. "For you, I won't, but still." She turned back to Sister Mary Rose. "What should I say instead? Is there another way to say 'screw 'em'?"

"You are holding up the line. Remember, my office, young lady. Now move along." The nun gritted her teeth before taking her hole punch in hand and reaching for Teresa's lunch ticket.

Teresa didn't know whether to follow this wild girl or if she should simply find some other plain, boring girls to have lunch with. She scanned the cafeteria and decided Sophia was her best bet.

They sat at the end of a long table in the back of the cafeteria. The orange plastic chairs looked new and out of place in the otherwise old lunchroom. Brick walls, which undoubtedly held secrets of sinners past, took up an entire side of the room, while across from it was another entire wall of windows with a view of the side of the church. Teresa wasn't sure if this was a good sign or not, but wouldn't worry about it just now. Sophia motioned for her to eat, and her stomach gave up a low growl as she picked up her fork.

"Eat," Sophia told her. "You sound hungry."

She laughed. "Yeah, I didn't have much for breakfast." For some reason she didn't have a problem admitting this to her new friend.

Lunch consisted of meat loaf, mashed potatoes with brown gravy, and mixed peas and carrots. Warm yeast rolls with a pat of butter on a little piece of white cardboard. Then, of course, there was the red Jell-O. Teresa thought the meat loaf much tastier than her mother's, but didn't say this out loud. She didn't want to seem weird or stupid. Her dad always told her it was best to keep one's mouth shut when you didn't really have anything to say, and that's what she was doing.

For the next five minutes, both girls ate heartily, drank their white milk, and kept their thoughts to themselves. When they finished they took their trays to the kitchen window, where they dumped what little was left on their plates into an industrial-sized gray garbage can, then placed their flatware in a large tub of soapy water. Then Sophia motioned for Teresa to follow her outside.

Not sure this was a good idea, Teresa spoke up. "Aren't you supposed to go see the Sister after lunch?"

Sophia stared at her as though she had two heads. "Are you kiddin' me? Tell me you ain't serious? Hell no, I am not going to see Miss Virgin Mary Rose!" She pulled a pack of Camel unfiltered cigarettes from the inside of her blouse, then removed a pack of matches from the inside of her shoe. Without looking to see if they were being watched, Sophia lit up and inhaled like this was something she did all the time. It had to be, Teresa thought, because she blew the smoke out of her nostrils just like some women did on television, only Sophia lacked the swanky, long cigarette holder many of those women used.

Sophia held the pack out to her. "You want one?"

"Uh, no . . . not here. I will later." Hopefully, later would never come.

"Really? I don't see how you can be a smoker and not want to smoke after you eat. It's the best time for me. I don't give a shit where I'm at. When I wanna smoke, I'm gonna." She continued to hold the pack out to her.

What the hell, Teresa thought, she drank coffee like an adult, and she was in the seventh grade. She might as well take up smoking, too. "I hear ya," she said, trying to act as nonchalant as possible. She'd never put a cigarette in her hand, let alone in her mouth. If her mother found out she'd tried smoking, she would have a heart attack. "I think I'll have that cigarette now."

Sophia lightly shook the pack and took a cigarette between her full lips, and used the end of her own cigarette to light Teresa's. She took a drag, then passed it to her. Knowing that Sophia was watching her, Teresa held the cigarette between her middle and index fingers, brought it to her lips as she'd seen in the movies, then took a big puff. Before she knew what had hit her, she began to cough, her eyes watered like a garden hose, and the taste was about as bad as anything she could remember. Through all the hacking and coughing, she managed to keep her hold on the cigarette. Sophia grinned, but kept quiet. No way was she going to pass herself off as a serious smoker if she kept this up. Drawing in a shaky breath, she took another puff, though this time, she just held the smoke in her mouth rather than inhale. A couple seconds later, she blew the nasty smoke from her mouth in the shape of a nice, neat grayish white cyclone.

"Well done," Sophia said.

Teresa gave up a slight cough before nodding, then said in a gravelly voice, "Uh, thanks." She really didn't know why she was thanking her since this new habit was beyond disgusting. But no way was she going to voice her thoughts. She'd get used to the taste. Just like the coffee she consumed at Woolworth's. It was too bad she couldn't lace the cigarette with cream and sugar.

Leaning against the brick wall on the side of the building, Sophia motioned for her to look at a pair of girls lingering near the steps that led to a door that would take you to the main office. "Think those two are in deep shit or what?"

Teresa followed Sophia's gaze to the two. "They look like they're lost. I don't know about the deep . . . *shit* part," she said.

"Let's go rescue 'em," Sophia instructed, not giving Teresa a chance to reply.

Teresa eyed the two girls as they walked across a small patch of grass, then a few feet down the sidewalk. One girl was short and a bit pudgy. Her hair was cut so short that if she hadn't been wearing the required skirt, Teresa would have thought her a boy.

The other girl looked like a goddess. Her platinum blond hair was as straight as a ruler, her blue eyes the color of the sky. She was neither too tall nor too short, neither too heavy nor too thin.

They approached the girls, and Teresa could see that they were completely scared out of their minds.

Chapter Three

"You let me tell her. I don't want you involved in my lies any more than necessary," Sophie told Goebel on the last leg of the drive to Abby's house.

He shook his head as he turned into the driveway. "I won't. This is your gig, sweet cheeks."

"Sweet cheeks? Where in the hell did that come from?" Sophie asked, as they got out of the car.

"I was remembering something, that's all," Goebel said. "I don't think now is the time to get into all the details."

"Sure, you say that now, but just so you know, I won't forget," Sophie added, as they walked up the steps leading to the front door.

"I'm sure you won't," he said just before the door opened. Apparently, Abby had seen them pulling into the long driveway.

"Sophie, Goebel," Abby said as she stood aside to let them enter. "What brings you two over?"

Like her mother, Abby had made Chris's father's plantation into a true home despite its size and the fact that they were running Dogs Displaced by Disaster, a major veterinary clinic, on the grounds now. Seen from the outside, one would not know that the insides of the former slave quarters were equipped with the latest medical devices, used by top-notch vets from across the country and a team of volunteers that would make the Peace Corps envious. Abby walked with Sophie and Goebel past the chairs and side tables, which were strategically placed in what they used for the main living area that led to the kitchen, which, again, as in her mother's house, was the heart of the Clay household. Toys were scattered about the floor, but this only increased the feeling of hominess.

"I just put the twins down for a nap," Abby said as she indicated their two high chairs, covered with the remnants of an early lunch.

Goebel spoke first. "Yep, I think we both would like to see those rascals, but we understand. Right, Soph?"

"Uh, sure. Little ones need all the rest they can get," Sophie commented.

Abby took a wet cloth from the sink and began wiping down the high chairs. "Sorry, if I don't get this stuff off here now, it sticks, and it's a real pain to clean up once it does that. If you all want some sweet tea, I just put a fresh pitcher in the refrigerator."

"No, I'm fine," Sophie said, wanting to get this over with as quickly as possible. "Your mother came by this morning."

Abby stopped what she was doing, tossing the damp rag across the back of the high chair she'd been cleaning. She focused all her attention on Sophie. "And?"

Sophie cleared her throat and glanced at Goebel, who gave her an encouraging nod. "The other day when you came by the house"—she saw that she had her goddaughter's undivided attention—"I was rude, and I apologize for that. And I am so very, very sorry the twins were frightened; your mother told me they were terrified of something. I just wanted to tell you the day you stopped over I'd just learned the house was full of carbon monoxide. I wanted to get you and the little ones out of the house as quickly as possible."

Abby sat down on a chair opposite Sophie. "Then why didn't you just tell me that? I thought something weird was going on in the house."

Sophie took another breath. *Keep it simple, remember. Keep it simple.*

"I'd just found out and was . . . embarrassed that neither Goebel nor I had thought to have the place checked before we moved in."

Abby looked at Goebel for confirmation. "Yes, we really didn't even give it a thought," he added, further adding to the believability of Sophie's lie.

"We think it's coming from one of the fireplaces, but we can't be one hundred percent sure until we have the place thoroughly checked out. It could take a couple of weeks to do this, and then, of course, depending on what they find, it could be much longer with repairs and all. I just wanted to tell you this so you and the kids would be safe."

Abby smiled. "Why do I feel like you're not telling me everything?"

Because I'm not a very good liar, Sophie thought.

"You are just like your mother, you know that?"

"And you're stalling, you know *that*?"

"No I am not! I just wanted to stress the importance of you all staying away from our house until we get the clearance from the . . . company."

"Where will you two be staying while the repairs are made?" Abby asked.

Shit! She hadn't even thought of that. Of course, if there'd truly been a carbon monoxide leak, they, too, would have to leave the house.

"We're staying at a new bed-and-breakfast in Charleston," Goebel interjected. "We thought it would be a good idea. The B and B is right around the corner from our office."

"Yes, and we are about to go there now," Sophie informed her. "So kiss and hug the kids for us, and I'll keep you posted." Sophie stood up and walked to the front door, Goebel and Abby trailing behind.

"Sure," Abby said to their backs as they practically ran out the front door. "Call me when the coast is clear," she shouted.

Goebel turned to give her a final wave while Sophie raced to the car.

Once they were safely ensconced inside the car, Sophie started talking a mile a minute. "I can't believe I didn't think of that. What the hell are we going to do now? I don't know of any new bed-and-breakfast by the office. I'm sure that Abby will check, too. She knew I wasn't telling the truth. The girl has a lie radar just like her mother and me. I need to call Toots so she can cover our asses should Abby call." Sophie took her cell phone from her pocket and punched in Toots's home phone number. Toots answered on the first ring.

Toots spoke without bothering with a greeting. "Abby just called and said she was coming over as soon as the twins wake up from their nap."

"Damn! I knew she would call you the second we left. I can see I was right. Listen, we told her we had that carbon monoxide leak, and now we've added to the lie."

"Oh shit, what is it this time?" Toots asked.

"Damn, you sound like I go around telling frigging lies all the time! Don't make me remind you that you're the liar in our group," Sophie hissed.

"You know what I mean," Toots said. "Now tell me what I need to know so I can keep Abby and my grandchildren safe. Listen, if we think of it this way, lying doesn't really seem all that bad. Plus, we really don't want to put them in harm's way no matter what the source of the harm is, right? Doesn't have to be carbon monoxide. It can just as easily be something . . . unknown."

"Damn, Toots, you have this all figured out, don't you. Now listen and don't interrupt me. Goebel and I are in the car now. We just left Abby's. She thinks we have to stay out of the house until this so-called leak is found and repaired. Goebel"—Sophie gave him her best evil eye—"told Abby we were staying at some new bed-and-breakfast that just opened up around the corner from our office. When she comes over, you have to cover our asses. Tell her you just called and insisted we stay with you. This way, we can still remain close by in case we are needed. Does that even sound half-assed plausible to you?" She spoke so fast she was out of breath. Sophie paused, waiting for Toots to come up with a better plan.

"I think it will work, but what if she drives by your place and sees that no one is there? No repair vehicles in the drive?"

"I hadn't thought of that. I should have just told her the truth . . . no, forget I said that."

"No, I won't. You haven't told *me* the truth, Sophia; I can't imagine why you would even consider telling Abby, given what you say is at stake."

Goebel turned into the gates that led to Toots's mansion. "We're at your house. I'll finish this conversation inside." She hit the END button on her cell phone.

Sophie focused her gaze on her husband. "Toots mentioned something about repairmen, said Abby might drive by the house, and what will I tell her if she asks why there are no vehicles in the drive?"

Goebel parked directly in front of Toots's house. "The woman thinks of everything."

"Yes, she does, and for once, I am glad. Now let's go inside and figure out our next move."

Chapter Four

"This is the expensive coffee you two hate, the two-hundred-dollar-per-pound stuff I get from the Philippines. Want me to scrounge through the pantry and see if I can find some of that cheap stuff you drink?" Toots asked while she waited for the coffee, *her special coffee,* to finish brewing.

"No, we can lower our standards, but just this once," Sophie said as she grabbed Toots's pack of Marlboros from the counter. "I'm going to smoke first. Want to join me?"

"Sure," Toots said, then followed Sophie out the back door, and, as was becoming the norm, Frankie, Toots's dachshund, followed her outside.

As was customary, they sat on the steps, and Sophie lit two cigarettes and offered one to Toots, just as she had since they were girls.

"So, is there something you want to tell me that you don't want Goebel to hear?" Toots asked after she'd taken a long draw from her smoke.

Sophie thought for a few seconds before answering. "Not really. Why would you think such a thing? Goebel and I don't have secrets, at least none that I know of."

"I just thought you might have something to tell me, you know, something about the house that you didn't want him to hear. Let's just say I was hoping," Toots added.

"I don't, that's just it. I have a very strong suspicion about what's going on." Sophie crushed her cigarette out in the sand-filled coffee can that was in its usual place beside the steps. "The thing is, if I voice what I suspect, it will only make it worse."

"Good grief, Sophie, do you realize what you just said makes absolutely no sense whatsoever?"

"Yes, and that's what I'm trying to say without saying just what the problem is. This kind of . . . wickedness shouldn't be spoken of, because it only makes what I suspect even stronger. I really wish I could tell you more, but trust me on this, I am keeping quiet for your own good, and, of course, for Abby and the twins. Hell, it's for everyone's own good."

"Even Ida's?" Toots asked, her voice tinged with humor.

"Even that old biddy," Sophie replied. "Seriously, this is bad, probably the worst . . . phenomenon I've been up against since all this ghostly stuff started. I just wish I knew what to do." Sophie's last words communicated her insecurities, her lack of experience in handling this new situation.

Toots turned to stare at her, lit another cigarette, handed it to Sophie, then lit another for herself. She took three long puffs, blew the smoke in Sophie's face, then spoke. "Okay, I think I may know what you're referring to."

Sophie shook her head, "Somehow, I doubt it, Toots. This isn't ghostly stuff."

"Let me just say this, and you don't have to say a word because I will know by your expression whether I'm hitting the nail on the head or not." She took another puff, then tossed the butt in the can. She didn't bother to crush the cigarette out because there wasn't much left to burn. She knew she was stalling, but she wanted to get this out of her head, *needed* to get it out of her head. "This issue, that's what I'm going to call it for lack of knowledge, okay? Now, this issue you think you may have at your house, would it require the services of a . . . clergyman?"

Sophie stood up, surprised and more uncertain than Toots ever remembered seeing her. She appeared to wrestle with some inner demon. "Let's go have that coffee. It smells good even if it is that expensive shit you pay a small fortune for."

Toots reached for her arm and pulled her away from the door. "I'm right, aren't I?" she inquired, and she knew it. Instantly, she felt Sophie's fear.

"Please, Toots, let's not speak of this again. Not until . . . I'm sure. Can you swear to me right now that you will not mention the word *clergyman*, *reverend*, *preacher*, *priest*, or anything remotely close to a religious scholar to anyone? Not even your friend Phil, Bernice, or God help us, Ida. Mavis, too. This would only frighten her." That was putting it mildly, Sophie thought, but for now, it is what it is, and she didn't have time to pussyfoot around.

"I promise." Toots placed her hand over her heart, something they used to do back in high school when they knew that they were being entrusted with something of such great importance that there had to be a physical show of their comprehension. The hand-over-the-heart gesture had been the choice then, and Toots could only hope that Sophie remembered what it meant.

"I'm glad you understand. Now, let's go inside and have that coffee. Do you have any pralines from the bakery?" Sophie asked as she stepped back inside the kitchen.

Ever since Toots had purchased the Sweetest Things, a down-on-its-luck bakery owned by Jamie, a young woman without a family whom they'd all taken under their wings a few years ago, they all expected Toots to have a variety of sweets when they came for coffee. Pralines were their specialty. The bakery, rather Jamie, had won numerous awards for her pralines, and it was all they could do to keep up with the supply and demand. The bakery's success far surpassed any of their expectations. The Food Network had called last month, inviting Jamie to bake on one of their shows. Another thriving business, thanks to Toots.

"If Bernice didn't take them all to Robert's, I'm sure we must have a few."

Inside, Goebel was seated at the table with two cups of coffee, one for Sophie and one for Toots. He had the half-and-half, the sugar, and he'd found the pralines she had stashed in the pantry in a large plastic container. "Something tells me you two need something sweet to go with this caffeine."

"As usual, you're right on the money," Sophie agreed as she sat down next to her husband. She took a praline off the plate, then took another and placed it on the plate across from her. "Eat this, Toots. You look like you've just seen a ghost. Scratch that. You *have* seen a ghost. More than once. You look like you could use a stiff dose of sugar." She pushed the plate across the table so that Toots could reach it. "Go on, your blood sugar needs a spike."

Toots took a bite of the praline, then washed it down with a gulp of sugar- and cream-laced coffee, just the way she liked it. "Yes, that was just what I needed."

Toots watched Goebel and knew that he was watching how she and Sophie were interacting with each other. "I don't think I've had anything to eat since dinner yesterday," Toots said, just to make conversation. "Of course, I had all that booze at your place last night, probably way more than a woman of a certain age should have, so this is good. I need sugar. Lots of sugar."

"You're rambling, Toots. It's not like you to ramble on and on," Goebel acknowledged. "Are you sure you're all right?"

Toots observed Sophie as she glanced back and forth between her and Goebel, as though she feared what Toots might say.

"Yes, I'm fine. Shit, Goebel, I haven't had anything in my system but alcohol and caffeine. I'm just a bit shaky, really. Sophie saw this when we were outside smoking. That's why we came in, right?"

"No, we came in because I smelled coffee, then when you sat down and I looked at you, I decided you needed a pick-me-up because you really look your age right now."

Had the situation not been of such importance, Toots would have flipped her the bird. But this was not the time to act like . . .

themselves, she thought. No, it was the time to let Sophie do whatever she needed to do, but because Goebel was watching her, she stuck her tongue out, then said, "Kiss my old wrinkled ass."

In a voice that reeked of false bravado, Sophie said, "Hey, isn't that Bernice's line?"

"If it is, then I'm claiming it as mine right now; that is, if you, Mrs. Blevins, approve?"

Toots was trying for lighthearted and fun, but she wasn't sure if she was successful because no one was laughing.

"I suppose Bernice wouldn't mind, but I know for a fact your ass isn't wrinkled," Sophie added, catching on and trying to keep the conversation from getting too serious.

"When did you see my ass?"

"More times than I care to remember."

"Gawd, that's really disgusting, Soph. Have you been spying on me or something?"

Out of the corner of her eye, Toots saw Goebel grin as they bantered back and forth. This was good, this was what she'd been striving for.

"No, I haven't been *spying* on you. I've lived around you long enough that I've had a few peeps. Now, let's leave it at that, okay?"

"What's okay?" Bernice called out as she and Robert entered through the back door.

Sophie shot Toots and Goebel the *look*. "Nothing that concerns you."

Frankie came trotting downstairs, searching for the source of the noise. Coco, Mavis's Chihuahua, trailed behind him. The two were best buds when Chester, Abby's German shepherd, wasn't around.

In her late seventies, and two years after major heart surgery, Bernice looked better than she had in years. And she knew it, too. Robert, her newfound love interest, followed her around like a lost puppy. "You are rude, Sophia. Did anyone ever tell you that?"

"Never," Sophia replied in her best smart-ass voice.

"Then let me be the first," she retorted. "What's going on?" Bernice took the empty carafe from Goebel and brought it to the sink, where she rinsed it out, then refilled it. She emptied the coffee grounds, then refilled the basket with more of Toots's premium blend.

Robert, ever the dutiful boyfriend, remained by the back door. "Get in here. You look silly just standing there like a statue," Bernice ordered. "Sit down for a minute. We're going to have a cup of that fine coffee you like so much." She shot Toots an I-dare-you-to-say-a-word look while waiting for Robert to sit down.

"Yes, do make yourself at home, Robert. What's mine, after all, is Bernice's," Toots said sarcastically. Toots was sure Bernice caught the dig. When Robert and Wade had purchased the house next door, Bernice had led them to believe that she owned this house, and that Toots was a guest. They'd cleared that up quickly, if she remembered correctly.

Bernice gave Toots the bird, a habit she'd picked up when the girls came for their first visit to Charleston all those years ago. It was their version of a kiss-my-ass sort of salute.

"No need to bring up the past, Toots. If it weren't for me, this place would be a mess. I don't remember the last time I saw any of you load the dishwasher or mop these hardwood floors, or shine all these windows." She finished her speech, then turned her back on them while she waited for the coffee to finish. "And I know you took the stash of pralines Jamie brought over last night, too. Those were for a special occasion."

"Stop your whining, Bernice. Jamie makes pralines daily, and we can get them anytime. And what was your special occasion, anyway?" Sophie singsonged.

"I'm not telling anyone just yet. Right, Robert?" She looked at Robert, who just sat there with a grin as wide as the moon.

"Yes, dear," he said obediently, and the grin on his face got even wider.

Toots shot up out of her chair like she had springs on her derriere. She grabbed the pot of coffee before Bernice had a chance to pour Robert and herself cups. "You're not getting any of this stuff until you spill the beans. I hate keeping secrets."

Goebel and Sophie looked at her as if she'd lost her mind.

"Yes, Bernice, you know how we all deplore keeping our private lives private," Sophie added.

Toots brought the pot of coffee to the table. "I didn't mean it that way. I meant we always tell one another when there's something special going on in our lives." She circled the table, refilling their mugs with coffee.

"Don't say one word, Sophia," Toots murmured as she filled her dear friend's cup. "Got it?"

Sophie rolled her eyes, taking a sip of her coffee. "This is disgusting. It tastes like elephant poo."

"How would you know what elephant poo tastes like?" Toots innocently asked.

Goebel snickered, and Robert joined in. Bernice shook her head disapprovingly.

"It can't be any worse than this crap. It amazes me how some people think of something as gourmet, like this stuff, and another, such as myself, classifies this as crap. And, no, I have not tasted elephant poop, but had I, I'm sure it would taste like this coffee."

Goebel spoke up. "Ah, Sophie, don't be too hard on Tootsie. Remember those slimy raw oysters you eat. I, for one, am sure they taste like snot."

When Toots had envisioned lightheartedness, she truly hadn't thought of elephant feces, but it took the attention away from the malevolent force that lurked in Sophie and Goebel's home. "I agree, Goebel. You couldn't pay me enough to put one of those nasty-looking things in my mouth," Toots said, just to keep the diverting conversation rolling along. "Now, Bernice, are you going to tell us what your secret is, or are we going to have to beat it out of you?"

"You're so darn nosy, Toots. When the time is right, Robert and I will tell you. For now, just forget it," Bernice said.

Toots wasn't going to argue with her or try to drag it out of her, at least not now. There were far more important issues to deal with. Whatever Bernice and Robert's secret was would simply have to wait.

The back door slammed, and they all turned to see Ida, minus Daniel. "What things are we putting in our mouth today?" she asked, clearly having been there for a few minutes, or at least long enough to hear that part of their conversation.

"I think we should be asking you that question," Sophie said. "And speaking of things, where is your boy toy today?"

As was the norm, Ida was dressed to kill. Not a single strand of platinum blond hair dared to stray from her perfectly cut bob. A walking advertisement for Seasons—her line of cosmetics and skin-care products that had put her name alongside such icons as Estée Lauder and Coco Chanel—she looked svelte, confident. Today she was wearing a mint-green sheath dress that hugged curves that would rival those of a twenty-year-old, and matching high-heeled sandals. A slim coral wristlet dangled from her slender arm. The only mar on her otherwise unblemished appearance—her coral lipstick was smeared on her lower lip.

"I see you've got sex on the brain as usual," Ida commented dryly. "Goebel, is she not woman enough for you?" Ida asked, then winked.

"I see you're still a slut," Sophie shot back. "Don't even think about coming on to my husband, Ida. He doesn't like women like you anyway," she added with a smirk.

"Women like me?" Ida chirped. "Exactly what would that be?"

Toots took control of the conversation before the two started another verbal war. "Both of you put a cork in the festering holes beneath your noses, okay? We've heard all of this before, and it never, ever leads to anything positive."

"She's right. You two need to kiss and make up," Goebel said.

Sophie's eyes about popped out of her head. "Make up, maybe. Kiss, never!"

Ida sat in a chair next to Toots. She took a praline from the plate in the center of the table, crammed it in her mouth, oblivious to the shocked expressions on everyone's face, then repeated herself. "What are you all staring at? Haven't you ever seen a woman enjoy something sweet?" Ida asked, then, before they could answer, she took another handful of pralines and proceeded to cram them in her mouth, one after another, barely chewing them before she swallowed. She reached for Toots's mug of coffee, downed what remained, then slammed the mug down. "What? Why are you all staring at me?"

Sophie was the first to speak. "I've known you for more than fifty years. In all those years, I have never, *ever* seen you display such a lack of manners. What in the hell has come over you?"

With pieces of praline stuck to her chin and mouth, Ida seemed to really consider Sophie's question. "I think I should be the one asking you that question. I was just at your place, and it looked like a tornado had gone through it. The kitchen cabinets were open, broken dishes were scattered all over the kitchen floor, and the smell was atrocious. You should take more pride in your home, Sophia, but now that you mention it, ever since I left your house, I've felt strange, a bit disoriented. I hope I don't catch a bug from your nastiness."

Chapter Five

Tuesday, September 6, 1955
Bishop Verot Catholic School
New Jersey

"What makes you think they want to be rescued?" Teresa asked her new and only friend.

Sophia dropped her smoke on the sidewalk and stomped on it. "Look at 'em. They look like they're scared shitless."

Teresa laughed. Sophia sure had a way with words. For this reason alone, she wouldn't invite her home. At least not yet. Tomorrow, she might change her mind. One thing was for sure—seventh grade wasn't going to be nearly as boring as she had thought only that morning.

"If you say so," was the only reply she could come up with. She watched the pair. They did look a little frightened. Maybe, like her, they were new to this school.

"Follow me," Sophia instructed.

Together, they strode across the schoolyard, stopping when they reached the two girls. The tall blonde with perfectly even features recoiled in obvious fear when she saw them. The other girl, short with strawberry-blond hair, a round face, and eyes that sparkled with mischief, grinned, then took the tall blond girl's hand in hers. "Hi," she said in such a friendly way that Teresa liked her immediately.

"Hey," she said, then held out her hand the way her mother taught her to do when introductions were made. "I'm Teresa Loudenberry and this"—she nodded to Sophia, who was busy scrutinizing the two—"is Sophia De Luca."

The girls stared at one another for a few seconds before the strawberry blonde broke the silence. Following Teresa's lead, she held out her hand. "I'm Mavis Chapman, and this is Ida. This is our first day of Catholic school."

"Mine too," Teresa said, just to reassure the pair. They did look a bit on the shaky side.

"Yeah? Well, it ain't all it's cracked up to be. I mean that in the worst way. The nuns suck, the curriculum is way behind the public schools, and the boys are mostly stupid, except for Kip Alderson. He's smart and will help you cheat on math exams if you pay him enough. Last year his going rate was two bucks. Might be more this year since we're gonna study algebra." Sophia smirked, then went on, "The only decent thing about this crap hole is the food."

The blond girl's mouth dropped open, and the other girl, Mavis, placed a hand over her mouth to muffle a soft giggle. "I'm not very good at math," she replied in a sugary-sweet voice.

"Then you'll want to hook up with Kip before he's bombarded with all the class cheats. There's a lot of 'em, too," Sophia said. "What about you?" She looked at the tall blonde. "You got a last name?"

Ida rolled her eyes. "Of course I do. It's Spencer. Like the actor, Spencer Tracy."

"Well, that sure as hell makes you special," Sophia blurted.

Ida Spencer's already pale features turned a shade lighter. "That's a mean thing to say."

Sophia laughed. "Ah hell, I'm just messin' with you. Look, take my advice. If you wanna get by in this shit-hole school, you're gonna have to take a few punches. You hang with me, and I'll show ya the ropes. Of course, if you'd rather hang with the likes of Kip and his gang of pantywaists, then by all means, do, but everyone will think you're a lezbo."

Ida's face went from pale to flaming red in a split second. "Why would you say such a thing?"

Teresa wondered why, too, but waited for Sophia to explain herself.

"Hey, I'm just tellin' you girls how it is. You're either with me, or you're not. I ain't gonna force any of you, that's for damned sure!"

Mavis spoke up. "You've always gone to Catholic school?"

"Yep."

"Then I think we need to follow Sophia's advice. Let her show us the ropes. What about it, Ida?" Mavis asked in the most adult-like manner.

Ida looked to Teresa, then back to Mavis. "I suppose it's okay, but I just want you to know I am not a . . . *lezbo* and just because you're friends with someone . . . like that, doesn't mean you're the same way!"

Sophia clapped her hands and laughed. "Well said, my new friend, well said."

Teresa thought Sophia acted like a girl twice her age, and she liked that. The girls in her sixth-grade class had all acted like babies. Suddenly, she was very glad that her parents had insisted on sending her to Catholic school. Somehow, she just knew these girls would all play important roles in one another's lives. But there was no way she would ever reveal this to her parents. Let them think she hated school. If they thought she liked Catholic school, they might insist she return to her old school. Well, not really, she thought, but she wasn't taking any chances.

Taking charge of the conversation, Sophia asked, "Any of you have math class next period?"

They all looked at the schedules they'd been assigned and nodded.

"Then you're about to meet the meanest nun of them all. Sister

Clara Marie. She's older than dirt and can't hear, or at least she acts like she can't. But try whispering in the old bat's class, and her hearing is supersonic. And forget passing a note. She has eagle eyes and can see even when her back is to the class.

"She thinks she's Isaac Newton, or maybe even Einstein, but her class has been the same forever. She's an easy A if she likes you; if not, well, you're fu— . . . screwed."

"Why do you use such foul language? Aren't you afraid one of the nuns will hear you?" Mavis asked Sophia.

They all laughed, except for Ida.

"I think it's very tacky to use profanity," Ida remarked.

"Frig 'em," Sophia said. "They all cuss. I've heard it. Whore. Bastard. Ass, though minus the hole. They're not the perfect creatures they pretend to be, trust me on that. Wait till you spend a few days in detention; you'll hear all of them cussing."

Ida spoke again. "I don't plan to get a detention, so I will have to take your word for it. You didn't answer my question, though. Why do you curse so much?"

All eyes were on Sophia as she contemplated her answer.

With a mischievous glint in her dark brown eyes, Sophia said, "Because I can, and I like to see the reaction I get." She laughed out loud.

Teresa joined in, and couldn't help but admire her new friend. She had guts, she'd give her that.

Taken aback at Sophia's honest answer, Ida spoke up, but in a friendlier tone this time. "Oh, well, don't expect me to join in. I find it very distasteful." Ida raised her perfectly shaped eyebrows.

"Five bucks says you'll be cussin' like a sailor before the end of the term." Sophie held out her hand to Ida, which Ida quickly shook before yanking her hand away as if she'd been burned.

"I don't have germs," Sophia said. "You need to relax that Miss Manners shit. It ain't gonna score any points with the nuns, if that's what you're thinking."

Teresa and Mavis giggled, then the bell rang, letting them know they had exactly three minutes to get to math class.

Sophia hid her cigarettes and matches while Teresa blew her breath on her hand to see if she smelled like smoke. Ida and Mavis followed them as they rushed to their lockers, all located within talking distance of one another. Sophia grabbed a well-worn book from her locker, then turned to the three girls, who seemed to want to follow her lead. "Let's meet here after school. We can walk home together."

For a few seconds, the other girls said nothing, then all three nodded their agreement. Little did they know this would be the beginning of a friendship that, literally, would last a lifetime.

Chapter Six

"What were you doing in my house? I didn't give you permission to just . . . go inside and roam around! What the hell did you think you were doing?" Sophie flew out of her chair and began pacing the length of Toots's large kitchen, almost tripping over Frankie. "Dammit, Ida, you should know better! I swear, I can't trust anyone these days!"

Frankie ran around in circles, barking up a storm. He knew that Sophie was very upset. After she leaned down and gave him a pat on his long back, he wiggled over to his favorite spot under the dining-room table.

Goebel, knowing why Sophie was acting like she was losing it, raced around the table and took her hand. "Soph, you're not being reasonable. Calm down." He gave her back a reassuring pat, mimicking what she had done with Frankie, then kissed the top of her head. Whispering in her ear, he said, "Remember, we don't want to divulge what you suspect."

Sophie nodded, then pushed away from Goebel. "Why were you at my house in the first place?" She *had* to know.

Ida, who appeared more out of sorts than Sophie felt, shrugged, hoping to hide her confusion. "I can't seem to remember. I had to . . ." She searched the faces around her for guidance. "I'm not sure." Stunned by her own words, tears trailed down her cheeks like two silver ribbons. "What is happening to me?"

The kitchen became so quiet, you could've heard a pin drop. Sophie knew what Toots was thinking and vice versa.

"You've had too much sugar," was all Toots could come up with. "Whatever the reason you went to Sophie's, it doesn't matter. You're here now, and I think we need to . . ." Toots hesitated. "We need to propose a toast. Yes, that's it, so let me find that good bottle of booze I put away." She hurried to the pantry, knowing all eyes were on her as she hustled around in search of the booze. Seconds later, she was back with a bottle of Glenfiddich, a bribery gift she'd received via FedEx the day after George Spector made his offer on the *Informer*. She tucked the bottle beneath her arm and grabbed a stack of red Solo cups off the shelf. All eyes were on her as she lined up six cups in a neat row. She opened the bottle of whiskey, filling the cups with a generous amount of the smooth single malt.

"Robert and I will not be drinking that stuff this early in the day, so don't bother," Bernice said casually as she sipped her premium-blend coffee. "We have an appointment this afternoon. I don't want to show up drunk as a skunk."

Robert just smiled and nodded his agreement.

For once, Toots was glad for Bernice's crudeness. "And I suppose this has something to do with the secret you're not quite ready to share with us?" Toots inquired.

"Who cares?" Sophie said, then winked at Toots. "I say let's get snookered and forget about Bernice's stupid secret."

Both Toots and Sophie knew what Bernice's response would be.

"I'll sew my lips shut before I tell you now," Bernice shot back. "Robert, don't you say one single word!"

"Yeah, Robert. Don't think for yourself. Let Bernice. She knows everything," Sophie added before taking the red Solo cup and another for Goebel. "Ida, are you going to share our toast?"

Again, Ida appeared befuddled and confused. "What are you talking about? *Toast?* I don't eat carbs, you know that!" She crammed the last praline down her throat and reached for the red cup.

Clueless as to what she'd planned to toast, Toots held her red cup high in the air, and announced, "To Phil. May his new medical thriller be a bestseller!" *Lame, lame, lame*, she thought. It would happen, just as Sophie predicted, but he didn't know this. Two weeks from now, when it hit the stores, he would be in for the surprise of his life.

Sophie and Goebel raised their cups high in the air.

"To Phil," they cheered.

Ida chugged her scotch in one long swallow as if it were water, then slammed her cup down. "Give me another one."

Sophie glanced at Toots. Both knew things were getting way out of hand.

"You don't need another drink, Ida. We're going to . . . to . . ." At a rare loss for words, Toots searched her mind for something, anything to explain herself. And she hadn't a clue what the hell she was trying to explain. "Sophie is going to read for us. Right?" Toots winked at Sophie, and she nodded.

"Read a book?" Ida asked. "Why in the world would she do that? We're not children!"

Toots's eyes doubled in size. "Ida, I want you to listen to me, okay?"

Ida nodded.

"Have you had anything to drink this morning, other than this?" She nodded at the bottle of scotch. "Any pills or anything?"

Again, Ida appeared confused. "Not that I recall. Look, I don't know what has come over me! I felt fine this morning when I drove Daniel to the airport." She ran her hands over her face. "I feel just fine!"

"Bernice, call Dr. Pauley and tell him I need him to make a house call. And make sure you say STAT!"

"Oh for Pete's sake! You don't need to call the doctor. There isn't anything wrong with Ida. She's just pretending to be stupid— no wait, maybe she's not," Bernice cackled. "But then again, Daniel seems to think she's the greatest, and I want to agree, but I don't know." She let her last words dangle in the air.

"Dammit, Bernice, why do you have to be so . . . ornery? Sophie, should we have Dr. Pauley take a look at Ida?"

Sophie's dark brown eyes circled those seated around the table, stopping on Ida. "No, not now. I'm going back to the house to check on that mess Ida mentioned. I think it's a good idea if we all meet back here, let's say in"—she glanced at her wristwatch—"an hour. I have some leftover lasagna Goebel stuck in the freezer. We can have lunch together."

"Good idea. Bernice, why don't you make a salad? Robert, you're good with bread. Find a loaf in the freezer and make us something tasty. Jamie keeps us loaded with breads, and it's time we started eating the stuff. Ida, I need you to . . . help me upstairs. I need your advice on what to wear to Phil's book-launch party. Do you feel up to that?"

Ever indignant, Ida replied, "Of course I do! I am an expert!"

Toots, Sophie, and Goebel all smiled. This was more like the Ida they all knew and loved. But they'd never tell *her* that.

Chapter Seven

Sophie wished like hell that her old spiritual mentor, Madam Butterfly, was still alive to advise her. She hadn't given much thought to the good-versus-evil stuff, except for where Walter, her deceased husband, was concerned. While he was a bastard of the highest order, he wasn't evil in the true sense of the word. He was just a nasty old jerk who'd delighted in tormenting her. No, this was something far greater than being mean in spirit.

There were signs to look for, and so far she didn't see any that were totally off the rails. Ida was acting beyond strange, and Sophie knew this was just a small physical change, and that in itself wasn't too alarming at this point. Ida could just be whacking out, too. She was over seventy years old. Not that that was old, but Sophie didn't know if early dementia, or early-onset Alzheimer's ran in Ida's family. Before she jumped to conclusions, she had to investigate further.

She'd converted the *spandrel*, the empty space beneath the staircase, into a home office of sorts. Though she would have liked more space, she liked the total privacy the area offered. She kept all of her psychic reading materials here, along with a few treasured items she didn't want to display to anyone. One of those private treasures was a book given to her by Madam Butterfly. It didn't have a title or a known author. Sophie had never opened the book's yellowed and fragile pages. When she'd received the book as a gift all those years ago, she'd known without Madam Butterfly's telling her that it was to be put aside, and she would know when it was time to open the well-worn brown leather cover and read its contents.

Handwritten, in a spidery scrawl, the first page read: *The Roman Ritual.* Of course, she thought as she carefully turned the page. Being Catholic, she'd heard of this book, but had never really given it much thought. She knew it contained rituals that were hundreds and hundreds of years old, rituals that were performed daily in the Church, such as Baptism, Communion, and Mass. She held the ancient book, handwritten in both Latin and English. Cautiously, she turned the page, and began to read. Half an hour later, she was startled by a light tap on the door, and she quickly closed the book, returning it to the mini-safe where she'd kept it since her move to Charleston.

"You ready to take this lasagna over to Toots's?" Goebel asked.

Sophie turned off the desk lamp and gave the narrow space one last look to make sure everything was as it should be. She felt creepy now, as though she had somehow been tainted by a source of true evil. "I'm ready," she said, and stepped out into the formal living area. Sophie had yet to see the disaster in the kitchen, and had told Goebel just to get what he needed and get out. As soon as she felt ready, she would tackle whatever entities had destroyed their kitchen.

Goebel held a green reusable Publix shopping bag in one hand and a jug of unsweetened tea in the other. He refused to drink sugar-sweetened tea since he'd lost so much weight. He didn't force his good eating habits on Sophie the way Mavis tried to, but she now found herself a bit more conscientious about her eating habits since they'd married. Grateful for the interruption, Sophie hurried out the front door, with Goebel following close behind. "Make sure you lock the door," she called out to him as she headed for the car. If by some odd chance someone had broken into the house, at least with the doors locked, they would have more of a challenge this time around.

She watched as Goebel juggled the bag and the tea so he could lock the door behind him. He swiftly made his way to the car, then placed the items on the backseat. "You don't look so hot, Soph. Did something happen that I need to know about?"

She took a deep breath before answering. She'd never told him about Madam Butterfly's gift, and wasn't sure if it should be revealed or not. Didn't matter, she thought. She would simply wing it, and whatever she said would be said and not taken back. "I got super creeped out when I was in my office. You know that little safe I have?"

He nodded. "Yeah, I've seen it but figured if you wanted me to know its contents, you would've told me."

"There's nothing in there but a few keepsakes, really. Nothing important, well, except for this book." She waited a sec for him to ask what book. He didn't, so she continued. "You remember my telling you about Madam Butterfly?"

Backing out of the drive, Goebel looked in his rearview mirror. "Wasn't she that psychic woman who told you all those years ago that you had the gift?"

"The one and only," she said, looking at him as he drove. "She gave me a book—actually it looks like more of a journal than a book. Leather-bound, and the pages are much bigger than normal."

"You're stalling, Soph. What gives with this book?"

"Have you ever heard of *The Roman Ritual*?"

"Yeah, sort of. Isn't that a book used in the Catholic Church, something to do with sacraments?"

"Something like that. Madam Butterfly gave me this book, and it's all handwritten, in both Latin and English. It contains the Holy Sacraments, the Sacrament of Baptism, and Confirmation. In chapter thirteen there are four sections on exorcism." She actually whispered the last word.

Goebel took his gaze from the road and looked at her like she'd lost her mind. "Sophie, did you just say what I think you said?"

She had known that this was going to happen. No one liked

that word—hell, it scared the bejesus out of her—but it is what it is, and she had to tell someone. "I did. Madam Butterfly told me that I would know when the time was right to read this book. As soon as Ida started acting like . . . like an idiot," she said because she didn't dare voice what she really wanted to call it. "Well, let me just say that I thought it was time for me to take a peep at that book. I did, and it frightens me, Goebel. Truly. It scares the living daylights out of me." Sophie took a deep breath, hating that she'd burdened him with this evil, but she had to tell someone.

He didn't say a word, yet she knew he was thinking about what she'd just told him. When he didn't have answers, he wouldn't say a word until he'd thought things out. She liked this about him because it made her feel as though whatever she said must mean something to him as well.

"You don't want to voice what you're thinking, am I right?" he asked as they arrived at Toots's.

"You know me well, don't you?" she asked.

He pulled the car around to the back of the huge Southern plantation home, then shut off the engine. "I like to think so. I am your husband. Isn't it part of my job to know what's going on in that beautiful little head of yours?" He took her hand in his and gave a reassuring squeeze.

She was so damn lucky to have this man in her life. She smiled. "It is. And you're very good at it, I might add."

"I am a work in progress," he said. "Seriously, Sophie, are you okay with this? Do we need to see a priest or something?"

"No!" she exclaimed, perhaps a little too emphatically. "Promise me something, okay?" She had to fight to control her emotions just then.

"Anything," he agreed.

"Don't use that word around Ida and the others. It brings up . . . bad images when . . . just don't mention anything about *this*."

"You don't want me to talk about priests because . . ." Goebel appeared confused, too.

"Damn, I don't want to say it out loud, but it looks like I need to. Toots said the same words earlier, and I warned her not to voice this . . . evil to anyone until I came up with an answer. Priests, evil, the Roman Ritual. I don't need to spell it out for you, now, do I?"

"Exorcism? Is that the word you don't want to hear?" Goebel asked.

Trembling, all she could do was nod.

Chapter Eight

Goebel's cell phone rang. "Hello? Yes, this is he. I appreciate you calling. Of course. I'm not sure. Let me ask my wife." He covered the cell phone with his free hand. "This is Ted Dabney, the great-great-nephew I told you about. He's in town for the night. Said he wants to meet with us, and asked if we would join him for dinner tonight?"

A million thoughts swirled through her brain. No, she did not want to see this man, but she had to. "Sure. It's not like I have much of a choice, is it?" she answered.

"I can go. You stay here with the girls if that will make this easier for you."

It would, but that would be taking the coward's way out, and she was a lot of things, but she was not a coward. "No, tell him we'll meet him for dinner. Just name the time and place. I need to talk with this man."

Goebel spoke into the phone. "Yes, we can meet for dinner. How about seven o'clock at Cristof's? Sure, see you then." He clicked off and took her hand. "Look, you don't have to do this. I can ask whatever needs to be asked. It's not like this has anything to do with . . . Ida. We want to know the history of our home, right? That has nothing to do with Ida's problem."

He was so wrong, and she told him so. "That's where I think all of this is originating. My dream, then the crushed smokes, the twins' being frightened the other day. And now Ida's acting so out of character after a visit to our house. I'm afraid it does have something to do with the history of the house."

"If you say so, then I agree. You're rarely wrong with this stuff. Now, why don't we put it out of our heads for a bit? Let's go inside and have lunch, okay? We'll deal with this together, I promise."

Again, she couldn't believe how lucky she was to have this man by her side, especially at her age. She leaned across the console and cupped his face in her hands. "I love you. Have I told you this today?"

He smiled. "Now that's the girl I know and love. For the record, I can't remember if you told me or not, so why don't you tell me again?"

"I love you, Goebel Blevins."

"Ditto, Sophie Blevins. Ditto. Now, let's go inside before they come looking for us. Toots will accuse us of having sex in the car."

"Nothing she herself hasn't done a time or two, trust me on that," Sophie observed as she opened her door.

"I'll take your word for it."

Goebel grabbed the tea and lasagna from the backseat. Sophie whipped out a cigarette, took a few puffs, then crushed it out in the coffee can next to the back-door steps. Before she opened the door, she turned to Goebel. "Remember when you referred to me as 'sweet cheeks'?"

He nodded his head. "I do."

"Exactly what did you mean?"

Goebel chuckled. "You have a nice rear end."

"Oh," was all she said before entering the kitchen.

The kitchen was a hubbub of activity. Bernice was at the sink washing lettuce leaves while Robert smeared a loaf of French bread with fresh cloves of garlic and olive oil.

"Get that in the oven if you want to eat before three. It's pre-heated," Bernice called out.

Goebel took the dish of lasagna from the bag and slid it onto the middle rack in the oven. "Done," he said. "What can I do to help?"

Robert, normally quiet as a mouse, spoke first. "You want to find some garlic powder in the pantry for me? I looked and can't find it, though Bernice swears it's there, except that she can't find it, either."

Sophie laughed at Robert's sudden burst of words. "Wonders never cease. Goebel, have a peep. You're taller than Robert, so you can see what's on the top shelf."

Goebel nodded and headed to the pantry.

"Where are the others?" Sophie asked Bernice.

"Ida is supposed to be helping Toots look for something to wear, but they've been up there ever since you left. I called up the stairs about fifteen minutes ago, but they never answered. They probably got lost in the closet. I've never seen a woman with so many clothes. And shoes, too. Every time she runs to the store for something, she comes back with another pair of shoes. She's gonna have to build another place just for her shoes if this keeps up."

Tapping her fingers against the countertop, Sophie couldn't wait to rush upstairs to see for herself what was going on. "That's nice, Bernice. I'm going up to check on them." Sophie raced up the stairs before Bernice could stop her.

She stopped when she reached Toots's bedroom. The door was closed, so she gave a light knock. If they'd decided to take a quick nap, she didn't want to bother them. She knocked a second time, then Toots opened the door. She held an index finger over her mouth, indicating silence, but motioned for her to come inside.

"Follow me," she mouthed.

Sophie trailed behind Toots as she led her to the master bathroom. Whispering, she said, "She won't come out and doesn't want me to come in, but I can see inside. You need to take a look at this." Inching away from the door, Toots stood back so that Sophie could peer inside the huge master bath. From her position just outside the door, she could see Ida. She was in a fetal position in the middle of the floor, surrounded by a puddle of urine. When Sophie saw this, she knew there was no time for questions. She had to act, and she had to do it now. "Ida, let's get up now!" She entered the bathroom and hooked her arms under Ida's as she tried to lift her.

"Come and help me, Toots. She's as limp as a rag doll."

Toots raced to her aid. "I've been trying to coax her out, but she's been totally unresponsive but not in a 'call the medic' way. This isn't good, is it?"

Together, they hoisted Ida into the Jacuzzi tub, uncaring that they were both standing in urine. "No, this is not good. Help me get her clothes off."

Sophie was remembering a time when just the thought of anything unhygienic near Ida would cause her to freak out and disinfect everything around her. She did not want her to fall back into her old OCD habits.

"You get the shoes," Sophie instructed. "I'll work on the dress." Together, they removed Ida's clothes, and neither of them spoke. When they'd finished, Toots took the cup she used to rinse her mouth out with after she brushed her teeth and filled it with warm water. "Let me rinse the tub out first," she said. A few cups of water later, Toots closed the drain and began to fill the tub with water. During all of this, Ida hadn't said a single word, hadn't moved a muscle. *The living dead*, Toots thought, but didn't voice the words. She didn't know if Ida's ability to hear was affected at this point.

"Hand me a washcloth," Sophie instructed.

Toots raced to the closet, where she kept a full supply of large, fluffy bath towels and washcloths. She handed one to Sophie, amazed at her ability, but remembered that she had been a nurse and this came natural to her. Later, she would tell her how impressed she was.

"Do you have any bath gel?"

Toots reached across the Jacuzzi tub for the bottle of gardenia-scented bath gel she used. She squirted a large amount in the center of the washcloth. "This will make her smell human again."

Sophie nodded, then proceeded to bathe Ida as if she were a

newborn. Her ministrations were precise and gentle. Toots observed how efficient and caring her dear friend was. Someday, she would have to tell Ida how Sophie cared for her, but not today.

After she rinsed the gel away, Sophie gently pulled Ida into a sitting position. "Help me get her feet over the tub, then, on the count of three, let's lift her out. It's okay if we put her in your bed?"

"Of course it is," Toots said.

Five minutes later and a bit short-winded, they had dried Ida, and Sophie managed to put one of Toots's nightgowns on her.

"So, what's next?" Toots asked, knowing this was just the beginning.

"I want her to wake up, and I'm not really sure how to go about doing this. I think we should allow her to wake up naturally, see if she's in her own mind, then go from there. You're okay with leaving her here for a while?"

Toots shook her head. "I can't believe you'd even ask me such a stupid question. Ida's one of us even though she is a bit on the weird side. Of course she can stay here. Forever, if that's what it takes."

Sophie rolled her brown eyes toward the ceiling, then genuflected. "And let's pray that it doesn't. A day with Ida is pure hell."

Toots laughed. "I'm sure you'll remind her of that when she wakes up. Seriously, Soph, shouldn't we be doing something? I don't want to say the word, but don't you think it's time we called in a . . . specialist?"

Sophie whirled around so fast she jarred her neck. "We are doing something, and if you so much as whisper that word, I will kick your ass from here to California and back. Round-trip. I'm going to take care of . . . this"—she nodded at Ida, who had remained motionless on the bed the entire time—"as soon as she's awake. Now, aren't you supposed to be helping out with lunch?"

"Is this your way of telling me to get out of my own room?" Toots asked.

"Yes, now go. I have a few things I need to do, and I really do not want an audience." Sophie stood by the bed, one hand gently resting on Ida's head.

"Okay. Give me a shout if you need anything. And I mean anything, Sophie," Toots said, the last words filled with total sincerity.

Drawing a deep breath, Sophie shook her head. "I know that. I just need to spend some time alone with Ida right now. I have an idea, and I need to focus."

Toots understood and left the room.

As soon as the door closed Sophie walked to the opposite side of Toots's big bed and hoisted herself onto it. After propping the pillows up and leaning against them, she took Ida's hand in hers and began to pray.

Chapter Nine

Bernice served the lasagna, giving Toots a portion that would feed three people at the very least. Toots, unsurprisingly, didn't have much of an appetite. But for appearances' sake, she took a few bites. "When will Daniel return? He might be the only one able to reach Ida at this point." As soon as she came downstairs, Toots had explained Ida's condition without giving away what they really suspected. She didn't want to frighten Bernice or Robert.

"I'm not sure. He's going to that attorney thing, a conference or something. Abby said Chris was going, too," Bernice explained.

Toots looked at Goebel. "Is that true?"

"I think he mentioned something about going the other day when we spoke. Said if he wanted to offer pro bono services, attendance was required for those practicing in the state of South Carolina."

"Abby told me that Chris was going—at least I think she did. It doesn't matter now. What matters is . . ." Toots wanted to say something about Ida's soul, but knew this wasn't the time or the place. Instead, she said, "I think now would be the perfect time for Bernice to reveal her big secret, don't you?" She aimed her question at Goebel.

"I told you I wasn't going to tell any of you," Bernice shot back. "You're all too darn nosy, I swear."

Robert cleared his throat, wiped his mouth with a paper napkin, then reached for Bernice's hand, and said, "Dear, I think maybe we should let them in on our little secret. They will know soon enough, don't you agree?"

Bravo for Robert, Toots thought. About time he spoke up for himself. Still, she couldn't help but smile. He and Bernice were such an unlikely pair, but apparently their love of recipes and one another was much stronger than she'd first imagined. They were an adorable couple, but Toots wasn't about to tell them that.

"Oh hell, I suppose we should," Bernice offered up. "I think we should at least wait until Daniel returns."

Goebel chuckled. "Makes one wonder what you two are up to, that's for sure. Don't you agree, Toots?"

She couldn't help it. She wore a grin the size of the moon. "I do. They're not very subtle, if that's what you mean. Just tell us and get it over with, Bernice. You and Robert plan on getting hitched, am I right?"

Robert's eyes twinkled like shiny stars. Bernice's face turned a deep shade of rose.

"All right, I might as well spit it out," Bernice said. "Yes, we are 'getting hitched' as you so graciously put it. We wanted to get our marriage license this week. Robert wants to get married in the garden. Here. That is, if you don't mind."

Toots's eyes filled with happy tears. There was nothing she liked more than planning a wedding. She was quite experienced. She walked around the table and leaned over and gave Bernice a hug, then did the same to Robert. The pair beamed like lasers.

Goebel got up and walked around the table to congratulate the pair. "This is the best news I've heard all day. Congratulations to you both." He shook Robert's hand and kissed Bernice on the top of the head. "You know, this gal here is about the best cook in the world. She makes a mean Southern fried chicken with white gravy."

Goebel remembered his first visit here years ago. He'd been

more than a hundred pounds heavier, and never missed a meal back then, and most of them were fried and heavy. This group of women had worked their magic on him, and now Robert was about to succumb to the headstrong Bernice, and in doing so, he would gain the love and respect of the godmothers and their leader, Toots. He chuckled at his thoughts. These women were life changers, of that there was no doubt.

"So," Toots inquired, "when do you two want to hook up? I'll take care of all the arrangements, if that's all right with you two?"

Robert looked at Bernice. "Whatever you want, dear."

Bernice rolled her eyes. She was getting as ornery as the rest of the women. "You've certainly had enough experience, that's for sure. How many times has it been?" Bernice asked, then waved her hand in the air. "Don't answer that. I'm afraid it will jinx me. And yes, Tootsie, you can plan my wedding. I don't have time. Robert and I are planning to self-publish a cookbook. We've been taking computer classes at night to learn about the formatting."

So *that's* where they'd been all those nights, Toots thought. "I think it's delightful. We'll have three authors in the group now. So, when do you want me to make this blessed event happen? I can have Jamie design the cake; she's quite the expert at that."

Toots was rambling. Of course Bernice knew Jamie could bake. She'd practically adopted her. Jamie had lived in the guesthouse for three years before purchasing a beautiful old house in Charleston, and when she wasn't at the Sweetest Things, she could be found at her new house, scraping paint off the solid oak floors. Being in a relationship with Mike, a pilot she'd met and who appeared to be madly in love with her, and she him, completed her. Once lonely and down on her luck, she'd put every bit of her energy into the bakery, had opened another one, and now landed an occasional guest spot on the Food Network since rising to fame in the world of pralines. Toots was proud of her and never forgot to tell her so. Jamie was like a daughter to her. That

Jamie and Abby were practically best friends pleased Toots immensely.

Life was good. Except for the issue with Ida, but she wouldn't think about that until Sophie came downstairs with a plan to rid Ida of whatever evil being had taken possession of her.

"So, just tell me when you two want to get hitched, and I'll take it from there," Toots said, struggling to keep her thoughts from returning to the negative but worried sick over what was happening in her bedroom.

Bernice turned to Robert. "It's his choice, but it can't be on the evenings we have classes. Tuesdays and Thursdays are out."

As usual, Robert smiled and agreed. "A weekend would be best for all of us, unless Toots thinks it's a bad idea." He looked to her for an answer.

"You're right. Weekends are perfect. Most of the time. I'm assuming you've a lengthy guest list?" Toots inquired of Robert.

"No, just Mavis and Wade on my side. And Daniel. He's almost like my son now. It is okay if I refer to him as my son, isn't it?" he asked Bernice.

"Shit! He's old enough to be a grandfather himself, but to answer your question, yes, you may consider him a son." Daniel's own father had taken off when he was very young. "He likes Daniel very much, you know that?" Bernice directed her question to Toots as if she needed her approval.

"Daniel is crazy about Robert, too. I think you all will make a nice little family, but first things first. You said you were planning to get your license. Would you like me to take you to the courthouse this afternoon? I don't have anything scheduled. Abby might stop over with the twins later, but I can call her and tell her I won't be here. Plus, I can share the good news. Or would you rather tell her together?"

"Let's tell her together. Can you call her now and invite her over?" Bernice asked excitedly.

Toots was about to agree to this when she remembered the situation upstairs. It wouldn't be wise to bring those children in this house with Ida still lingering in a state of semiconsciousness upstairs. She wasn't about to tell Bernice what they suspected, so she went with the first thing that came to mind. "I just remembered. Abby told me she had to take the babies to see Dr. Pauley today. Something about their one-year checkups." There. That sounded perfectly feasible to her. She was becoming quite the liar these days.

"Well, we can fill her in the next time she pops in. It's not like this comes as a big surprise, right? It was obvious to all of you that we were eventually going to end up getting married." Bernice stated this in a very matter-of-fact way.

Goebel piped in. "Sophie and I suspected there was something in the works, but you never know about these things. I thought Tootsie and Phil would be making an announcement when Abby was kidnapped, but I was wrong about that."

Toots squinted her eyes like two arrows. "I barely knew the man then! I know I have a bad record in the marriage department, but I'm not going to up and marry the first man that comes along!"

"Shit! I've upset you. I didn't mean to," Goebel apologized.

Toots got up and started clearing the table. They'd barely touched their food, but it didn't matter. Lunch was just a reason to stay in the same room together. "No need to apologize, Goebel. I do have a track record. Some I'm ashamed of, some I'm not. I am old enough to acknowledge my mistakes and wise enough to know when to laugh them off. Two of those marriages were real. Six were not."

They all knew that John Simpson, Abby's father, had been the love of her life. He was husband number one. He'd died in a car accident when Abby was just a baby. Chris's dad, Garland Clay, ranked high on the list, but, like all the others, he'd died too soon. Only the good die young, she thought.

"Let's stop all this talk of bad marriages, okay? You win some, you lose some. Right, Toots?"

"You're absolutely right. Personally, I consider myself to be a winner. The day I met Abby's godmothers, and, of course, the day I met Bernice, were two of the best days of my life."

No one said a word as Toots carried a stack of plates to the sink.

Chapter Ten

"So, what did you think of Sister Clara Marie?" Sophia asked Teresa.

"Not much really. This math is too easy, so I guess she is a bit behind in her curriculum. I learned this stuff in fifth grade. I don't think I'll need to cheat on the exams."

"She's an old biddy. I would bet my last smoke she's ninety years old if she's a day. Can you imagine being *that* old? Try not to get too close to her. Her breath smells like rotten cheese. I don't think she bothers to brush her teeth."

Teresa laughed. "I'll try not to."

They walked down the hall together and out the front door. The end of their first day of seventh grade. "You wanna hang out and wait for the other two?"

"Ida and Mavis?" Teresa asked.

"Yeah. I think they want to hang out with us. What about you?"

Teresa wasn't sure what Sophia meant and asked her. "Do I want to hang out with them, or do I mind if they hang out with us?" She wasn't sure. She probably came off like a total jerk, but she'd just met this girl today. She was still feeling her out.

"Both," Sophia answered immediately.

Teresa thought about it. They seemed like nice girls. Her mother would let her invite them over, that much she knew. Ida seemed a bit uppity, but Teresa knew girls like her were really just scared and acted all haughty just to cover up their fears. They were new to Catholic school in general and this one in particular, just like her. Yes, she thought they deserved a chance to become friends. "I like them. Mavis is funny."

"She's a sweet girl, but Ida . . . I ain't so sure about her. She's kind of a bitch, don't ya think?"

Teresa laughed, then felt bad for doing so. It was wrong to poke fun at others. Her mother reminded her of this at every opportunity. She wouldn't mind being friends with the other two girls. "I think she's a bit . . . unsure of herself, that's all." She didn't want to talk about a girl she hardly even knew.

"She thinks her shit don't stink, but I like that about her. It takes a lot of balls to carry around an attitude that big."

The girls both laughed.

"Here they come." Teresa pointed to a cluster of kids coming out of the main entrance.

"You sure you wanna invite them to walk home with us?" Sophia asked before they made their way over to the edge of the sidewalk, where a group of kids had gathered.

Not wanting to lose what little ground of coolness she'd gained, she held her hands out as if she were palming the world. "Shit." She laughed. She sort of liked using that word. "Well, shit, I think we should invite them to walk home with us. The more the merrier." Did she really just say that? She sounded exactly like her mother.

"I think so, too. Who knows when the uppity girl might come in handy? Something tells me the nuns are going to like her," Sophia said, "and it certainly can't hurt to have a friend they approve of, especially given what they think of me."

Teresa saw Mavis and motioned for her to come over. Ida was with her, so Teresa would assume she'd follow Mavis. She did.

Sophia took charge of the girls the second they entered their circle. "Where do you guys live? We need to figure out the best way home, meaning the longest route. That'll give us plenty of time to smoke and plenty of time for the smell to wear off before we're home."

"Smoke?" Ida whispered. "Are you serious?"

Sophia removed her cigarettes from the inside of her bra. She shook the pack, catching a cigarette with her full lips. She removed the pack of matches from her shoe, lit up, then whipped another smoke out, lighted it off the glowing red tip of hers and held it out for Teresa.

Looking left and right, then behind her, Teresa took the cigarette, her hands shaking like dry leaves in the fall. She didn't live that far from the school. Just one more reason her parents had decided to send her here instead of Our Sacred Angels of Mercy. Her mother had suggested she could walk to the school in the afternoons, and they could walk back home together. The look of mortification on her face must have spoken volumes because her mother never mentioned walking her home again. She looked around again just to make sure her mother wasn't lurking in the shadows. Seeing that the coast was clear, she took a puff from her cigarette but didn't inhale. She would practice that when she was alone. For now it was enough just to hold the smoke in her mouth, then blow it out in one long, silvery stream.

"You two ain't gonna smoke?" Sophia asked them.

"No, I don't think so, but you go ahead. I don't care one way or the other," Mavis said.

"Well I do, and I won't be sticking those nasty things in my mouth." Ida raised her chin a notch higher than she normally carried it.

"Look, Ida, I don't give a flying fuck if you smoke or not, okay? I'm tryin' to be nice here, show you the ropes, you get it?" Sophia's Jersey accent was more pronounced when she raised her voice.

Ida nodded, then took Mavis's hand. "We'll follow you two."

In pairs, they walked to the end of Conway Street, where the road split. "I'm to the right, and down a street," Sophia announced.

"Me too," Teresa added.

"That makes three of us. I just moved into the neighborhood. Spring Street, last house on the right," Mavis told them.

"Well, I am one street over from Spring Street. Eucalyptus Avenue. So I guess this means we're all walking home together?" Ida said, though her tone was much friendlier this time around.

"I guess it does," Sophia said. "Okay, if we're gonna be friends, let's stop this formal shit. Call me Sophie. I hate being called Sophia. You got any nicknames?"

Teresa did but wasn't sure if she should tell them or not. Most likely, they would never meet her father, so they wouldn't hear his stupid nickname, but then again, she did like the new secretiveness Sophie seemed to inspire. "My dad calls me Toots. If any one of you tells anyone else, I will personally . . . beat your ass."

There! She was starting to sound more and more like her new best friend, *Sophie.*

Sophie cackled with laughter. Ida rolled her eyes. Mavis smiled, showing the most perfect set of teeth Teresa/Toots had ever seen.

"I won't say a word," Sophie promised.

"Me either," Mavis added.

"I suppose I will keep that horrid name between the four of us, too." Ida said it as though she were doing them all a favor.

Sophie stopped when they reached the end of the street, where they made a right turn for their respective homes. "We need to do something to seal this . . . oath. We need a . . . handshake."

Teresa liked the idea immediately.

"I think that's a fantastic idea! I've never had a secret handshake before," Mavis said excitedly.

"Oh, I suppose I can join in. It's not like we're under oath or anything," Ida added in her know-it-all way.

"Listen up, Ida. This is going to be better than taking an oath. This bonds us all together. We have to swear on our lives that whatever we shake on will always remain between the four of us unless we decide differently." Sophie watched the others, wanted to make sure they knew she wasn't acting silly. This was serious shit. She'd never had a close friend before, let alone three close friends. Billy Watson didn't count.

"Are you in or not?" Sophie asked them.

"I'm in," Teresa said.

"So am I," Mavis repeated.

"Of course I will join in. It's not like I've had a better offer," Ida disclosed.

"Then let's do it," Sophie announced.

Toots held out a hand. Sophie covered it with hers. Next came Mavis, and lastly, Ida. They repeated the process in the same order.

They looked at one another, then rested their gazes on Sophie since this was her idea.

"On the count of three . . ."

"One. Two. Three."

"When you're good, you're good!" Sophie shouted, and they all joined in. "When you're good, you're good!"

The handshake couldn't have gone off any better. It was as though they'd been doing this all their lives.

"Well, that was fun! Do we have to keep our secret handshake a secret or just what we're shaking on?" Mavis asked.

Again, they all looked to Sophie. "I think we should keep both a secret. What about it, Tootsie?"

She laughed. "I do like having secrets, so I agree with Sophie. Let's keep this between the four of us."

"Then let's swear with our secret handshake that we'll keep the secret handshake a secret." Mavis was giddy when she spoke.

They all laughed, then went through the motions again. The only difference was that this time when they said, "When you're good, you're good," they really meant it.

Chapter Eleven

"What in God's name am I doing in Toots's bed?" Ida demanded, looking around her as though she were in another world and hadn't a clue how she'd gotten there. And she was, in a way.

"You whacked out in the bathroom," Sophie explained. She needed to see what, if anything, Ida remembered.

Ida looked down. The shock of what she discovered hit her full force. "Why am I wearing this?" She touched the pale pink gown Sophie had dressed her in. "I know I did not have this on when I came here this morning." She paused as though trying to recover a memory. "Is it still morning?" she asked in a childlike voice. Sophie felt a stab of pity for her friend, who placed so much of her self-worth on her appearance and what others thought of her.

Sophie plumped the pillows behind Ida's head. "You don't remember anything, do you?"

Ida considered her question. "I remember stopping by your house. I knocked, but no one answered, so I went inside. Your place looked like a cyclone had gone through it. I always thought you were so neat and organized."

"Do you remember why you stopped over?"

Ida gave her a dirty look. "Of course I do. I need you to model for another brochure for Seasons. We're planning the fall line now. I thought you could be the model of the month."

"I'm flattered, really. But isn't that your position?"

"Yes and no. You're dark. I'm fair. Dark is better for the fall look. Plums, purples, and rich reds, they look much better against your skin tone than mine."

Was it really that simple? Sophie knew the answer, but it didn't matter now. Something much darker than Ida's fall shades of makeup had touched her friend. She would fix this; she had to because it was her fault. She knew something wasn't right in that house. She knew it the day Abby brought Jonathan and Amy over. She knew it the other day when she'd felt all that cold air, knew it from the dream that really wasn't a dream. This was on her shoulders, and she was not about to allow some evil spirit to possess Ida, even if Ida was a bitch most of the time. She was her friend no matter what. And friends didn't let friends . . . well, she knew what she needed to do. Now all she had to do was convince Ida to be a willing participant.

Taking a deep breath, Sophie turned so that she faced Ida. "When you came searching for me this morning and didn't find me in the house, did you see anything unusual?"

"You're unusual, Sophie. Why don't you just come right out and ask me whatever it is you want to ask. We've been friends for too many years to beat around the bush, wouldn't you agree?"

"I do, but there is a bit of a problem. You see, I think there is something . . . well, I believe there to be an evil spirit in my house. A soul who hasn't crossed over. I've had dreams . . . or visions of a woman who had a horrible accident in the house." Surely Ida could deduce what she was telling her? "I believe there is a man involved, too." Ida would like this addition to her story, that she was sure of.

"Why am I undressed in this bed? Did I faint?"

Sophie relayed the events to her. "I stuffed pralines in my mouth?"

"And washed them down with scotch."

"And this scene in the bathroom?" Ida looked in the direction of the master bedroom. "I actually lost control of my bladder?" The shock was still evident on her face.

Sophie wanted to laugh, but there was nothing funny about what was going on. Yes, Ida pissed all over the floor, but Ida wasn't in control of herself. "You did, but it wasn't like you could control yourself. What I'm trying to tell you is this— I think that something evil, a spirit or an entity of some kind"—this was the part she'd been dreading—"entered your body when you were at the house this morning." She gave Ida a few minutes to absorb her words and what they meant.

Her mouth opened, but no words came out. She blinked rapidly as if trying to dispel the images Sophie had just revealed to her. "I don't understand. Tell me again."

Damn, this was much worse than she'd thought. "I think there is a very strong possibility that an entity, an angry spirit, may have, well it might've . . ." Shit, this wasn't easy. As much as she normally delighted in messing with Ida, she didn't like this one bit. "There's a chance that you might be . . . possessed."

Ida fell back against the pile of pillows, her face as pale as the white silk pillowcases she was leaning against. Her lips had a bluish tint, as if the oxygen were being sucked out of her body. Her hands gripped the light blanket Sophie had placed over her. Sophie feared she was about to lose her again. She leaned across the bed, placed her hands on Ida's shoulders, and gave them a light shake. "Stay with me, Ida. Can you hear me?"

She squeezed her thin shoulders a bit harder than normal, hoping to get a response from her. "Ida?"

Snapping back into the moment, Ida rubbed her forehead with one hand and pulled the blanket up under her chin. "I'm here," she whispered.

There was nothing more to be said. Sophie needed a minute to think of her next move. She felt sure Ida would appreciate a few moments of silence. She really needed to go home and study the book that Madam Butterfly left her, but she couldn't leave Ida like this. She *wouldn't* leave Ida like this. She might be here for the rest of the day and into the night. It didn't matter. She was not going to let Ida out of her sight until she purged her of the evil that was trying to take over her mind and body.

"Listen to me, can you hear me?" Sophie said in a strong, firm voice. Not the soft, almost melodic voice she used when she was performing a séance. This was her voice, the voice of Sophie, her friend.

Ida nodded that she did.

"Can you talk?"

Ida rolled her eyes. This was good; she was being a smart-ass, Sophie thought. Smart-ass was very good under these circumstances.

"Yes, but I would like something to drink. Could you get me something to drink?"

Sophie had never felt so sorry for Ida. Not even when she'd been obsessed with germs. She had no control over this, and certainly had done nothing to deserve it, but it is what it is. "Yes, I'll get some water."

She hurried to the master bathroom. Spying Toots's mouthwash glass they'd used earlier to clean the urine out of the Jacuzzi tub, she rinsed it a couple of times, then filled it with water and returned to the bedroom.

"Drink this." She held the glass to Ida's mouth, fearing that if she let her hold it, she'd drop it and spill the water all over herself. Ida drank the entire glass.

"More," she said, somewhat out of breath.

Sophie refilled the glass, and this time, Ida held it. Though her hands were still shaky, she didn't spill the water. Her color was coming back. That was a good sign. She needed Ida to talk, to tell her how she felt.

"Want some more?" Sophie asked.

"No, that's enough. I want to know why this is happening! I don't practice that voodoo magic, or that psychic stuff you live for. I want an explanation, Sophie, and I want it now!"

This was much better. Ida was returning to her old bitchy self. "I do, too. I am going to try to help you, but you can't act like a bitch, Ida. You need to listen to me and do what I say. Do you think you can do that?"

Ida considered her question. "I don't have a choice, do I?"

"Yeah, you could let it go and who knows what would happen to you, maybe to Daniel, quite possibly the twins, so sure, if you want to let it go, that's your choice."

"Of course I will not let this go! Do you think I'm insane?" Ida said, her tone almost back to normal.

Well, yes, she did often question her friend's sanity, but now wasn't the time to bring up the past.

"Do you feel like going downstairs?" Sophie didn't know what she was going to do once they were downstairs with the others, but she'd figure it out when and if.

"Is there something for me to wear, other than this?"

"I'm sure I can find something in Toots's closet. Sit tight," Sophie said before entering Toots's huge walk-in closet. Five minutes later she came back with black silk lounging pants and a matching top. She took a bra and panty set from Toots's lingerie drawer, then found a pair of sandals next to the bed. "This should fit. You want me to help you dress, or step out for a minute?" She really didn't think it was wise to leave her alone right now, but if Ida insisted, she'd step into the hallway and leave the door cracked open.

"You can stay put. I have a feeling it was you who put this awful gown on me, so you must've seen the full view, not that I care. I'm not ashamed of my body."

Sophie grinned. The bitch was back. At least for a while.

Chapter Twelve

Sophie saw that everyone was still in the kitchen. "Toots, come over here a second, I need to talk with you in private," she said, then waited at the bottom of the staircase.

They all focused their attention on Sophie.

"Just Toots, okay?" she said to Goebel, Bernice, and Robert. "I'll fill you guys in on the details later."

Toots hurried to the bottom step. "Wanna go out and have a smoke?"

"Yes, but I can't. Follow me upstairs. I don't want to leave Ida alone any longer than I have to."

Toots followed behind. When they stood outside Toots's bedroom door, Sophie put a finger to her lips indicating they should be quiet. In a hushed voice, she said, "I don't want Ida to know we're out here. I need to observe her for a few minutes, to see if she's really back to herself, or if this entity that seems to have taken over is screwing with me."

Toots's eyes got as wide as saucers. "Are you serious?"

"Yes. Evil lies and tries to draw you into its grasp so it, or they . . . hell, I don't know how to refer to this shit, but I do know that we can't let our guard down. We might think Ida is fine when in reality, she's not."

"I don't get it. How can we distinguish the real Ida from this *thing*? This is almost too bizarre, even for us."

"I'm not sure. I've read on the topic but not enough to completely understand it. I have a book at my house. I keep it locked in a safe in my office. Madam Butterfly gave it to me years ago when I was having her read for me. You remember her, right? She's the woman who told me I had *the gift*. I think those were the words she used. This book she gave me wasn't really a book. It's a journal of sorts, and it's handwritten, in both English and Latin. Inside the cover it reads *The Roman Ritual*. Have you ever heard of this book?" Sophie whispered.

"Maybe. As you know full well, I spent six years going to Catholic school, so I think I heard it mentioned. Why? What does this have to do with anything?" Toots spoke softly and quietly, very much disturbed at the thought of Ida's having been possessed by some evil demon or whatever.

Sophie peeked through the crack in the bedroom door to make sure Ida wasn't in trouble. She appeared to be sleeping, but Sophie knew that right now nothing was necessarily as it appeared, nothing was as it should be. She needed to get to the bottom of these goings-on, and fast.

"This book contains instructions for those in the priesthood on how to perform an exorcism."

Toots's face turned chalk white. "That is horrible!"

Sophie nodded her agreement. "I know, but I don't believe Ida's at that stage now. She's acting weird, yes, but I don't think there's a full-fledged possession taking place. Remember that dream I had about the woman?"

Toots nodded.

"I believe it has something to do with her and what I saw happen in that house. I know this doesn't make any sense right now, but I need someone to confide in other than Goebel because I don't want to move Ida right now. I think it's best if she stays here where you can keep an eye on her while I figure out what the hell I need to do."

"I agree. Though I have to be honest, this scares the living daylights out of me. I don't want Abby and the kids around while this . . . crap is going on."

"I don't either, but you'll have to make that your mission. Keep her and those babies away from your place and mine for now. It might be a good time to suggest she and Jamie take the kids to the beach for a few days. Isn't Chris out of town this week?"

"He's at the same conference Daniel is attending. I don't know if I can convince her to leave. She told me the other day that she wanted to get more involved with her Dogs Displaced by Disaster program, and asked me to keep the kids while she worked. I know how important that is to her. Hell, it's important to all of us. If Abby and Chris hadn't started the organization after those horribly destructive forest fires in Colorado, who knows what would've happened to all those animals? I think of little Frankie and how much I love him." Suddenly, Toots stopped and cleared her throat. "I'm babbling again, aren't I? Sophie, stop me when I do that. I'm beginning to sound like a senile old lady."

"Well, you're at least half-right since you are an old lady. In point of fact, we're both old ladies. We are all in our seventies now, including you, my dearest friend," Sophie had to remind her.

"How could I forget? I just hate it that we all turned seventy last year, but then I think of the alternative, and it sounds wonderful. You have to admit none of us act—or, thanks to Ida—look our age."

"Right now, looking our age is unimportant. I need you to watch Ida while I go back to my place."

"Do you think it's a good idea for you to do this alone? I know you said not to mention the clergy in any way, but wouldn't it be best to leave this to the pros? A priest or someone who's experienced in this?"

Sophie peered through the bedroom door again. Ida still appeared to be asleep. "I don't think it's needed at this point. Don't ask me how I know that when I don't know much of anything else right now, but I'm positive we're not dealing with the kind of demons that you think. This isn't a . . . satanic possession." She crossed her fingers. She was 99 percent sure. Thoughts and images whirled around in her head. She just knew that she had to get back to her house as soon as possible.

"I trust you," Toots said. "Go on then. I'll keep an eye on her," and she motioned to the bedroom. "Do what you need to, so we can put this behind us." Toots paused. "I probably shouldn't tell you this, but I'm going to anyway. While you were up here with Ida, Bernice and Robert told Goebel and me what their big secret is."

"They're getting married," Sophie said.

Toots looked at her and grinned. "Is this the psychic in you? Or were you eavesdropping while we were downstairs?"

"Neither. I've seen how they are with one another. It's a natural progression that they would tie the knot. Look at me. Did you ever think I'd marry Goebel that day he first walked into your house?"

Toots gave a quiet laugh. "No, I honestly didn't give it a thought."

"I thought you suspected there was something going on between us. Doesn't matter now. Though I'll make sure to offer up my congratulations to Bernice and Robert, I'll do it later. I'll let them tell me," Sophie added.

"That's a good idea. Now, go on and do whatever it is you're planning. I'll keep watch over Ida, and I'll call Abby and suggest that trip. Now, go."

"Okay. You'll call me if Ida acts out of the ordinary in any way?"

"Cross my heart," Toots said as she placed her right hand over her heart.

"Good. Remember, call my cell phone if you think you need to," Sophie instructed as she headed downstairs.

In the kitchen, Bernice, Robert, and Goebel were still gathered around the kitchen table, each with a steaming mug of coffee in front of them. A plate of cookies, probably from the Sweetest Things, sat in the center of the table.

Bernice was the first to speak. "I called you for lunch. You didn't answer, so you're shit out of luck, unless you want an oatmeal-raisin cookie."

"That's okay. I'm not hungry," Sophie answered, then turned to her husband. "I need to go back to the house for a while."

He jumped up, almost knocking his cup over. "Then let's go."

"No, I mean just me. I need you to stay here with Toots. Just in case." She gave him *the look*, which she knew he would understand.

He sat back down. "You're sure?"

"One hundred percent. I'll have my cell turned on, so don't worry. Just sit tight while I'm gone. I'll be back in time to go to dinner with that Dabney man," Sophie said before practically running out the back door. Seeing their car parked so close was an added bonus. She slid inside and cranked the engine, not bothering to look back.

Ten minutes later, she pulled into her driveway. She took the keys out, remembering that Goebel had locked the front door. Normally, they parked in the back of their long drive and entered the house through the back door just like they'd done at Toots's place.

Her hand trembled as she inserted the key into the lock. Why she felt so nervous was understandable, but it was so unlike her. She felt rushed, as though she needed to hurry and find out exactly what was going on in this house and with Ida. A sense of urgency coursed through her like a jolt of electricity.

Inside, the house seemed empty and dark. Lost, as though all the life once living inside had been extinguished like a flame. She stuffed the keys in her pocket, checked to make sure she had her cell phone, then headed upstairs.

As soon as she reached the top of the stairs a cold gust of air greeted her. She looked up, but there was no air-conditioning vent above her. Taking a deep breath, she proceeded to walk to the room that she called her séance room.

The door was closed, and that was unusual. Sophie always kept this door open because the room always smelled like mothballs to her. Goebel had tried to open the window once so she could air the room out, but the window would not budge. As far as they could tell, there was no reason for that either. Goebel had suggested breaking the glass, but Sophie wouldn't allow him to.

The window was original, and though its beveled glass made her a bit disoriented when she looked at it, she liked the added charm it gave the room.

Sophie reached for the doorknob but stopped. She felt a slight movement. She whirled around, but no one was there. Her heart rate increased, and she felt a bead of sweat forming above her mouth. "Who's there?" She stared down the long hallway, hoping to catch a glimpse of something, anything that would explain the movement she'd felt, but there was nothing. Taking another deep breath, she put her hand on the doorknob and turned it. The door creaked open without any push from her. *Weird*, she thought as she stepped inside the room.

The odor of mothballs was thick, but there was something else. She inhaled, trying to pick up a scent the way a bloodhound would. Something familiar—a floral scent that she couldn't name exactly could be sensed through the mothballs. It didn't matter. She walked over to the chair she'd used when she held the séance the other night. Sitting down, she carefully placed her hands on the old wooden table, then closed her eyes.

Relax, she thought. *I need to relax, to let go of the fear.* Inhaling, then slowly exhaling to try to calm her pounding heart, Sophie spoke, her words soft and still. Her séance voice.

She closed her eyes. "I can do this. I don't know who you are, and I don't know what happened to you." She paused, allowing herself a few minutes to gather her thoughts. Remembering that Madam Butterfly always told her that when in doubt, she needed to be positive, she spoke again. "I'm here to help you. I mean you no harm." The words she always used when trying to contact the other side.

Opening her eyes, Sophie searched the room around her. Nothing seemed out of place. The room was as it should be. Other than the door being shut and the cold air, she had not picked up any psychic vibes at all. Highly unusual for her. Again, she closed her eyes, thinking that this spirit, whatever it was, needed calm and quiet. She remained still for a few more minutes. Nothing.

Rubbing her hands across the old wooden table in hopes it would act as a conduit, as she believed, she began to speak. "Someone hurt you a very long time ago. You don't know where you are. You are"—she paused—"caught." Knowing she was on the right track encouraged her. "You're stuck between worlds. There is no need to be afraid. When you enter the bright side, you will be whole again."

Sophie felt a disturbance in the air. A shift. "Are you with me now?"

Unsure of what she expected, she closed her eyes again. Waiting for a sign, a movement, anything to let her know she wasn't losing the spirit, she leaned back in the chair and relaxed. Maybe she was too uptight, trying too hard to focus. Maybe it just wasn't the right time.

Ready to call it quits for the moment, Sophie stopped dead in her tracks when the door to the room slammed shut.

Chapter Thirteen

"You should have called first," Toots said as she took Amy from Abby.

Her daughter adjusted Jonathan on her hip with one hand and slung the diaper bag over her shoulder with the other as she walked to the kitchen. "Mother, are you serious? I've never had to before. Why now?"

Toots chose not to answer Abby just yet. "Bernice, help me get the high chairs set up. The babies are here," she called out. Bernice and Robert were on the veranda trying to decide on a wedding date. Goebel had wandered outside to check out her dying magnolia tree. For now, Toots, Abby, and the twins had the kitchen to themselves. Toots hoped that Sophie wouldn't show up. She didn't want to have to explain why Sophie had been in a house that was supposed to be poisoned with carbon monoxide. Hopefully, Abby wouldn't ask where the godmother who was supposed to be living at Toots's for a while was.

Holding hands like two teenagers in love, Bernice and Robert returned to the kitchen and set up the high chairs. Toots prayed they wouldn't mention that Ida was upstairs. If Abby thought she was ill, she would want to check on her. And Toots could not let Abby upstairs. If anything, she needed to do something to get her out of the house. Sophie had warned her to keep the twins away from this . . . evil, and she would. She just had to figure out a way to get them out of the house without raising Abby's suspicion.

Abby's reporter instincts were always there, just waiting to pounce on anything fishy. It was hard to pull anything over on her daughter, but she remembered she *had* kept her in the dark when she'd purchased the *Informer*. Unfortunately, motherhood had only increased Abby's intuitive feel for what was happening around her.

"Mom?" Abby said. "Are you all right? Is there something going on that I should know about?"

Amy started crying, and Toots was thankful for small favors. "Ah, now look at Gramma." Toots peered inside Amy's mouth. "Oh goodness, Abby, have you seen this?"

"What?" Abby practically leapt across the kitchen.

"Amy has teeth, or at least she's getting them," Toots said.

"You scared me. For a minute I thought something was wrong. And to answer your question, of course I've seen her teeth. It's what happens when they're a year old. She *is* my daughter. Jonathan has them, too. Just not as many. See?" Abby held Jonathan's mouth open for Toots to look at and admire his new teeth.

"This makes me sad, Abby. Very sad."

"Mom! What is it with you today? You're not acting like yourself at all. I think you're up to something."

Toots adjusted the high chair, placed Amy in the chair, then buckled her in. She took the matching high chair and placed it next to the other. "Bring Jonathan here." Toots held her arms out for her adorable grandson. She kissed his soft little neck, and he giggled. "This one is going to be a lady-killer for sure." After she finished securing Jonathan in the seat, Toots asked Abby, "Can I give them a treat?"

Abby plopped down in a chair. "Sure, as long as it's not laced with sugar. What do you have?"

"I have some of those baby things they chew on. They look like dog bones. I hope they taste better than they look. Let me get them." Toots hurried to the pantry in search of the baby bones. That's what she was going to call them. "These." She held out the box for Abby's inspection.

"Those are fine, we have them at home. They're very messy though," she added.

"I don't care, as long as they enjoy them."

Toots positioned her chair so she could watch the twins and keep an eye on the stairs. If Ida decided to make a trip downstairs, she would be there to guide her right back up. She'd worry about an explanation when and if. For now, though, she really did want to admire her beautiful grandchildren.

"Tell me, what's making you sad?" Abby asked.

"Oh, I meant the babies and their teeth. It's just another sign they're growing up. Before you know it, they'll be in school, then they'll want to drive. I'm sure they'll both be highly pursued by members of the opposite sex. It's only natural—just look at them. I do believe they are the most perfect babies I've ever seen. Except for you, Abby. I spent days and weeks after giving birth to you looking for something, anything that marred what your father and I knew was complete perfection. To this very day I am happy to announce I still haven't found a thing." Toots smiled at her daughter. Abby was almost perfect. At least to her.

"Aw, that is so sweet of you to say. Why do I think you're trying to butter me up? Are you keeping secrets again?" Abby went to the refrigerator and took out a bottle of water. Bernice came up behind her, having left Robert out by himself on the veranda. "Darn! You scared me," Abby said, then gave Bernice a hug.

"How've you been?" Abby asked. "Mom said you were here. Sit." She pointed to the two chairs across from her.

"Not until I give this little king and queen a kiss." Bernice kissed both babies on the top of their heads. "They're growing like weeds, Abby. Before you know it, they'll be in college and having babies of their own. Time is moving too fast these days."

"I hope they do it in a different order. Maybe college, then marriage, then babies"—Abby laughed—"but if they choose to do it the other way, Chris and I would be okay with that, too," she added.

"Have you put their names on any of the lists for private schools? Some parents do that even before they have their children."

"Mom! I think you're losing it. To answer your question, no. I haven't even thought about sending them to private school or public school. I want to enjoy them every minute I can. Like you said, they're growing up so fast. They'll be on their own, and I will be the saddest mom in the world."

"Don't think you've got the take on sadness. The day you left for college, it took me exactly three weeks to stop crying. I even cried in my sleep—right, Bernice?" Toots asked.

Bernice rolled her eyes. "I do recall you bawling a lot, but I don't think it was three weeks. I can almost guarantee that I would've strangled you by then. Though you were not happy; none of us were. It was so lonely without Abby around."

"Stop it, you two! This is the happiest time of my life. I want to share it with you. And for the record, I've been thinking about homeschooling."

"I thought you said you didn't want to think about that now. Abby Clay, I do believe you've told me a fib."

"Yeah, right. And you never have, right? What about the *Informer*?"

Toots went to the sink, grabbed a paper towel, and ran it under lukewarm water. She waited for the twins to finish their bones, then began wiping the mess from their pudgy little hands. "Let's not talk about that now, okay? Homeschooling, don't you think that would be a bit hard to do?"

"Yes and no. I thought maybe Chris and I could either take turns, or we could hire a teacher to come to the house. Isn't that the way they used to do things in the old days, Mom?" Abby teased. "Back when you and my godmothers were growing up?"

"Yes, but not in our old days. We all went to Catholic school—Bishop Verot, as I am sure you remember from all the stories you've heard about it."

Goebel chose that moment to come in through the back door.

"That old magnolia tree looks like it's on its last legs, but I'm certainly no expert. I have a guy I met at the nursery, he calls himself the tree whisperer. Says he can revive any tree. I could give him a call if you'd like." Goebel washed his hands at the sink, then made his way over to the twins.

"Yes, call him. That tree is as old as this house. I believe it was planted by the original owners. It would be a shame not to try to save it."

He spent a few minutes making faces and tickling the twins, then seemed to realize what that implied, with Ida upstairs. Toots gave him the don't-say-a-word look.

"I'll call him now. I saved his number in my cell phone. Better yet, I'll take a picture and send it to him so he'll have an idea what I'm talking about. Good seeing you, Abby, and those two little stinkers."

"Later," Abby said, and waved goodbye.

For some reason seeing their mother wave her hand in the air made the twins giggle. "Oh, you two are little rascals, you know that?" Abby took a package of baby wipes from the diaper bag and wiped their faces.

"They're very good with this, Abby. I remember when you were little, you hated having your face washed. It didn't matter how dirty you were, either."

"Trust me, this is just a lucky wipe. They usually put up a fight, but they're at Gramma's, and I think that makes them happy."

"Of course it does, and it makes Gramma happy, too. More than you'll ever know. I am so blessed to have you living so close to me. Just think how many sets of eyes you'll have on these two when they really need it."

"Toots, are you going to shut up for a second so I can tell Abby what you wanted me to tell her?" Bernice interjected.

Toots almost flipped Bernice the bird but caught herself just in time. She wouldn't want to corrupt her grandkids before they were ready to be corrupted.

"Go on, I'll keep quiet."

Bernice scrunched up her face when she looked at Toots, then gave the most beautiful smile when she returned her gaze to Abby. "It's probably not a big surprise, but Robert and I have decided to get married. Tie the knot. Hang the noose around our necks. And we want to seal the deal next week."

Abby felt tears in her eyes. "Oh, Bernice, I think this is the best news I've heard in ages. I'm so happy for you two." Abby leaned down and wrapped her arms around her godmother.

"Did I hear you correctly? Did you say you wanted to get married next *week*?"

"You did, and we are. Is that enough time to plan a big event?" Bernice asked.

"No! I mean, yes, but don't ever, *ever* call a wedding an event! Events are *funerals*, Bernice. You should know that by now. You've helped me through eight of them."

"Oh yeah, I forgot. So, what do you think?" Bernice asked Abby.

"If you and Robert are happy, I think that's what matters most. Right, Mom?" Abby looked at her mother, who had a very strange look on her face. "Mom? Are you all right?"

"Abby, I want you to take the kids outside right now. Do not ask any questions. Just go! Hurry!" Toots shouted so loud, the twins started to cry. "Bernice, help her get them outside immediately! Move it!"

Hearing the urgency in Toots's voice, Abby and Bernice practically yanked the little ones out of their high chairs and ran out the back door. Another second, and they would have been exposed to Ida, who stood on the bottom step. "What in the world was that all about?"

Chapter Fourteen

Still in the séance room, Sophie crept back to her chair. "I mean you no harm. I want to help you. Your staying here isn't going to change what happened to you. Do you understand what I am saying?"

She was talking to an entity. It was quite normal for her to do so, but for some reason, this time she was frightened. Maybe this *was* a demonic spirit. Maybe she should call a priest or a member of the clergy.

No, she needed to calm herself down. Closing her eyes, she tried to slow her breathing to a normal pattern. That would still the rapid beat of her heart, help her to gain control of herself.

In her séance voice, she began to speak softly, encouragingly. "If you left this world unexpectedly, I know you must find it hard to let go, but you must. If you want my help, you need to show yourself." Sophie paused, looking around the room to see if anything appeared changed. Other than the door slamming shut, there was nothing at all. "Is this your former home? Did you have an accident while living here?" She thought of the dream and the woman at the bottom of the stairs. Maybe she lingered because she wanted to . . . to *find out who pushed her!*

The image was so vivid that Sophie drew in a breath. "Somebody pushed you down that long staircase, and you want me, need me, to find out who did this to you. If that is what you're trying to tell me, show me a sign acknowledging that it is." Sophie waited for a few seconds, then saw the knob on the door turning. The door opened so slightly that, had she not been watching for any changes, she wouldn't have noticed.

"You're here now?"

The door opened again, but this time it moved at least a foot. Sophie knew she was taking a chance, but there wasn't much to lose at this point, so she went with her gut instinct. "Are you a member of the Dabney family?" The words barely escaped her lips when the door slammed again, only this time it was with such force the window behind her shook. She turned around, expecting to see an apparition, a wisp of something, but still she saw nothing remotely otherworldly in the small room.

Sophie scanned the room again, really looking at it this time. There had to be a clue, something about this room that would aid her in releasing this . . . *spirit* from its earthly bonds. Nothing. She stood up and went to stand by the window. The beveled glass gave the images outside a distorted look, almost like one of those mirrors in a fun house. Sophie blinked, then looked outside again. She gasped, then took a calming breath, letting it out slowly.

The gardens that she and Goebel had worked so hard to bring back to life were gone, replaced by dirt paths. The giant trees, which were as familiar to her now as her own image, were small and scraggly, as if they'd only been planted recently. She shook her head to try to clear the visual, but it remained. Looking through the window and squinting her eyes, Sophie saw a man on a . . . *horse?* "Dear heavens," she said, and strained to see the details. Though this time all she saw were the gardens, the giant trees. The gardens appeared as they should. Stepping away from the window, Sophie realized she'd just seen her home and how it had looked in the past. Not having a lot of experience with the past in the sense of actually seeing it as it was in real time, Sophie decided this wasn't leading her where she needed to be led. Without another thought, she raced out of the room and downstairs to the kitchen.

What she saw almost sent her into a state of shock.

Ida's description of the mess in the kitchen didn't begin to cover the devastation she observed. This was not an entity trying to get her attention. No, this was something much more wicked. Carefully, she walked through shards of broken glass, splinters of what once were her cabinet doors, and the detritus from several jars of jam that had been smashed on the wood floor. "Goebel needs to see this." She removed her cell phone from her pocket and dialed his number. He answered on the first ring. "You need to come home right away. Borrow one of Toots's cars, and hurry." Sophie clicked off, not giving him a chance to respond. She knew he'd understand the urgency behind her call when he saw the disaster in their kitchen.

A buzzing sound coming from their pantry made her turn around. A few feet away from the kitchen island, Goebel had enlarged and redesigned the pantry, telling her they would never have an issue storing food, paper towels, odd-sized platters, and the usual kitchen items that never fit in a normal-sized cupboard. He'd customized it just for her. What she saw now brought tears to her eyes. It wasn't the loss of the food; she didn't care about that as it could be replaced. But she did care that the custom-built shelves were split into tiny pieces. The handcrafted porcelain knobs looked like someone had taken a hammer and smashed them into tiny pieces. Boxes of rice were ripped apart, peanut butter smeared on the floor, and the canned food they had was destroyed, crushed. Several antique platters and bowls she and Goebel had collected during their short marriage were now nothing more than colored shards of glass. A swarm of flies buzzed through the pantry, hovering above each pile of spilled food. "There is no way a spirit did this," she said out loud. While she was no expert, she knew this much destruction had to come from a source so evil, so foul and unholy, that she feared its malevolence and its power. This was not the woman in her dreams, or her vision. In all likelihood, Sophie was staring at the work of the devil or someone who had the devil inside them. Most likely the latter.

With that thought in mind, she knew she had to get to Ida, and if she needed the aid of a member of the clergy, then so be it. Still, there was that small, still voice in her head that told her, no, this was not demonic in the sense of needing a priest but demonic in the sense of the evil quality of a person who hadn't managed to find their way to the other side. Sophie knew better than to ignore her gut instinct. This entity who'd destroyed her house was powerful, but not as powerful as she.

"I'll send you to the other side, you son of a bitch, and when I do, I hope you burn forever in the fires of hell."

"Sophie." She heard Goebel call out to her. He'd used the front door, too.

"In the kitchen," she answered.

"My God! What on earth happened?" he asked as he observed the destruction. "Are you all right?"

"I'm going to find out, trust me. I'm a bit shook-up, but I'll be okay," Sophie said, as they both stared at the mess.

"Think we should call the police?" Goebel asked her. She knew he wasn't asking her because he didn't know what had happened, but because he knew she would know if this was a supernatural event or just another break-in.

"You are the police, and no, we don't need them here. I would hate to try to explain this to them. Even though they know we do psychic investigations, I'd rather keep this between us."

"I hate to tell you this, but there's more bad news. Abby brought the twins over to Toots's, and Ida came downstairs. Toots said she was sure that Abby and the kids didn't see her, but she rushed them out of the house so fast that she knows Abby isn't going to forget about it or let it go."

Sophie felt her heart sink to her feet and back. "That's not good. I need to keep Ida somewhere safe until I find out exactly what I'm dealing with. When I saw this"—she pointed to the kitchen—"I felt sure it had to be some demonic thing, but it's not. It's connected to that woman in my dream, or vision, whatever. I went to my séance room when I arrived and just sat there, waiting to see if I could make contact with . . . well, you know the routine, but I had the oddest experience." She told him about the door and what she'd seen when she looked out the window. "I think it's imperative that we speak with this Dabney man tonight. Maybe he can tell us something that will send me in the right direction."

"Would another séance help?" Goebel asked as he trudged through the unholy mess that had once been their beautiful kitchen.

"No. At least I don't believe it would at this stage. Later, I'm just not sure." Confused by the turn of events, Sophie wandered through the kitchen, careful not to step on the glass.

Goebel frowned, his eyes taking in the scene around them. "I need to start cleaning this up. We'll have bugs if I don't." He headed for the pantry, where they stored the cleaning supplies.

"Stop!"

He did.

"Don't go in there, okay? It's much worse than this," she said, gesturing at the mess surrounding them.

For once, Goebel didn't listen to her. He stepped inside the pantry. "Son of a bitch!"

Sophie stood next to him. "I told you not to go in there."

"Soph, get real. I live here, too."

What was she thinking? That she could hide this from him? Take care of it without his knowing? *Stupid, stupid, stupid*, she thought. "I know. I'm sorry. It's just that you worked so hard in here. I know how proud of it you were. I was too, and now look at this." She splayed her hands out in front of her. "Totally destroyed."

A loud crashing sound caused both of them to look up. "It's coming from the attic. Follow me," Sophie called out as she rushed through the debris in the kitchen and up the staircase.

She'd been meaning to get Goebel to do whatever was necessary in terms of safety so that she could return to the attic and look in those trunks she had located in the corner. But after the lack of results with the séance and everything else that had been happening, she had forgotten to mention it to him. And she had almost forgotten about what had happened when she had gone up there.

But there was no more time to spare. Someone or some*thing* was insisting that she go back inside the dark, dank space and find whatever it was she was supposed to find.

Remembering that the light had been too dim to navigate safely around the floorboards that had been prepped for whatever remodeling was to take place, Sophie grabbed a flashlight before starting up into the attic. Pushing the heavy door aside, the late-afternoon sunshine penetrated the dusty panes of glass only enough to illuminate particles of dust dancing in the air, suspended for a few seconds before settling on the old wooden beams. She stepped inside the small space, stopping when she was greeted with such a foul odor, unlike anything she'd ever known, that she was forced to cover her mouth and nose with her hand. Suddenly, Ida flashed around the edge of her thoughts, and she knew then that, without a doubt, the key to finding out what or who had possessed her lay here, somewhere in this pile of ancient dust and rotting wood.

Now all she had to do was find it.

GETAWAY

Chapter One

Chester greeted Abby at the back door, sensing that she needed his assistance. He leaned against the heavy frame to keep it open when she entered with Amy on one hip and Jonathan on the other. Once inside, she stooped down, allowing the twins to wiggle out of her arms. "Thanks, Chester," she said before giving her long-time best friend a rub between the ears. "I swear you're more human than animal."

"Woof! Woof!"

Once inside and seeing that Amy and Jonathan were occupied with a scattering of toys they'd left on the floor this morning, she found her godmother Mavis's cell phone number written on a notepad next to the phone. Quickly, she punched in the digits. Mavis picked up on the third ring.

"Yes, dear." She didn't bother with hello. Abby smiled. She knew Mavis was fascinated with the ability to see who was calling.

"Did I catch you at a bad time?" Abby asked.

"Of course not, Abby. Wade and I were getting ready to close up for the night."

Abby could only imagine what closing up for the night consisted of since Mavis and Wade operated a funeral parlor. There was no way that she was about to ask.

Peeping around the corner to make sure the twins were safely occupied, her voice grew serious. "Is there anything going on with Mom that I need to know? I stopped over earlier, just to say hi and let the twins visit, and we were no more settled in than, the next thing I know, she's practically tossing us out. She didn't bother with an explanation, either."

Abby was more than concerned. Normally, her mother would practically have to beg her to stay longer just so she could play with her grandchildren, but that hadn't been the case today.

She could hear Mavis's intake of breath across the ether. "I haven't seen your mother since we attended the séance at Sophie and Goebel's. She did have a little too much to drink that night. Wade insisted we drive her home even though she said she was fine. Of course, I knew better. I haven't spoken to her since then, so as far as I know, everything is fine. She and Phil were talking about their upcoming trip to New York for his book launch."

Mavis was so kind, but sometimes she could be a bit long-winded.

"Yes, she mentioned the trip the other day," Abby said. "Do you think Sophie or Ida might know what's going on with Mom? It's just so unlike her to act . . . well, never mind. Mom does act weird, a lot, but I've never seen her act this way around the twins."

"I'm sure everything will be just fine. I wouldn't worry too much, dear."

Abby thanked her and ended the call. She punched in Sophie's cell phone, and it went straight to voicemail. She tried her home number, and no one picked up. "Weird," she said to herself. With Ida next on her list, she punched in her number. It rang at least ten times, then Abby hung up. That left Bernice. She called her mother's house, knowing the odds of Bernice's answering the phone were in her favor.

And, sure enough, Bernice answered on the first ring. "Thank goodness you called," Bernice said.

Abby's heart raced. "What in the world is going on?"

"I've been sworn to silence, but your mother told me if you called to tell you she was just fine, and not to worry."

"Oh, great. That's just great. Seriously, Bernice, is there something going on with her that I should know? She tossed me and the kids out so fast, I was too shocked to question her. Now I know something is wrong because she would insist on speaking to me if there wasn't." At least that's what Abby thought. She and her mother didn't keep secrets. At least none that she knew of. Of course, there was the matter of the *Informer,* but Abby hadn't cared that her mother had purchased the struggling tabloid behind her back. She thought it truly proved what lengths a mother would go to for her child. Had the situation been reversed, she was sure she would have done the exact same thing for her kids. Like mother, like daughter.

"Abby, your mother is fine. Physically, at least. Now, as far as her mental state goes, I've questioned it for the past thirty-plus years."

Abby grinned. Leave it to Bernice. "Yeah, I understand where you're coming from. But still, this isn't like her at all, and I need to know what's going on so I can help fix whatever it is."

She heard Bernice's sigh. "Do you think the twins are old enough to be in the wedding? I was thinking ring bearer and flower girl."

Abby pulled the phone away from her ear and looked at it. Maybe Bernice was the one she needed to be concerned about. "I'm not falling into your trap, Bernie," Abby said, knowing she hated being referred to as "Bernie."

"Look, I understand where you're coming from, but I really don't know what's going on with your mother. Ida's upstairs in your mother's room, Sophie and Goebel went home. Well, I think that's where they're at. She left in a rush, and he wasn't far behind her. I'm as much in the dark as you, and you know your mother. When she wants us to know something, she will tell us. If it were life threatening, she would have told us. I wouldn't worry if I were you," Bernice said. "I was serious when I asked you about the twins being in the wedding. Since they're practically walking, I thought it might be fun to see them in action."

The visual of Amy and Jonathan walking down any aisle without her trailing behind made her laugh out loud. "We'll see, Bernice. I'm not sure if they're steady on their feet enough yet, but they change daily, so I will give it some thought."

"Good. I'll tell your mother to call you as soon as she's able," Bernice said. "She's going to do my wedding. What do you think of that?"

"God knows she's had enough experience, so it should be perfect. She loves doing that stuff, so I can't wait. I'm happy for you, really. You've been alone all your life," Abby said, then felt a bit sad.

"No I haven't, kid. I've had you, your mom, and my son Daniel. You're my family, and that will never change, you got that?"

Abby's eyes filled with tears. "I feel the same way, and I know that Mom does, too. Now"—she knuckled her eyes—"before I start blubbering, let's stop this lovey-dovey stuff. Just know you're loved, and make sure to tell Mom to call me as soon as she thinks it's appropriate to let me in on what's happening over there."

"Will do," Bernice promised, then hung up.

"Sure you will," Abby said.

Her reporter instincts had been dormant too long, she thought as she observed the twins still playing on the floor. It was high time she did a bit of investigating of her own.

Chapter Two

"Who's there?" Toots asked.

"The police," Bernice answered sarcastically. "Who were you expecting?"

Toots peeked out of the small crack between her bedroom door and the door frame. "What do you want?" she asked none too nicely. "I've got a . . . situation in here." She wasn't about to tell Bernice the full version of what Sophie suspected, at least not until she was 100 percent sure. In the meantime, her job was to keep Ida occupied, and that was almost impossible. She'd given her a double dose of an antihistamine to knock her out. The last thing she wanted was the entire gang asking questions.

"Abby is worried about you," Bernice told her. "She thinks you're mentally deranged. She's considering having you committed."

Toots yanked the door open and stepped out into the hallway. "Shhh, I don't want to wake Ida." She inched her bedroom door almost shut, leaving just enough of an opening to see Ida lying on her bed. "Repeat what you just said."

"Abby's worried about you," Bernice repeated. "And frankly, I'm beginning to worry myself. What in the hell are you and Sophie up to now? Don't tell me nothing, because I don't believe it for one little second. You're hiding something from me, and I want to know what it is. And I want to know right now, this very second."

Toots considered telling her the truth, but sure as shit Bernice would mention it to Robert. It would scare the poor old guy half out of his mind, and who knew what could happen then. The old guy could have a heart attack or something. She trusted Bernice to the ends of the earth; she'd been like a sister to her for almost all of her adult life. But right now just wasn't the time to tell the whole truth and nothing but. Time for a little bit of embellishment. "Ida's having some of her old issues resurface and doesn't want anyone to know." There, that should cover them, at least until Sophie came up with a plan.

Incredulously, Bernice asked, "You mean that germ stuff?"

Toots nodded. She hated lying to Bernice, but right now it was for the best. She didn't want to frighten her or Robert, or anyone else for that matter. And she would do whatever it took to keep Abby, and her beautiful grandchildren, safe.

"Please don't tell me I have to Clorox this place down now? I can't stand the smell, plus I'm too old to get down on my hands and knees to scrub the floor."

"No, no, don't even go there. I wouldn't expect you to clean like that anyway. I'd send her to a nuthouse first." Toots smiled. "If Abby calls again, explain this to her, but make sure she keeps it quiet for now."

"No, I am going to do no such thing. When Abby calls again, and you and I both know she will, I'm going to insist she talk to you. And you can tell her whatever lie you want."

Bernice had a way of cutting right through the flesh and hitting the bone. Toots had taught her well. She grinned. "Bernice, I'm doing this for her own protection, and the twins', too. You are going to have to trust me on this one," she added.

"I suppose I can. What about the wedding? Are you going to be able to fit this in between all of your mysterious callings? I would hate to have to hire one of those overpriced wedding planners."

"Damn, Bernice, you're acting like a virgin bride! Of course I can fit this in. As you can't seem to stop reminding me, I am quite experienced. Once the date is set, I'll take it from there." Toots had connections all over Charleston. For that matter, she had connections all over the country. She could whip up a wedding in a matter of hours if she had to, but she wasn't about to tell that to Bernice.

"Two weeks? Robert and I discussed it, and at first we thought we wanted to get hitched next week. But then we changed our minds and decided on two weeks. Is that enough time for you, Miss Planner of Weddings?" Bernice asked.

"I'll arrange for you and Robert to get your marriage license tomorrow. Once that's finished, why don't you set the date then? Just in case there's an issue, you know, red tape and all," Toots added.

"All right, I guess I can live with that. But I am not fielding any more telephone calls for you." Bernice shook her head and headed downstairs.

Toots took her cell phone from her pocket. She'd missed several calls from Abby. Before she had time to rethink her decision, she dialed Abby's cell.

"Mom," Abby said. "What is going on now? You scared the daylights out of me. Why the need to toss us out?" Abby did not sound like a happy camper.

"Dear, I didn't mean to scare you or the twins. There is a . . . situation that requires my and Sophie's undivided attention. It's one of those psychic things, just a little closer to home." This explanation didn't make one bit of sense to her, and she knew damn well that Abby wouldn't fall for it, either, especially given the cockamamie story about carbon monoxide at Sophie and Goebel's house that Abby had been told.

"As long as you and Sophie aren't being hurt in any way, I'll accept your explanation. For now. I just wish you would trust me enough to confide in me."

"Oh, Abby, I trust you more than anyone in the world. You need to trust me when I say this isn't something you need to involve yourself in. The outcome could be very . . . let's just say you're better off not knowing right now. When and if the time is right, and you need to know, or there is no reason for you not to know, you have my word I'll fill you in on everything. Can you live with that for now?"

Toots took a peep at Ida. *She's sleeping like the dead*, Toots thought. *Uh-oh, bad choice of words.*

"I suppose I don't have much of a choice," Abby relented. "Just be careful, okay? I know you and Sophie."

"What do you mean by that?" Toots asked, wanting to keep the conversation going just to hear her daughter's voice. She'd felt incredibly guilty for tossing her and the twins out earlier.

"I know how the two of you are when you're concocting one of your schemes."

Toots heard a rustling noise coming from her room. She sneaked a look inside. Ida was thrashing about. Sophie had told her to watch for signs of odd movements. "I need to go, Abby. I'll call you later. I promise there isn't anything for you to concern yourself with. Kiss the babies for me." Toots ended the call before Abby had a chance to respond. She hated doing this to her daughter but made a mental promise to make it up to her.

Inside her room, she dialed Sophie's cell phone. "Ida is moving around like she's trying to fly."

"Shit," Sophie said. "Is she talking weird, saying anything out of the ordinary?"

"No. I can't believe she's even capable of moving after I gave her all those antihistamines."

"How many did you give her?" Sophie asked.

"Two, just like you said. Phil might stop by later if he gets back from New York. I'll have him check her over."

"Don't do that, Toots. She's okay. Remember, I was a nurse. It's not going to cause her any trouble. She might have a bit of a dry mouth when she wakes up, but that's about it. I don't want Phil to ask questions. We don't need anyone asking questions."

Toots should have been offended, but she wasn't. Phil didn't need to know about this, and besides, he had enough on his plate preparing for his book-launch party. "I won't breathe a word."

"I'll keep my cell phone on all night. I'm not sure if I'm going with Goebel to meet with that Dabney great-great-nephew, but if I do, I'll let you know. Any more changes with Ida, let me know."

"So you just want me to sit in my bedroom and watch her sleep? What should I tell Phil if he asks why?"

"You'll think of something, Tootsie, you always do. I'm in the attic right now, I have to go."

Okay, Toots thought. She didn't want to know why Sophie was in the attic, though she assumed that it probably had something to do with Ida's dilemma.

Resigning herself to spending the evening watching Ida, Toots pulled a chair up next to the bed. Something told her it was going to be a very long night.

Chapter Three

"Hey," Goebel called out from the entrance to the attic. "You want me to get a flashlight?"

"No," Sophie said. "I already have one. Don't come in here, stay back. The smell is sickening. It could be a dead rat. Just stay put." Sophie spied the old trunks she wanted to look through, still stacked in the corner where she had last seen them. She instantly changed her mind. "You better come inside. I might need some help with these trunks."

Goebel stooped as he made his way across the attic. "It smells awful in here. If I didn't know better, I'd swear there was a dead body in here. It certainly smells like rotting flesh."

Sophie turned around so fast she had to grab one of the low-hanging beams to steady herself. She'd also thought the odor was the smell of death, but hadn't wanted to put words to her thoughts. She remembered working in the hospital morgue all those years ago, when she'd been in nursing school. Once you smelled a decomposing body, the odor stayed with you forever.

"I want to look in these trunks. Help me move them to the hall-way. And be careful where you step. When I came up here a few days ago, there was not enough light and I stepped on a floor-board that cracked under my feet. See where someone started a remodeling project up here and never finished it? I want to see what, if anything, might relate to what's going on in this house."

For the next fifteen minutes they dragged the dusty trunks

across the attic floor and out into the hallway, pushing them against the wall. "Do you want to go through these now?" Goebel asked, wiping a stray cobweb from his face.

"Yes. I need to," she said.

"You want me to stick around and help? Remember, we're meeting Dabney at seven."

Sophie glanced at the time on her cell phone. "There's enough time to look through a couple of them."

"Then what are we waiting for?"

Sophie swiped her hands over the top of one of the trunks, trying to remove who knew how many years of accumulated dust and what looked like mouse droppings. "Let's get an exterminator up here, and soon," she said. "God only knows what else we might find."

Luckily, the trunks weren't locked. Sophie took that as a good sign. Brushing her hands across her slacks to remove some of the dust, she hooked her fingers under the edge of the trunk and lifted. Hundreds of tiny dead spiders clung to the faded pinkish silk that lined the trunk's lid. "This is disgusting," she complained, but didn't let a few dead spiders alter her plan. She had to do this, no matter how gross she thought it was. To date, nothing could ever compare to what she'd done for Ida and Mavis in that embalming room in California. No, this was a piece of cake compared to slicing off a dead man's penis. She'd promised them she would never tell a soul, and to this date, she hadn't. Clearing her mind of the image, she focused on the contents inside the trunk.

"You want me to get some cleaning rags?" Goebel asked. "Wipe the stuff down?"

"Sure, that's a good idea," she answered. Actually, she didn't care one way or another.

Knowing she had to get down to business, Sophie removed a stack of old newspaper clippings. Hardened with age, the print was barely visible, but she was able to make out a date:

Saturday, August 13, 1983.

Okay, this meant nothing to her until she skimmed to the bottom of the page. A wedding announcement. Theodore Dabney and Nancy McCartney were married on that date. This had to be the great-great-nephew they were having dinner with. Why would they keep something this significant in an old, dusty trunk? Why hadn't they taken this whenever they'd sold the place? Lots of questions, and hopefully, she would soon have the answers. She placed the stack of papers on the floor. Leaning over and peering down into the trunk, Sophie spied a small black box. She wiped away the dust, and a smattering of something she didn't want to put a name to, and opened it. Inside was a tiny cuff-like bracelet, no more than two inches in circumference. To Sophie the bracelet looked like sterling silver. An elaborate bit of scrollwork surrounded the outer part of the bracelet. She shined her flashlight on it and saw what appeared to be writing. "Goebel, run downstairs and get the silver polish."

"I'll be right back," he said.

She nodded. This must be a baby bracelet. Given its size, it couldn't be anything else. Straining to read the name engraved on the inside, she thought the first letter was an M. She rubbed the inside of the bracelet with her sleeve but still couldn't make out the rest of the letters. Goebel's pounding footsteps told her she was only seconds away from finding out exactly what the name was.

"Here, I brought some extra rags, too," he said as he handed her the container of silver polish and a rag. Sophie squeezed a small amount onto the rag, then rubbed it on the inside of the bracelet. Using the end of the rag to buff away the polish, Sophie drew in a deep breath when she read the name.

Margaret Florence Dabney, 1923.

"Look at this!" Sophie exclaimed. "This must've belonged to one of the Dabneys."

Goebel leaned down for a closer inspection. "It has to," he said. "Maybe Ted can tell us who Margaret is."

She nodded, then finished cleaning the bracelet as best as she could. When she finished, she looked at her husband. "I'm going with you tonight. I think I've seen enough dust and mouse droppings for now." Sophie stood up and brushed away the dust that had fallen on her slacks. "Let's get showered. I can't wait to find out . . ." She stopped when she remembered Toots's phone call. Ida thrashing about was not a good thing. Not at all.

She had a decision to make. Did she meet this Dabney fellow, or should she return to Ida's bedside? Knowing the importance of both, it was a tough choice.

She followed Goebel to the master suite, the bracelet safely tucked inside her pocket. Thankful their room hadn't been mysteriously vandalized like the kitchen, Sophie brushed her slacks off again and sat down on the bed. "You okay?" Goebel asked her before heading to the shower. "You don't mind if I go first? Or you can join me if you like," he added with a wicked grin.

She laughed, but her heart wasn't in it. "I'm good, you go ahead."

Since acknowledging her psychic abilities, Sophie had never felt so unsure of herself and her skills. She'd had misgivings here and there, but nothing like now. Being pulled in two directions by an unknown force was new to her. She needed to make a decision and be quick about it. This wasn't a Hollywood starlet, or a frantic mother in search of her children. This went back almost a hundred years. Ida's soul was virtually at stake, Sophie's home was uninhabitable, at least for today, and she hadn't a clue which way to turn. For the millionth time, she wished she had Madam Butterfly, her former spiritual mentor, to advise her. The book of Roman rituals she'd given her was completely useless to her now.

Wanting to clear her mind, she lay down on her bed, feeling the need to close her eyes for a few minutes. She hadn't had a decent night's sleep in what seemed like forever.

Chapter Four

*S*he could not move, nor could she feel her legs when she tried to move them. Her arms were on fire, the pain so intense she feared she might die. Florence tried to move her head but couldn't. Tears filled her dark blue eyes as she searched frantically from left to right. She wanted to scream, but when she tried, her words came out in a whisper.

The baby! Dear God, what is happening to me? *She tried to call for Ruth, but still could not speak loud enough to be heard.* Where is Theodore? *She tried to remember, though it was quite difficult. She did recall some of the evening's festivities.*

The Hamiltons had stayed for dinner. She enjoyed the evening but wanted to rush through their after-dinner drinks in the parlor as she had news to share with her husband and couldn't wait to have him to herself. But Theodore had been drinking heavily. He'd been boisterous, and cruel to Cook, and Florence had been terribly embarrassed by his behavior. Beyond that, her memories of the evening were vague.

She tried to wipe the tears from her face, and when she did, another stabbing pain seared the length of her arm. And then there was nothing but darkness.

Florence opened her eyes, uncertain how long she'd been lying at the bottom of the staircase. Again, she tried moving her legs. Nothing. They were useless to her now. Using her right arm,

she struggled to drag herself to the kitchen. Cook would be clean-
ing up from tonight's dinner.

Piercing, knifelike pains coursed throughout her upper body,
though she could feel nothing below her waist. Gasping for breath
from the effort, she tried to turn her neck to calculate how far
away the kitchen was. Her head throbbing, she used all of her
strength to strain to see her location. Tears continued to fall down
her face when she realized she'd only moved a few inches.

Dear Lord, *she prayed,* please help me!

"Ruth," she called out again, her voice not more than a hoarse
whisper. "Help me."

Suddenly, blackness engulfed her again. Relieved, she gave in
to the shadowy tunnel beckoning her. She smiled when she realized
that nothing hurt anymore. The feeling was back in her legs, and
her arms no longer felt as though they were on fire. She was dream-
ing again. In her semiconscious state she knew this.

Now standing at the top of the stairs, whole and complete, she re-
membered why she had been in such a hurry for the evening to end.

The baby!

She had to tell Theodore about the baby, felt it urgent that she
do so tonight before he retired for the evening, and before he
passed out from the large quantity of liquor he had consumed.

Then she was hit by a pain so sharp, surely she would die if it didn't
stop. She opened her eyes and saw she was still at the bottom of the
staircase and had only moved a few inches! How could this be possible
when only moments ago she felt perfectly normal?

"Sophie, wake up!" Goebel coaxed. "It's your turn to take a
shower."

She bolted upright so fast she bumped her head into Goebel's.
"Damn, that hurt," she said as she rubbed her head. "You okay?"

"I've had harder knocks than that one," he said. "You fell asleep."

She recalled her vision or dream. "I saw the woman crumpled
at the bottom of the stairs just now. Rather, I think I dreamed of

her this time. Goebel." She paused, trying to remember details from her dream. "I've been assuming that the woman in my visions, dreams, whatever we're calling them now, died! But she did not die from falling, or being pushed, down the stairs. I'm sure this is what she's been trying to tell me all along!"

"Okay, if that's what you believe, I'm with you. So, what do we do next?" he asked.

Sophie got off the bed, preparing to take her shower. As she unbuttoned her slacks, she felt the small bracelet in her pocket. Taking it out, she looked at it again. "This is the key, the bracelet. Don't ask me how I know that, I just do." Feeling a renewed sense of purpose, Sophie hurried to the master bath, where she continued to talk to Goebel as he trailed behind her. "I'm not sure if I should leave Ida with Toots any longer than necessary." She stepped into the shower while continuing their conversation. "Toots isn't equipped to handle her if Ida totally flips out. I should go see her first, before dinner. There's plenty of time."

"You don't have to go, I told you that. I'm sure I can question Dabney without any trouble. I was a cop, remember?"

Sophie turned the shower off. Goebel handed her two towels. She wrapped herself up with one, then twisted the other towel around her wet hair. "Yes, I remember our first stakeout in Chicago quite well."

Goebel chuckled. "That was the best stakeout I'd ever been a part of. Really wasn't all that long ago."

Sophie went back to the master bedroom. She removed underclothes from her dresser, slipped them on, picked out a slinky black dress that clung to her curves, and added low-heeled black sandals. Back in the bathroom, she twisted her wet hair into a topknot. A few swipes of blusher, mascara, a smear of lipstick, and she was good to go.

Goebel wore a pair of navy blue Dockers with a pale blue shirt. His thick, dark hair was combed back from his forehead. She inhaled his manly scent. He smelled divine. He was so handsome,

Sophie couldn't believe this was the same man that she'd met that first night at Toots's place. Weight loss and marriage definitely agreed with him.

"Why the big grin?" he asked her.

"Just looking at you makes me smile, Mr. Blevins. That's it, and nothing more. Now let's get out of here before I rip your clothes off." Sophie raced out of their bedroom and down the stairs as quickly as possible. She didn't bother looking behind her to see if Goebel followed because she knew he would. She also didn't stop to look at the disaster that awaited them in the kitchen. She'd call a cleaning crew first thing in the morning. For now, the flies could continue to enjoy their feast.

Once they were out of the house, Sophie relaxed even more. Goebel drove Toots's Lincoln, with her close behind in their SUV. No news from Toots since her last call, so hopefully she could get by with a few more hours before Ida flipped out again. She really needed her to be okay. Her need to speak to Dabney had quadrupled.

Ten minutes later, they were pulling through the gates at Toots's place. Sophie parked in the back, and Goebel drove the Lincoln around the side to the garage. They met up at the back door. Sophie stopped and took a smoke from her pocket. "I just now realized I haven't smoked all afternoon. I can't believe I haven't suffered from withdrawal symptoms." She lit up, took several drags, then smashed the butt in the coffee can on the side of the steps.

Sophie entered the kitchen. "Hey, you two," she called out when Bernice and Robert didn't bother to acknowledge her and Goebel's presence.

Bernice held a hand in the air. "We're trying to decipher this recipe. Wade found this in some dead woman's brassiere, and thought we might want to use it for the cookbook. Take a look, see if you can figure it out."

Sophie looked at the yellowed page. Beautiful cursive handwriting had faded with age, but she didn't have too much trouble reading the recipe. "You two need new glasses. This is a recipe for white chicken stew." She gave the paper back to Bernice.

Bernice held the page out as far as her arm allowed. "I guess these dollar-store glasses need to be replaced with the real thing." She continued to scan the old paper. "Says here it's from Dabney House. Isn't that what they used to call your place?"

Sophie stopped dead in her tracks. "Where did you say you found that recipe?"

Robert spoke up. "Wade found it in an older woman's . . . the upper part of her unmentionables."

Goebel laughed so hard tears welled up in his eyes. Sophie's eyes looked as big as saucers.

"I'm assuming the woman he took it from is dead?"

"Yes, she is. I'll ask Wade if he can poke around and find out more about her if it's that important. Shit, this is just an old recipe," Bernice said. "You can have it if you want."

"No, I can look at it later if I need to. It just reminded me of something, that's all. I take it Toots is still upstairs with Ida?"

"Haven't heard a peep from either one of them. A small miracle." Bernice laughed.

"I'll be right back," Sophie said, and headed for the stairs.

Upstairs, Sophie peeked inside Toots's room. Toots sat in a chair by the bed, reading a magazine. Ida was dead to the world. She gave a light tap before entering.

"Shhh," Toots said, holding an index finger against her lips. "She's sleeping sound as a baby now. Hasn't been moving around at all."

Sophie breathed a sigh of relief. "Thank God. I was concerned but knew you could handle things. We're meeting Ted Dabney for dinner at seven. Maybe he can tell us more about our house's history. I had sort of a breakthrough a while ago. I had another dream about the woman I tried to contact in the séance the other night. If my dream is to be believed, and I think it is, this woman fell down the staircase but survived the fall. My gut tells me this is what she wanted me to know."

Toots walked over to the window that overlooked her magnificent gardens. Sophie stood next to her. "That's it? Surely there's more to the story. If Ida's possessed"—she whispered the last word—"then where does this woman factor in? You don't think she's evil, do you?"

"Of course there is more to the story. I just haven't figured that part out yet. I'm sure the woman isn't evil, but there is an entity in the house. You wouldn't believe your eyes if you saw the disaster in my kitchen. The cupboards are ripped off the hinges. My pantry has been totally demolished, food and all. It made me sick when I saw it. Goebel put so much hard work into designing that room. It is a room, too. No one I know has a pantry that large."

"Mine is close, but I agree, the design is ingenious. Do you want me to round up the gang to come help with the cleanup?"

"Hell no. I'm hiring a cleaning crew for this. I might need to use my old room at your place for a few nights, if that's okay. The house smells awful, plus there's something dead in the attic. Speaking of attics, what do you think of this?" Sophie took the tiny silver bracelet out of her purse. "I found this in one of the trunks. It was totally tarnished before I cleaned it. Does that name ring any historical-society-lady bells with you?"

Toots took the small bracelet from Sophie and held it close to the window. "Margaret Florence Dabney, 1923. Other than your place being called Dabney House, no. But it makes sense. Though I can't understand why the family didn't take this with them when I bought the place. This is good silver, from what I can tell."

"It is. They don't make baby bracelets like that anymore. As long as you're okay with Ida, I'm going to dinner with Goebel so I can meet this great-great-nephew of the original owners. Who knows what he'll tell us?"

"I bought your place for practically nothing, and there has to be a reason they were in such a hurry to sell. Places like yours are going for three to four million dollars these days. Had I not been so wrapped up in the *Informer*, I would've researched its history more thoroughly."

Sophie sighed. "It doesn't matter now. I'm sure the great-great-nephew can fill us in on whatever gory details there are. Bernice has a recipe Wade gave her. It's for chicken stew. The recipe originated from the Dabney House. Is that weird or what?"

Toots moved away from the window and spied Frankie, her dachshund, hiding in the corner. She picked him up and carried him across the room. "Nothing seems weird to me anymore, Soph. These past five years have been so full of strange incidents and coincidences, I feel quite odd when nothing out of the ordinary takes place. Maybe it's time for me to make some changes, add a bit of spice to our lives, now that we're all settled in the South."

Sophie sat down on the edge of the bed, careful not to disturb Ida. "Please tell me you didn't say you needed to add 'a bit of spice' to our lives? How much spicier do you want it? My house is haunted, Ida's probably possessed by some poor soul who can't or won't cross over to the other side, and you think we need to make changes?" She paused, a look of bewilderment on her face. "You and Phil. Is there something you're not telling me? Because if I find out you two plan on getting married after the fact, I will personally slice your tits off, as well as his nuts."

Now in her seventies and eight husbands later, Toots still blushed. "I can't believe you would even think of something so . . . so ridiculous! I have no intention of getting married again. Eight times was enough for me. I like my life just the way it is, thank you very much. I do not need a man telling me what to do and how and when to do it, like you and Ida do."

"By your reaction I can tell I hit a nerve. You've thought about it—don't lie. Remember, it's me, Sophie De Luca. You can't pull the wool over my eyes. Now, have you discussed marriage or not?"

"You're supposed to be un-possessing Ida. Why are we even talking about marriage? No, we have not . . . we haven't gone into great detail. Phil is busy with his book. He's almost finished with book two. Remember, you predicted his book will be a rip-roaring success? I know his second book will be as successful as his first. Like Robin Cook, he'll follow up with another book, and another, then maybe a movie deal. Where in the world would he find time to marry an old broad over seventy? I'm sure it's the last thing on his mind right now."

"Do I detect a bit of jealousy?" Sophie asked.

Toots began pacing the width of her large bedroom, maintaining a death grip on the little dachshund. "No you do not. Absolutely not! Phil and I have a wonderful . . . arrangement. He's happy, and so am I. So, to answer your question, no, I have no immediate plans to marry Phil. Nor he me."

"Good grief, you sound like a prim old bitch who hasn't had a piece of ass since losing her virginity. I was just asking. You don't have to get so defensive. Forget I mentioned the M word, okay?"

"Just because you and Goebel have the perfect marriage doesn't mean it's right for me, or Ida, or Bernice, for that matter. We're all happy and busy. All of us have so much money, we're practically giving it away. No, scratch that, I am giving it away. We're in a good place, Soph, so why would we, rather I, want to mess with things when they're this good?"

"If you weren't my best friend in the world, I'd smack you. I simply asked you a question. I get that it's a touchy subject with you. Eight times is a frigging world record, but who's counting?"

"Apparently you are. And Bernice. And Ida. The only one who doesn't remind me of my marriages is Mavis. She's the kindest woman I know. I need you to know that, okay? Mavis is *much nicer* than you. Or Ida." Toots felt her blood rush to her ears.

"Bullshit. There is something you're not telling me. I'm not going to delve into it anymore tonight since I need to get out of here, but I will not forget this conversation. We'll finish this later."

Frankie chose that very moment to leap from Toots's arms and jump on the bed, where he proceeded to pee smack-dab in the middle of the bed.

Chapter Five

Cristof's was located in Charleston's historical district on Woolfe Street, near St. John's Episcopal Chapel. Formerly a plantation home, it now had the reputation as one of Charleston's finest places to dine. Each floor had a theme designed according to the menu. The first floor, the most sought after, served up Southern food with a modern flair. The second floor served sushi and some Thai dishes, and the third floor was strictly vegetarian. Something for everyone. Because of its diversity, securing a reservation was considered an accomplishment.

A hostess dressed in a black pencil skirt with a crisp white blouse led Goebel and Sophie to a table on the first floor. Apparently, Ted Dabney dined at Cristof's often enough that getting a last-minute reservation wasn't as difficult for him as it was for most others.

"Mr. Dabney is running late and asked that we suggest a bottle of wine." The girl couldn't be a day over twenty-one. When she smiled, she revealed unnaturally white teeth. Her bleached blond hair hung perfectly straight. Sophie was positive that she had ironed it. No one's hair was that straight. "No, we'll pass on the wine, but thank you."

The girl nodded, smiled again, and stepped away from the table. Two seconds later another young woman, dressed in an identical black-and-white outfit, arrived at their table. Sophie concluded that this restaurant was not going to be conducive to discreet conversation. "May I bring you a drink?" she asked in a rehearsed voice.

"We'll have iced tea, one sweet and one unsweetened," Goebel said, then winked at Sophie.

As soon as the waitress left the table, a man in his late fifties or early sixties came to their table. "You must be Mr. and Mrs. Blevins. Sorry about the lateness, but I had a meeting that lasted much longer than I'd anticipated." He held out his hand for Goebel, who stood up to shake his hand.

"Mr. Dabney, nice to meet you," Goebel said, then sat down.

Sophie remained in her seat, but like the typical Southern woman, she held out her hand for Mr. Dabney. "Pleased to meet you," she said in her most professional voice.

Ted Dabney was an ugly man, Sophie thought as she observed him. Too tall and much too thin, he seemed uncomfortable with his size. His shoulders were rounded from years of stooping; he hunched in the chair, reminding her of someone who knew he was about to get slapped and was preparing for the hit. His eyes bugged out of his head. Maybe he had a thyroid problem. His skin was so pale it appeared translucent.

The waitress delivered their iced teas and took Mr. Dabney's drink order. He ordered a martini. Sophie would never have pegged him as a martini type of guy. She equated martinis with James Bond, and by no stretch of the imagination was Ted Dabney James Bond. No, had she been asked to guess what kind of drink he would order, she would have said a glass of white wine. Wimpy and light. But she knew better than most how much looks could be deceiving.

The waitress returned with his martini. "Would you care to hear the dinner specials now, or would you prefer to wait until you've finished your drinks?"

"We'll have our drinks. Please leave us for a while," he said with so much authority that Sophie knew that in this case, looks really were deceiving.

"Now, you want to know about the house." Ted Dabney's demeanor changed from sophisticated businessman to one who'd known fear.

Sophie took this as her cue to begin her story. Never one to mince words, she dove right in. "Why did you sell the house so far below its market value?"

Ted Dabney took a sip of his martini and traced the rim of the glass with his long index finger. He took a deep breath, as though the mere thought of talking about his ancestral home was painful. And maybe it was.

"I didn't care about the money. I didn't need it, so that was never an issue when I put the house up for sale. A Realtor friend of mine put it on the market. I'd had it listed for a few weeks when my friend called me to tell me that an offer had been made on the house. It was the first offer, and I told her to take it. She laughed and asked me if I'd lost my mind. Little did she know had I stayed in that house any longer, I probably would have. She said the offer was a joke, and added that if I took it, I was an idiot. She actually called me an idiot. Needless to say, I'm not friends with that woman anymore. Ms. Loudenberry offered three hundred thousand dollars, and I took it." He took another sip of his drink. "I hired movers to pack up the place and moved to Atlanta."

"Tell me what frightened you so badly," Sophie questioned. "I . . . well, I know things about people."

Ted Dabney nodded. "Yes, I know who you are. I . . . well, you understand I'm a businessman. It would be suicide to go into battle without investigating your adversaries."

Goebel took her hand and squeezed. She returned the gesture of affection.

Dabney took another deep breath. Sophie felt the fear radiate off him. He was truly afraid to talk about the house. She needed to reassure him that he shouldn't be.

"Then you know that I can see things that you can't. Ted—if I may call you Ted?" She paused. He nodded. "Ted. This isn't going to sound even remotely normal to you, but it does to me and my husband. We do psychic investigations and encounter people who fear the unknown, people who've been frightened simply because they've been conditioned to fear what they don't understand. However, there really isn't anything to be afraid of when you're . . . when you see life from the other side." Sophie wasn't quite sure how to explain her position to this frightened man. She didn't want to scare him any more than was necessary, but she also wanted to assure him that not everything paranormal should evoke fear.

"I'll have to take your word on that," he said.

"Good. Because I know what I'm doing. I was alarmed when I first discovered I had the gift. It isn't everyone's normal, but it is my normal." She couldn't remember when she'd been so conversationally challenged.

"What my wife is trying to say is that it's okay for you to be afraid of the unknown, but you shouldn't be frightened by whatever events took place in your house."

"I grew up in that house, and trust me, if you'd lived there as a kid, you would have been frightened. I remember how I hated having to go to bed at night. The long walk upstairs, the creaks, the coldness. I hated it. I begged my parents to leave, to move anywhere else, but there was nowhere to go then. They'd lost all the family wealth right after I was born. The only thing they owned was the house. My father gave piano lessons. Mother took in ironing. They were the complete opposite of their parents, my grandparents."

"Tell me about your grandparents," Sophie coaxed.

Dabney downed the rest of his drink. "What do you want to know?"

"You tell me. What are your memories of them?" Sophie didn't want to influence him in any way, yet she needed to know about the earlier generations that he'd lived with.

He lifted his glass in the air. Within minutes a second drink was placed in front of him. Both glasses of tea were discreetly refilled.

"My grandfather was the meanest old son of a bitch, pardon my French, I have ever had the bad fortune to know. I remember always being afraid of him when I was a kid. My mother—she was the youngest—was afraid of him, too. She never actually said so, but I could tell. I couldn't have been more than five or six, but I remember when he, my grandfather, was still alive and lived with us. I think he hated my mother because she was normal and her older sister wasn't."

"What do you mean by normal?" Goebel asked before Sophie could.

"Aunt Maggie was born blind. My grandfather never let a day pass that he didn't remind my grandmother how useless she was."

Sophie's heart raced. "Aunt Maggie?"

"She's still alive, if you can believe that. She's in her nineties now, lives in Charlotte, in an assisted-living facility for the blind. I had promised my parents I would take care of her if they couldn't. Of course, they both died in 1976, in an automobile accident, when I was away at college—they were only in their late forties when they died—so at the time it was a tough promise to keep, but I kept it." For the first time that evening, Ted Dabney's smile lit up his pale face. "Aunt Maggie never married, but she would have been a terrific mother had she had children."

Sophie reached for her purse. Inside, she found the silver bracelet and held it in her hand. Could it be possible that Aunt Maggie and *Margaret Florence Dabney* were one and the same?

She had to ask. "Was your Aunt Maggie's given name Margaret Florence?"

Dabney focused his gaze on Sophie's hand. "Yes."

Like a blooming flower, her hand slowly opened to reveal the silver baby bracelet she held in it. "Does this belong to your Aunt Maggie?"

He took the tiny circle of silver from her hand. "Yes. I've seen it before. I stored all of my wife's personal items in the attic after she died, and I remember seeing this. Why? Is there something significant about it that I should know?"

"I was hoping you would tell me," she said, hearing the defeat in her voice.

"Only that it belonged to Aunt Maggie."

"I was hoping you could tell me more about this. Possibly it meant something to your Aunt Maggie? Or your mother?" She couldn't explain to him what her feelings had been when she found the bracelet earlier that day, but she had immediately known in her gut that it was significant. She'd been counting on him to reveal some big secret, and so far, beyond what he had said about his grandfather, he'd told her nothing useful. Nothing that would lead her to believe any of his ancestors had taken possession of Ida.

"I do remember mother's telling me that anything that had belonged to Aunt Maggie was put away. Aunt Maggie was sent away when she was only a child. My grandfather hated her, at least this is what my mother said. Grandfather hated all women. I do not know why that was. My grandmother was a good woman, and a good mother. I remember her as always being sad."

Sophie knew she wasn't going to get any more useful information from Ted Dabney, but she had learned a great deal about the former residents of Dabney House. She would have to work at it, but she had a strong suspicion about the events that had taken place a little more than ninety years ago. And she planned on righting a wrong that should have never happened. With this in mind, Sophie relaxed and enjoyed the shrimp and grits she'd ordered.

Chapter Six

Ida awakened to the sound of the shower running. Disoriented, she fought for memories that were slow to surface. She'd needed to ask Sophie something, she couldn't remember exactly what it was, but that was beside the point. She pulled herself into a sitting position, stopping to plump the overstuffed pillows behind her. Toots's room. Yes, now she remembered. She switched the bedside lamp on. The clock said that it was ten fifteen.

The shower stopped running. Seconds later, Toots emerged from the en suite bathroom wearing a pink robe, with her hair wrapped turban-like in a towel. "You're awake. It's about time. How do you feel? Are you hungry? Thirsty?"

Ida cleared her throat. "Good heavens, Toots," she said, her voice scratchy and hoarse. "Why all the questions? And why am I still here?"

Toots went to the bathroom and returned with a glass of water. "Drink this."

She sat on the edge of the bed while Ida drank the water. She was tired of playing nursemaid and wished Sophie would call her with some news. She removed the towel and walked across the room and took a hairbrush from her antique vanity. Running the brush through her wet hair, Toots waited for Ida to finish her water. If she knew she'd been drugged, Ida would have a shit fit. And if she knew Frankie had pissed on the bed while she was sleeping, she'd have another shit fit. Luckily for Ida, Toots had mopped up the urine before it had a chance to soak through the heavy fabric. Frankie was not getting a treat tonight. Toots smiled at the thought.

"Why are you laughing?" Ida inquired in her best know-it-all-voice, the same one she had as a twelve-year-old when the four friends had first met.

"I'm not laughing. I'm smiling. There's a difference," Toots singsonged in her best smart-ass voice.

Toots saw Ida roll her eyes. That was a good sign.

"Of course there is. Now, tell me why I am still here in your bed? Daniel must be worried sick. He likes knowing where I am. He's crazy about me, you know," Ida added.

"All men are crazy about a woman when she puts out on the first date. I thought if anyone knew that, you would." Toots delighted in teasing Ida.

She was doing all that she could to keep Ida from whacking out. So far, so good. Ida was taking the bait and running with it.

"You're a fucking pig."

Stunned, Toots dropped the hairbrush. "What did you just say?"

"You heard me," Ida said, her voice rising several octaves higher than normal. "You're a fucking crippled pig."

Toots placed her hand across her pulsing heart. This was what Sophie had warned her about. Any change in behavior. While Ida was a conceited bitch, she rarely used foul language. Unsure what to do, Toots remained rooted to the floor.

Suddenly, Ida stood up on the bed, her hands splayed at her sides, her mouth turned downward. Her eyes glowed, as if a flame had been lit behind them. "Did you hear me, you pig? Answer me when I'm talking to you! You fucking bitch!"

Shit shit shit! Toots needed Sophie, and she needed her now! She scanned the room for her cell phone, then remembered she'd taken it into the bathroom when she'd showered. Racing into the bathroom as though her life depended on it, she found her phone next to the sink. With trembling hands, she punched in Sophie's cell number. One ring. Two. "Come on, Soph. Pick up the phone." Toots peeked out the door. Ida remained standing in the center of the bed, her hands rigid, her eyes glazed over. Whoever this was, it was not Ida.

"Hello."

Thank God. Finally. "Sophie, you need to get to the house as fast as you can. Ida is acting like that girl in *The Exorcist.* I don't know what to do!"

"What is she doing?" Sophie asked.

"Acting like a nut. She's standing in the middle of the bed. Her arms are stiff, and her eyes look like someone else's. I'm actually afraid of her. I'm in the bathroom now."

"Calm down. We're pulling through the gates now. Just stay in the bathroom until I get there, okay?"

The only time Toots recalled being this frightened was when Abby had been kidnapped by that bastard who had owned the *Informer.* "Hurry!" she said, then punched the END button.

Peering out the door, she continued to monitor the thing that had taken over Ida's body. Her hands shook, and she made fists to still them. Knowing the woman Ida was and seeing this evil creature, or whatever, inhabit her body, angered Toots. Why not possess someone else? Like her? Or Sophie. Ida wasn't as tough as they were. She was feminine and prissy and . . . she didn't deserve this. It was a cruel joke.

Toots heard footsteps pounding up the stairs. Sophie pushed open the bedroom door and stopped when she saw Ida standing like a statue in the middle of the bed.

"What the hell?" Sophie shouted.

Toots came out of the bathroom. "This isn't Ida. She called me a pig and a fucking cripple! What is wrong with her, Sophie? Can you do something? Please, help her!" Toots was almost in hysterics. She'd seen a lot of unnatural happenings in her lifetime, but this ranked at the very top of the list.

"Calm down, Toots. Listen to me. I need your help, okay? Can you help me?"

Toots nodded.

"Okay. Goebel went to the house to get some things I need. I want you to go downstairs and wait for him. As soon as he arrives, bring me the things I need. Can you do that?"

Again, Toots nodded. "I'm scared, Soph," she whispered. "Really scared. This shouldn't be happening to Ida."

Sophie shook her head. "And you should be. I am, too, but I'm going to take care of Ida. Now go downstairs and wait for Goebel."

Without another word, Toots raced out of the room and out the back door. She stopped when she realized she was outside in nothing but her robe. Totally nude beneath it, she closed the robe tighter, then stepped back inside. With hands shaking, she found her cigarettes lying on the counter. She shook one out of the package and lit up. Screw smoking outside. She stood by the door and blew the smoke through the screen door. "Come on, Goebel. Where the hell are you?"

She heard Sophie shouting upstairs. Taking another long drag off the cigarette, she was ready to go back upstairs when she saw headlights. Goebel parked the car, and quickly made his way to the house.

He shoved the screen door aside. "Good Lord, Toots, are you all right?"

"No. Give me the stuff. Sophie needs it now."

"Calm down, Toots. You're as white as a sheet."

"Give it to me, there isn't time. Come on." Toots yanked the small bag out of Goebel's hands. "Sophie needs us now!"

Without another word, they ran upstairs with the supplies Sophie required. Inside the room, Ida continued to stand in the center of the bed, her face ravaged, her eyes bulging from their sockets. "Good Lord, what is wrong with her?" Goebel asked.

"She's possessed. Now give me the bag." Sophie slowly walked to the edge of the bed with her hands out in front of her as though they alone could protect her from the evil that flowed from Ida's body.

"You bitch, get out of here!"

"No, I am not going anywhere, you son of a bitch!"

Toots listened in shock. Wasn't Sophie supposed to pray or toss holy water on her or something?

"I hate you! You ruined me, do you hear me? You ruined me!" The voice coming from Ida was not Ida's voice but the voice of something dark and wicked.

Sophie removed a small wooden cross and placed the bag on the side of the bed. She held the cross out in front of her but didn't speak. The thing that was Ida saw this and laughed. "That doesn't frighten me!" She kicked the bag, sending it flying across the room, where it landed on the floor next to the dresser.

With a sudden surge of bravery, Toots ran to the bed and knocked Ida, aka the Thing, down. She landed on the floor, and when she did, Toots sat on her. She grabbed Ida's hands, pulling them above her hand. Toots used her knees to keep Ida's hands in place. "Okay, Sophie, do your thing. I've got her down now!"

"Goebel, hand me the book, the journal. It's there in the bag! Hurry!" Sophie shouted.

From his position in the doorway, he sprinted across the room like a panther. Locating the bag, he removed the book and gave it to his wife. "Sophie, be careful."

She nodded. "Stay on top of her, Toots. She's full of fire." She flipped through the old journal Madam Butterfly had given her. Never in a million years had she thought she would ever use this, but she always said, "never say never," and now she was grateful she'd taken the book out of the safe and tucked it away with her special tools. She'd had a gut feeling she might have to use them.

"Tell the devil to leave her," Toots shouted, as Ida, aka the Thing, surged with energy. It was all Toots could do to maintain her position on top of Ida's body.

"This isn't the devil we're dealing with, Tootsie. This is one mean old son of a bitch, and he's just met his match!" Sophie squatted beside Ida and slapped her, *it*, across the face.

"Sophie!" Toots shouted. "Don't hurt her!"

"Be quiet!"

Suddenly, Ida went completely limp. Her expression changed from horrified to mystified. Toots quickly moved away from Ida, allowing Sophie to inspect her. "Ida?" she said in a calm voice. She gently patted her cheek. "Ida, come on, wake up. Toots, get me a glass of water."

Toots almost smiled. Once, a long time ago, when Ida was suffering with her OCD, Sophie had taken a glass of water and tossed it in Ida's face. And now she was doing it again. It wasn't really funny, but Toots started laughing. She tried to stop, biting the sides of her mouth and pursing her lips, but laughter tumbled out of her like a bubbling brook. Tears fell from her eyes. She could hardly see. Searching for her mouthwash cup and not finding it, she removed the cap from the mouthwash bottle and filled it with water. Still laughing, Toots stepped out of the bathroom, careful not to spill the water. "Here," she said between hiccups.

"Now's not the time, Tootsie," Sophie said between clenched teeth. She held her hand out for the water. Cupping the back of Ida's head in one hand, she lifted her just enough so that she could sip the water. "Ida?" she cooed. "Are you okay?"

Ida opened her eyes. Glazed, glassy as though she'd had way too much to drink. She shook her head from side to side.

"You're not okay?" Sophie continued asking in her nurse's voice.

"What is happening to me?" Ida croaked. "I feel strange, Sophia. I think I'm going to be sick."

"Oh shit! I'll be right back." Goebel raced out of the room. Less than a minute later he returned with a giant soup pot. His timing couldn't have been more perfect. Sophie had just repositioned Ida with her back against the bed frame, her legs out in front of her. Goebel placed the pot in front of her. Ida upchucked, making all kinds of nasty noises. Again, Toots was overwhelmed with the sudden urge to laugh. She backed away so Sophie and Goebel wouldn't see her. Toots tried to cram her fist in her mouth to quiet her laughter. More tears and the sounds of muted laughter. She couldn't stop laughing. Backing into the bathroom, she grabbed a large washcloth and tried stuffing it in her mouth, but it did nothing but gag her. This made her laugh even more. Her shoulders shook and her vision blurred with tears, but she couldn't stop. She wanted to stop, needed to, but try as she might, she continued to laugh hysterically. She turned the water on, cupped her hands beneath the flow, then took the water and tossed it in her face. Momentarily it took her breath away, but that only caused her to laugh even more. She sat down on the commode, head in her hands. Try as she might, she couldn't stop laughing. The more she tried, the harder she laughed. She recalled a television commercial about something called pseudobulbar affect; they'd referred to it as PBA, a condition of either uncontrollable laughter or crying. Just the thought threw her into a major fit of hysterics.

"Toots, are you all right in there?" Goebel asked as he stood outside the bathroom door.

She forced herself to walk across the small expanse and open the door. She knew her face was as red as a ripe tomato, her eyes rained insane tears, but she managed to nod in the affirmative. She wiped her eyes with the washcloth she had tried gagging herself with a few minutes ago. The memory of that forced another bout of insane laughter. She leaned against the wall, her head hanging to her chest, but no matter what, she could not stop laughing. In fact, the more she tried to stop, the harder she laughed.

Goebel stepped inside the bathroom and closed the door behind him. "Toots, you need to calm down, okay? Soph has Ida, our Ida, under control now. Just calm down, take a deep breath."

His words soothed her but she still found it difficult to stop laughing. She took a deep breath, then another, and was finally able to speak, though just in a whisper. "What's wrong with me?" She hiccuped again, then burped. Before another round of hysterical giggles could start, Goebel placed his hand over her mouth. She had the sudden urge to bite him, then stopped when she realized she wasn't acting normal at all. These thoughts had a much-needed sobering effect on her.

"You gonna stop now?" Goebel asked.

She nodded, and he took his hand away from her mouth. "You're having an anxiety attack. You know this, right?"

"I am?" She barely whispered the words.

"Yes. Now just take a few deep breaths. In and out. Easy, now." Goebel continued to calm her.

Toots finally stopped laughing. She stood in front of the mirror, and the image staring back at her looked like a woman who'd been to hell and back. "I don't know what came over me!" Suddenly, she had a terrible thought: What if *she* was possessed? Could Ida's demon have left Ida's body and taken root in hers?

"Take a few minutes and relax. Sophie has Ida under control, at least for now. She wants to hold a séance as soon as possible. She told me to ask you to call Mavis and Wade, ask them if they can come over. Bernice and Robert, too. She wants to do this tonight before—" He stopped abruptly, needing to rephrase his words. "She wants to stop this now while she's still able."

"What do you mean by that?" Toots asked.

"Those were her exact words, Toots. I'm not sure if she meant them literally, but I would guess she did. You want me to call Wade and Mavis?"

Shaken but in control again, Toots shook her head. "No, I'll call them. It's late, so it might take them a while to get here."

"They're both at Wade and Robert's place—there was a note on the dining-room table. Said Bernice was too tired to go to her condo."

"Good, then I'll just walk over there and tell them. Maybe I can prepare them for . . ." Toots stopped. "Robert won't participate in a séance. Sophie knows that."

"I'm just the messenger here. Tell them they're needed, then let Sophie take it from there. I know she wouldn't ask this if it weren't something that was necessary."

Toots nodded. "You're right. Give me a minute." She splashed water on her face, though this time she didn't see anything remotely funny. She ran a comb through her wet hair. In the closet, she dressed in an old gray sweat suit that had belonged to her first husband. She never wore it unless she was feeling extremely sad. Tonight, she was both very sad and frightened almost to death. The soft cotton comforted her. She closed her eyes, trying to bring up an image of John. Sadly, he was just a faded image, and his scent no longer permeated the old sweats. None of that mattered now. It was comforting to know her heart beat against the same fabric that had once covered John's beating heart. Those were the days, she thought, as she stepped out of the bathroom into her bedroom.

Ida was now on the bed with Sophie seated next to her.

"Feel better?" Sophie asked Toots.

"Sort of. I'm not sure what just happened to me, but I'm fine." She directed her gaze at Ida. "Is she going to be okay? Is she still . . . possessed?"

Sophie ran her hand along the length of Ida's arm, then patted her hand. "I can't answer that yet. I need to go to the other side. You'll get the others?" Sophie asked in a soft voice. "Ida won't be able to participate this time."

"No shit," Toots said, for lack of anything better. "I'll be right back."

As soon as she stepped out of the room into the darkened hallway, Toots forced herself to calm down and relax as much as one could under the circumstances. This night would go down in the record books, at least in hers. Just thinking about it gave her the chills.

Downstairs, she grabbed a cigarette, lighting up the second she stepped out into the warm night air. The sky was a bluish black, the

full moon illuminating the path through the trees and guiding the noc-
turnal creatures to their midnight feasting. Crickets chirped, frogs
croaked, and the call of a whip-poor-will sang in the distance.
Barefoot, Toots raced across the lawn, the wet grass clinging to
her feet. Stopping when she reached the shrubbery that separated
her property from Wade and Robert's, she knew the exact spot
where she could slip through the greenery without a scrape. As
soon as she slid through the narrow gap in the shrubbery, she
raced to the back door and up the small flight of steps. She
pounded on the door, not caring if she startled them awake. She
pounded on the door again and was relieved when she heard
Robert's almost cheerful words. "Be right there."

How the hell could he be so frigging nice? She didn't know,
but he was, and right now, she was grateful. He wore a maroon
robe and his gray hair, what was left of it, stood straight up on his
head, reminding her of the great and powerful Oz. She smiled.
"Robert, Ida needs you and Bernice, and Mavis and Wade, to
come over. There's a problem, and Sophie needs all of us to help
her. Can you get Mavis and Wade up?"

She heard Bernice pitter-patter to the door. "What in the name of
Pete are you doing here this time of night? Shouldn't you be in bed?"

"Ida is in big-time trouble. Sophie needs us now. Just come
over as soon as you can, and I'll explain everything later. Tell me
you can do this, as in right now?" Toots wasn't wasting time. She
needed to see this through, for Ida's sake and for her own sanity.
That laughing episode had truly frightened her, maybe even more
than Ida's possession.

"Oh, all right. Give us a few minutes to get dressed, and we'll
be there," Bernice said. "I'll wake Mavis and Wade. They were
late getting home tonight."

If the matter weren't so serious, Toots would have teased Bernice about being in Robert's bed, but now wasn't the time. She
mentally tucked the thought away for later. "Tell them to hurry,
okay?"

"We'll be right over, Toots. Relax," Robert said before turning away from the door and heading to the back of the house, where his bedroom was located.

"Go on, we're coming," Bernice said. "I swear."

Toots decided she didn't have any choice, she had to take them at their word and hope for the best. "Hurry," she called out one last time before turning away. This was not the time for any of them to be thinking of themselves. Time was not on their side.

Chapter Seven

Abby checked on the twins one last time before heading downstairs. They'd been antsy all evening and hadn't wanted to go to bed at their normal bedtime. Usually, she and Chris rocked them for a few minutes before putting them down for the night, but tonight, when she'd tried to rock them together, they'd wiggled out of her arms, whining each time she tried to pick them up again. Giving in, she'd let them play until their eyelids drooped. Lucky for her, they'd been content to play in their room, so when Abby saw they could barely keep their eyes open, she'd scooped them up one at a time and put them in their cribs. They missed their daddy; Abby was sure of it. Chris hadn't spent a night away since their birth. She missed him, too, even though she knew he'd be home tomorrow evening. The big house felt empty without him.

Downstairs, she let Chester out one last time for the night. As she waited at the back door, she saw headlights heading toward her mother's house. Alarmed, she went back inside and dialed her mother's cell phone. Toots answered immediately. "Abby, why on earth are you calling me at this late hour?"

"Why are you up at this late hour? I was out with Chester and saw car lights headed your way."

"You did?"

"I thought maybe someone was sick," Abby said. "You don't sound very good. Mom, are you sure you're okay?" Abby knew for a fact that her mother and the three Gs—as she referred to Sophie, Ida, and Mavis—were always up to something. Just because it was past midnight and they were over seventy didn't stop them from taking chances that most women their age wouldn't even consider.

A bit winded, Toots opened the back door to her house, more than a bit surprised when she saw Phil's car parked in the driveway. She smiled. "I'm just fine, Abby. Go back to bed."

"Who said I was in bed?"

"If you weren't, you should be."

"I can't sleep without Chris. Amy and Jonathan can't, either."

Toots did a complete about-face. "Should I come over? I can be there in three minutes flat if I run."

Abby giggled. "No, I'm all right, Mom, seriously. Just out of sorts, that's all. Now tell me why you're still up and who's at the house? I can see the lights through the trees. Your place is lit up like the Fourth of July."

Goebel or Sophie must have turned on all the lights downstairs. Probably Goebel, as Sophie had Ida to contend with. When Toots had left, the only light on in the house had been the bedside lamp in her bedroom. "I see that," she said, stepping inside the kitchen. Phil was busy making a pot of coffee and didn't see her when she came up behind him and wrapped her arms around his waist. He whirled around, his huge smile a welcome respite after the evening's events. "Abby, Phil is here. I'm guessing those were his lights you saw." She raised her eyebrows in question, and Phil nodded. He gave her a mug of hot coffee, her special grind. She mouthed the words "thank you," then took a sip. Just what she needed, she thought. A shot of caffeine with a large dose of sugar.

"As long as you and the gang are okay, I'm going to call it a night."

"If you need me, just call, okay? Something tells me this night is going to be a long one," Toots said. "Kiss the babies for me."

"I will, Mom, and thanks. I needed to hear an adult voice."

Abby ended the call, and for a moment, Toots wanted to race to her house but remembered that Abby *was* a big girl now. If she'd really needed her, she wouldn't have minced any words.

Before she had a chance to ask Phil why he'd returned from New York so soon, Mavis and Bernice, with Wade and Robert trailing behind them, entered through the back door. "Is everyone all right?" Mavis asked her in sweetest voice. "Where are Sophie and Ida?"

Toots spoke up. "There's a situation," and she proceeded to update them on the evening's happenings. "Ida seemed to have calmed down a bit before I left, so I'm assuming she's still okay." They gathered around the table, as was the norm for them. Phil poured coffee and started a second pot.

Goebel spoke up. "Ida's fine as far as I know. Sophie wants to sit with her for a while before leaving. Toots, is it okay if we have the séance here? I don't think it's a good idea to leave Ida, given what has been going on in our place."

"Of course," Toots agreed. "Mavis, will you help me set up in the formal dining room?"

Mavis wore a pair of brown slacks with a cream-colored blouse. Her strawberry blond hair was neatly combed, and she wore lipstick, even at this late hour. Toots couldn't help but smile. When she'd first contacted her dearest friends five years ago, Mavis had been so obese that Toots had feared for her life. Now, however, she was the picture of health. She rarely had a hair out of place and always adhered to her diet, rarely indulging in anything that wasn't good for her health. She thought of the song lyrics "We've come a long way, baby." And they had. Every single one of them.

"I'd be happy to. Do you still keep the candles and glasses in the same place?" Mavis asked. It'd been a while since they'd held a séance here.

"As far as I know, everything is where it was the last time we held a séance here," Toots responded. She followed Mavis to the dining room. She flicked the switch, and the overhead lighting warmed the room with its soft, golden glow. Toots rarely came in here anymore, and decided she needed to use this beautiful room that she'd spent so much time decorating when she'd purchased her home all those years ago. A brief thought passed through her mind: She would have Bernice and Robert's wedding reception here at the house. This room would be perfect for a sit-down dinner.

Mavis found the old purple sheet they'd used in California. It had been left behind at the beach house by a former pop star. Sophie swore by it, said many old souls had touched its silken threads. Toots wasn't sure about that, but she'd remembered to bring it along when she left California.

She removed the large floral arrangement in the center of the table. Mavis held the purple sheet in front of her, then shook it out and spread it across the table. Toots found several tapered candles in the drawer of the hutch, and put one where each point of the compass would be. Sophie said this helped guide the spirits in the right direction. At this point, Toots was willing to do anything to rid Ida of the evil that had overtaken her body. She removed a box of rocks glasses from the bottom of the hutch. They hadn't used this batch before. Almost every time Sophie held a séance and used glasses, they wound up broken. Toots made sure they always had a large supply, just in case. She closed the drapes even though it was dark outside. They knew to follow their routine. As Sophie explained time and again, sticking to the exact procedures each time only ensured success. She wasn't willing to risk anything at this point. The clock was ticking.

Toots found a legal pad and several sharpened pencils in the hutch drawer. She'd forgotten about them until now. They'd discovered who had murdered Thomas, Ida's first husband, through psychic writing. Looking around the room, Toots remembered the air-conditioning vent. Dragging a heavy chair to the other side of the dining room, she stood on it in order to reach the air vent. Pulling the small lever to the closed position, she gave an extra pull just to make sure. A lot of Sophie's work involved air movement, hence the need to shut all artificial, man-made sources of air.

Mavis positioned the chairs around the table. "I can't think of anything more we can do to prepare for this, can you?"

Toots perused the room. "It looks good to me. I'll let Sophie know we're ready."

A crash from the kitchen sent Toots and Mavis running. "What in the world?" Mavis asked when she saw Coco and Frankie on the kitchen countertop, cowering in fear. Mavis hurried over to her beloved Chihuahua, who huddled in the corner next to the canisters. "Be careful," Phil said, pointing to the broken glass on the floor.

Toots grabbed a shaking Frankie. "What happened?" she asked. "The dogs were in my room last time I checked."

"They both came barreling down the stairs, their hackles practically standing straight up in the air," Phil said. He took the little dachshund from Toots. "Maybe someone should check on Sophie and Ida."

Toots didn't waste one minute. She raced up the staircase so fast her hair whipped behind her. She entered her room. "Sophie! What's going on? We're ready for you downstairs."

Sophie and Ida were huddled together in the corner, and Toots watched Sophie as she urged Ida to look at her.

"Listen to me! You are not wanted here! Do you understand?" Sophie spoke in low tones, but Toots was still able to hear her.

"What?" she asked.

Sophie waved her hand in the air, indicating silence. Toots stopped when she realized Sophie was totally focused on Ida, and the words were for her ears only.

"I need to see your face, *Ida*. I need you to listen to me, *Ida*. Do you understand what I am saying to you, *Ida*? You may not touch the animals, do you understand me? I won't let you harm them, do you hear me, damn you!"

So *that's* why Coco and Frankie were cowering downstairs. A wave of anger coursed through her. She wanted to slap Ida's face. How dare she try to hurt those precious dogs? No wonder Sophie hadn't wanted to leave her alone.

"Fuck you, pig! You're an ugly, crippled pig! Do you hear me, damn you!" The words came out of Ida's mouth, but the voice wasn't Ida's. Angry and mean, the voice continued to pummel Sophie with filthy language. "Do you hear me, bitch?"

Toots couldn't stand it another minute. She raced across the room, filled with such an intense rage it scared her.

"Stop, Toots. Stay where you are," Sophie shouted. Her eyes never left Ida.

Toots stopped, then plunked down on the edge of the bed, her heart hammering so fast in her chest she feared she would suffer a heart attack. Taking a deep breath to calm herself, she watched in fascinated horror as Sophie touched Ida's face with the wooden cross she'd taken from her bag. When Ida failed to respond, Sophie lay the cross beside her. She whispered something Toots couldn't make out, then, right before her eyes, Ida virtually slumped into a pile of black silk, her body limp.

"Help me get her on the bed, quick!" Sophie shouted.

Toots grabbed Ida's feet while Sophie took her arms. "On the count of three, let's put her on the bed. One, two, three." Together, they hefted Ida onto the bed. Ida wasn't overweight, but she felt like she weighed a ton.

Ida, the real Ida, moaned when Sophie propped her head up. "What?" she asked in a soft whisper. "What happened?"

Sophie stared at Ida, her gaze never wavering. "Do you know who I am?"

"Sophia."

Ida almost always called Sophie *Sophia*.

She turned her so that she could see Toots. "And who is this?"

Pushing herself up on her elbows, Ida spoke. "Why are you asking me this?"

"Do you know her name?" Sophie persisted. "Tell me her *real* name."

"Teresa."

Sophie's shoulders sagged in relief. "Tell me what you remember of the past few hours. I know we've been over this before, but I need to hear it again."

Ida nodded, knowing her situation was very serious. Her face, void of makeup, looked haggard and worn. "I just wanted to see you, Sophia. The catalogue for the fall collection, you know this. I am so tired, I don't know if I can . . ." Ida struggled to continue. "I'm confused. This is the longest day of my life. I know that I'm"—she threw her hands out—"absent from myself. It makes no sense at all. What's wrong with me? Do you know? I can't go on like this!" Tears fell from Ida's eyes.

This was truly Ida, and Toots could see she was very scared and confused. She had a moment's guilt when she remembered how she'd wanted to slap her a few minutes ago. While Ida was stuck up and beyond arrogant, she did not deserve this. No one did.

"I'm going to help you, I promise. You have to do whatever I tell you, no matter what, okay? This is serious stuff, Ida, nothing like the OCD. Do you understand?"

"Of course I do. I'm not ignorant."

This was Ida, Toots thought, and smiled.

"No, you're not, and that's a good thing. I'm going to tell you what I suspect, and you have to promise me that you'll listen until I'm finished. Can you do that?" Sophie asked Ida, then looked at Toots. "And you, too."

Toots and Ida nodded.

"Remember the séance the other night and how I had trouble contacting the other side? I believe I was blocked by an evil entity." Sophie paused, then went on. "I'm sure this entity is a soul who hasn't crossed over. He may be hanging around because of some unresolved issue, maybe he feels guilty, or maybe there was a death that was tragic. Suicide, murder, who knows. Anything violent would prevent a peaceful crossing over. I've felt a strangeness in the house for a while now. Sudden bursts of cold air. Then the dreams, or the visions, I'm not really sure at this point, but I know that the woman in these dreams or visions is trying to tell me something. She's lingering, and wants me to find an answer so she can rest in peace. When you stopped by my house this morning and saw all the destruction, I believe this entity was so strong, he took possession of your body."

No one said a word.

"Are you telling me I'm possessed by the devil?" Ida asked, her face so pale her features were blurred.

"No! Not the devil. No, thank God, this isn't like that! Don't even have those thoughts, do you understand me? Remember how when I go into a trance, the spirits make themselves known and use me as a conduit to deliver their message? I believe this is what's happening now, only you didn't have a choice. This entity is using you as a portal, a means to torture those who he deems to be weak. This is nothing personal, Ida, but you're the perfect candidate for something like this. You've had psychological issues in the past, and this evil entity knows your weaknesses and is exploiting them. In a matter of hours, you've urinated on yourself, and the language you've been using is unlike you, and just a few minutes ago you tried to kick Frankie and Coco." She stopped. That was more than enough for now.

"I kicked the dogs?" Ida whispered.

"No, you didn't. I got to you before you could. And that's another thing supporting this analysis, Ida. We both know that you'd never hurt an animal when you're in the right state of mind, so given this, I'm sure we're dealing with an evil spirit."

"Should I go downstairs and tell the gang we're canceling the séance?" Toots had been silent much too long.

"No, we need to do this now while Ida is . . . herself. Do you think you can manage to come downstairs now? Are you too weak?" Sophie asked Ida.

"Of course I'm coming with you! I don't want to be left alone! I've got to call Daniel. He's coming home, and if I'm not at the airport to drive him home, he'll be worried. I don't want him to worry about me. He'll get tired and find . . . never mind. Yes, let's just do this and get it over with. I have too many good things happening in my life right now!" Ida's renewed energy spurred Sophie off the bed.

Sophie and Toots helped Ida to her feet.

"Then let's get this over with before this entity returns."

Chapter Eight

As they gathered around the large dining-room table to call up the dead, Sophie bowed her head in prayer. "To our highest power, we ask for your protection from benevolent spirits and we ask St. Michael the Archangel to watch over us and protect us from all malevolent spirits who might want to inflict harm upon us. We are here to summon the spirit of Theodore Dabney."

Sophie sat at the head of the table, with Ida on her left side and Toots on her right. Bernice was seated beside Ida, and Robert sat next to Bernice. Mavis and Wade sat opposite Robert and Bernice. Phil and Goebel sat at the end of the table opposite Sophie.

Mavis and Toots had set the table up as they'd done numerous times before. The rocks glass was in the center, and at each corner a candle burned, their flames dancing despite the lack of any air circulating.

No one spoke a word as Sophie continued her speech to the dead. "We're here to make contact with the other side. If there is a presence in this room who wishes to communicate with any of us, slide the glass in the center of the table to my right for yes. Slide the glass to the left for no. I ask you to enter this space peacefully, with no evil intent."

All eyes focused on the glass in the center of the table.

The glass remained in its place.

Sophie took a deep breath and tried again. "Theodore Dabney, make yourself known."

They waited for a sign, anything to let them know there was a presence in the room.

Suddenly, the candles were snuffed out, leaving the room in total darkness.

"Theodore Dabney, are you with us?"

An evil laughter spewed from out of nowhere.

"If you are Theodore Dabney, move the glass in the center of the table."

Again, they focused on the glass, even though the only light in the room was the fiery red wicks that continued to glow. The glass flew across the table, stopping in front of Ida.

"What do you want? Tell me so that I may help you," Sophie said in her séance voice.

The glass fell off the table, landing in Ida's lap. With shaking hands, Ida placed the glass back in the center of the table. Sophie nodded. "Are you with us, Theodore? Move the glass again."

For the second time the glass moved, but this time it didn't fall off the table. Sophie took another deep breath.

Finally, she made contact. "Was your death unexpected? Move the glass to the right if your answer is yes and to the left if your answer is no."

They watched the glass as it slowly moved to the left.

No one had expected this.

Sophie closed her eyes, focusing on the entity in the room. "Did a member of your family die in a tragic manner?"

They watched the glass move to the left once again.

"Then what do you want?" Sophie asked, knowing she would not get an answer in such a way that she and the others would understand. She needed questions that could yield concrete yes and no answers. There was no in-between.

"I want us to join hands, so lay your right hand over the left hand of the person seated next to you. This is called forming a chain. The spiritual energy of each of us, combined, should produce a higher level of energy." She hoped the combined force of the energy generated was powerful enough to evoke another response. Once they'd formed the chain, Sophie began to pray.

"St. Michael the Archangel, we ask you to guide this spirit away from its earthly bonds so that he or she may find the light, and in finding the light, may have eternal peace."

A few minutes passed, and when nothing happened, Sophie tried again. "Are you willing to accept my help? Please move the glass to the right if your answer is yes and to the left if your answer is no." Sophie didn't have too many more tricks left in her bag. Either the spirit of Theodore Dabney would make its wishes known, if it was the spirit of Theodore Dabney—and she was positive that it was—or it wouldn't. He needed to give her some kind of clue, anything that would give him that final push to cross over.

Slowly the glass moved to the left.

Defeated, Sophie spoke in her normal voice. "This son of a bitch is playing with us! Mavis, get the lights."

Mavis hurried across the room and switched on the lights. "That's better."

"What's wrong, Soph?" Toots asked, her voice laced with concern. "This isn't like you."

Bernice and Robert stood up at the same time. "We're out of here. This is bull." Robert's lack of belief was justified. He took Bernice's hand, and together they made their exit.

Sophie shook her head. "I don't know why I'm having such a difficult time with this spirit, but what I do know is that I am not going to let it bully me, or frighten Ida any more than it has already. Are you good, Ida? Can you stand on your own?"

All eyes focused on Ida. "Of course I'm good, and yes, I can stand on my own. I'm not that old."

This was the Ida they all loved and sometimes hated.

"I'll go make a pot of coffee. Phil, want to help me?" Toots asked.

"I thought you'd never ask. Sophie, let's call it a night," Phil said.

Wade hadn't said the first word until coffee was mentioned. "I could use a cup, maybe with a splash of whiskey added to it."

"I'll join you in a minute. I just want to clean up in here."

Mavis made sure the wicks were completely snuffed out, then she took the rocks glass and placed it on the hutch.

"I just don't get it. When we were in California, you could whip up a ghost on command, and now this. Any ideas?" Toots asked Sophie.

"None. But maybe . . . no, forget it," Sophie said.

Goebel had not uttered a word during the séance until now. "I probably don't want to know what's going on in that beautiful head of yours, but you're going to tell me anyway, right?"

Sophie nodded.

"Forget what? I hate it when you do that." Toots stood up and stretched. It was way past their bedtime, but sleep would come later.

"It's something Ted Dabney said at dinner tonight. I don't know if it's worth pursuing or not."

"If it will help me, then I agree with Toots. I want to know what it is," Ida declared. "I can't live like this."

"I found a silver baby bracelet in a trunk stored in the attic. I cleaned it enough to read the inscription. It had a name and a date. Margaret Florence Dabney, 1923. I showed this to Ted, and he said it belonged to his Aunt Maggie." Sophie paused. "She's living in an assisted-living facility in Charlotte. And she's blind."

"I get it now," Goebel said.

"And?" Toots coaxed.

"I'm thinking."

"Spit it out, Sophie. We don't have all night." Toots had had enough of the netherworld for one night.

"I think we need to make a trip to Charlotte, as soon as possible. Toots, do you still have that private jet on standby?"

"Of course. Do you want me to call Joe? He's used to being called out in the middle of the night. All those celebrities he flies around the world. It's your call. Yay or nay," Toots said, a new surge of excitement building in her. She needed to get out of Dodge. A trip to Charlotte was the perfect opportunity. Since they'd returned to

Charleston, Toots hadn't been out of the state. Though she hated the thought of leaving Amy and Jonathan behind, she wouldn't be gone long enough for them to miss her. "Well?"

"Yes, make the call. I'm dying for a cigarette. I have to go smoke now; I can't wait another minute," Sophie said. "Mavis, thanks for taking care of all of this." She gestured toward the table. "The candles and all."

"I'm more than happy to help out. I miss the four of us. We haven't been alone in quite a while."

"Then let's go to Charlotte. Just the four of us," Sophie suggested. "It's not like we can't just pick up and leave. We're big girls." For a minute, Sophie forgot Goebel was still in the room with them. She turned to him. "You wouldn't mind if I go to Charlotte?"

"If you're sure, then go ahead. Someone needs to get that disaster in the kitchen taken care of."

Mavis said, "I think that's a wonderful idea! Wade can run the funeral parlor without me. Of course, he doesn't do the makeup like I do, but no one really cares when it comes right down to the nitty-gritty. As Toots always says, 'dead is dead.'"

"I don't recall ever saying that."

"Maybe it was Sophie. It doesn't matter. Let's go tell the guys," Mavis said.

"Sounds like a plan," Sophie announced. "I need a cigarette, big-time. Goebel, are you sure you're okay with me leaving you behind?" She'd never spent a night away from him since they'd married.

"I'm okay with it, Soph. Do whatever you need to do. Ida is counting on you." He placed a hand on her waist and gently guided her out of the room.

With Ida between them, Toots and Mavis followed close behind.

Chapter Nine

A t precisely 9:42 A.M. the Citation X touched down at Charlotte Douglas International Airport.

Toots hired a limousine to drive them to Pine Shadows, the assisted-living facility where Margaret Florence Dabney awaited them. Once they'd made the decision to travel to Charlotte, Goebel contacted Ted Dabney, who then contacted the administrator at Pine Shadows and made arrangements for them to visit his aunt.

The drive from the airport to Pine Shadows took forty-five minutes, during which Sophie reviewed the list of questions she'd prepared on the short flight. Toots occupied herself by sending text messages to Abby and Chris. Mavis was content to view the passing scenery. Ida dozed, off and on.

As soon as they arrived at the facility, Ida perked up. She took a mirror from her purse and reapplied her lipstick, a soft pink from Seasons. "I do wish I'd had more sleep. These circles under my eyes are terrible. Do any of you have a tube of concealer?"

"I barely had time to shower and change," Toots said, rummaging through her purse. "Try this." She handed Ida a tube of Maybelline concealer.

Ida acted as though she'd been burned when she saw the brand. "Really, Toots."

"I'm not particularly fond of Seasons' concealers. They're too thick."

"I'll make a note for my chemists," Ida offered dryly.

Gone was the pathetic woman possessed by an evil entity. Ida had perked up as soon as she'd received a phone call from Daniel right before they left Charleston. As usual, a man made all the difference in her life.

The limousine pulled into the circular drive and stopped. Toots was paying the driver big bucks to wait for them. No one knew how long they would be.

"Let's get this show on the road," Toots cajoled. "I feel good about this, Sophie. What about you? Anything churning in your gut?"

"Not yet."

The four entered the reception area, where they were greeted by a young woman who introduced herself as Anna. She wore her dark brown hair pulled back in a low ponytail. Dressed in a dove gray business suit with a pale yellow blouse, she exuded professionalism. Her bright blue eyes were clear, alert. "If you all will follow me, I've arranged for Ms. Dabney to speak with you in one of our conference rooms."

They followed her through a maze of long hallways. Pine Shadows looked more like a luxury hotel than a retirement center. Thick gold carpet softened their footsteps. Plush chairs with side tables invited all to sit and relax. Vases of fresh flowers were placed at the entrance to each room they passed. Anna stopped when they reached the end of another long hallway.

"Ms. Dabney gets through her days by following a strict routine. It's about time for her lunch, so I've asked the staff to provide you with a meal as well. I hope you enjoy your visit. Now"—Anna held one hand with the other—"let me introduce you."

Margaret Florence Dabney sat next to a window overlooking the manicured lawn. She turned away from the window as soon as the door opened. "Anna?" she asked in a surprisingly strong voice.

"How are you today, Margaret?" Anna questioned.

"I'm the same as I was yesterday, and the day before that. At my age, very little changes." Margaret Florence Dabney had a sense of humor. She returned her gaze to the window.

Anna smiled. "Your guests are here. They're joining you for lunch."

"Then I feel sorry for them. Please introduce yourselves. I may be blind, but my sense of smell is excellent."

Sophie wasn't sure what she expected from Margaret Dabney. Certainly not the lively woman sitting in front of her. "I'm Sophia Blevins."

"Sit down then. And your friends? Do they have names?"

"Toots, Mavis, and Ida. We've been friends since we entered the seventh grade." Sophie motioned for the three to speak up.

"Ms. Dabney, I'm Teresa Loudenberry. My friends call me Toots." Margaret nodded.

"Mavis Hanover. I own a funeral parlor." Her eyes doubled in size when she realized how silly she must sound. Still, Mavis was proud of her success.

"A noble profession, don't be ashamed," said Margaret.

Mavis beamed.

"There is someone else here," Margaret stated. "She's wearing a musky perfume."

"Ida McGullicutty," she said as she walked toward Margaret, who was sitting by the window in her wheelchair, and took her hand.

"Pleased to meet you, Ida," Margaret said as she shook her hand. "I'm in this wheelchair because I've broken my hip— twice."

"I'm so sorry," Ida replied.

"It is what it is," Margaret said in a voice without an ounce of self-pity.

Anna cleared her throat. "If you all will excuse me, I will let you enjoy your visit. Lunch will be served at one o'clock."

"Anna is very efficient," Margaret explained. "Pine Shadows would not survive without her."

Toots sat down in a soft, butter-yellow chair. Ida and Mavis sat on a matching sofa across from her.

An awkward silence ensued. Margaret Dabney appeared unfazed by their lack of conversation, but Sophie guessed there weren't a ton of lively conversations that took place here at Pine Shadows. She removed the silver bracelet from her purse and rubbed her thumb against the intricate scrollwork. "Did your great-great-nephew explain why we're here?"

"Only that one of you lives at Dabney House."

Sophie thought of the phrase "like pulling teeth" as it applied to Margaret. When someone reached the ripe old age of ninety-four, Sophie supposed, she didn't have to speak up if she chose not to. "My husband and I bought the house from Toots. She purchased it from Ted several years ago."

Margaret turned away from the window to face them. Sophie was stunned. Her eyes were completely black, colorless. Thin gray hair barely covered her pale pink skull. Her hands looked dry and parched. Deep blue, purplish veins stood out against her white skin. Mentally vibrant, physically she was fading away. Sophie felt a well of pity gurgle up for this old woman who, according to Ted, had spent her entire life in one institution after another. Suddenly, she was glad they'd made the trip to Charlotte.

"What do you want to know?" Margaret asked.

Okay, Sophie thought, this isn't going to be hard. She removed her list of questions from her purse. "I wrote these down on the flight over, but I'd rather you tell me *your* story."

"Of course. After lunch, we will talk."

Sophie glanced at her watch. Lunch was ten minutes out. "If that's what you want."

Again that phrase "like pulling teeth" flashed through her mind. She walked over to where the others were sitting. "She only speaks in single sentences. We may be here for a while. She wants to eat lunch first."

Toots raised her brow, grinning. "We'll do whatever she wants, too."

Sophie nodded. "I'm in no rush as long as our evil spirit doesn't decide to take possession of Ida while we're here."

"Mavis and I will watch over her while you question old Ms. Dabney. You know, something tells me that if we whisked her out of this place, we could show her the time of her life. Can you imagine being . . . forget it. It's simply too depressing."

"Don't even think about it, Toots. She's blind and in a wheelchair. And way older than us, and we're already ancient." Sophie teased Toots about her age constantly, but they both knew they could easily take ten years off, courtesy of Seasons Miracle Cream.

The door to the conference room opened, followed by a woman pushing a rolling table. "Miss Maggie, I was so happy when Anna told me you had guests for lunch. I asked the kitchen to make your favorites today."

Margaret smiled, showing teeth that, while yellow and gray, were still hers. "Thank you, Dolly."

Dolly was a large black woman with a grin as wide as she was. Though she was at least three hundred pounds, she moved like a gazelle. Light on her feet, she ran around the table as fast as anyone half her size. She set out plates and napkins. Silverware, glasses. While she busied herself filling the glasses with iced tea, Sophie's stomach growled.

"I'm a-hurryin', ma'am." Dolly chuckled.

Sophie laughed with her. "I can't remember when I had my last meal." And she couldn't.

"You'll remember this one, miss, I can promise you that." Dolly removed the lids from the silver tureens. "You want me to serve now, Miss Margaret?"

"Yes. My guests are hungry."

Sophie assumed that meant that Margaret had heard her stomach growl. She did have a keen sense of hearing.

Dolly rushed around the conference table, filling each plate. When she finished, she wheeled Margaret to the head of the table.

"Y'all can set wherever ya want, okay? We ain't fancy in here, are we, Miss Margaret?"

"What is that?"

Dolly's smile was as bright as the sun.

As soon as they were seated, Margaret bowed her head. Sophie, Toots, and Ida lowered their heads, waiting for the blessing. When no one spoke, Sophie piped up. "God is great. God is good, and we thank Him for our food. By His hand we shall be fed, give us, Lord, our daily bread."

"Lunch is served," Margaret announced.

Lunch was chunks of white-meat chicken, plump purple grapes, thinly sliced Granny Smith apples, pecans, and crushed pineapple served on freshly baked croissants. Sophie bit into the sandwich, closed her eyes, and chewed greedily. "This is the best chicken salad I've ever tasted. Toots, we need to get the recipe for Bernice."

For the next half hour they forgot about entities, spirits, and demonic possession. When they finished the chicken salad, Dolly returned with dessert. Toots and Sophie eyed the blackberry cobbler with their tongues practically hanging out of their mouths. Toots would send Margaret some of Jamie's pralines.

After they'd stuffed themselves with the cobbler, Dolly brought in a freshly brewed pot of coffee. "That's just what I need," Ida declared. She'd had little sleep and too much food.

Dolly and another young woman cleared away the dishes when they finished. "If it's all right with you, Miss Margaret, I'm goin' home now."

"Of course, Dolly. Give your mother my love."

Sophie looked at Toots, Mavis, and Ida. From the expressions on their faces, it was obvious they, too, wondered just exactly what kind of relationship the two women shared. They didn't have to guess for long.

"Ted hires my staff from outside. Dolly's been with me for twenty-six years."

Apparently, money could buy a private staff in an upscale assisted-living facility.

Sophie looked at her watch again. A few minutes before two. She wanted to hear Margaret's story before it was naptime.

"Dolly's a great cook," Sophie said.

"Yes, and a friend, but I suppose one might think it odd to have a black woman as a friend."

Four sets of eyes stared at her.

"Why would you think that? We have friends of all different races—black, Hispanic, and Asian."

"My father came from a long line of people who owned black men as slaves. Even after those days, my father's attitudes were such that I was forbidden to speak to the black men who worked for him on the plantation."

"Tell me your story, Margaret. I need to know if anything"— Sophie didn't want to come out and use the words *murder* or *suicide*, so she went with the best she could come up with—"violent happened at Dabney House?"

Margaret's expression went from happy to dejected in seconds. She nodded. "I will tell you what I remember, but it's been so long, I'm afraid most of my recollections are simply fragments from bits and pieces of what I can remember. If you want to hear an old woman talk, then I have all the time in the world."

"Wheel me over there." She pointed to the sofa-and-chair grouping. Sophie pushed the wheelchair, surprised how easy it was to move. Poor Margaret was nothing more than a little bag of skin and bones.

"Where to start? I suppose I should start at the beginning. Or what I think is my beginning."

"Please do," Sophie begged. Toots, Mavis, and Ida gathered around Margaret, eagerly waiting to hear her story.

"Dabney House belonged to my father's family. Passed from one generation to the next. In its prime, we grew some of the juiciest peaches in the South. My mother made the best peach jam in the world. She was famous for her chicken stew, too. My father ran the plantation with a strict hand. Men who'd devoted their lives to my father were fired for no reason if it suited him. I never saw this. Poor choice of words. I was not living at home any longer. When Mother gave birth to a second child, Ted Dabney's mother, my father sent me away to live in Massachusetts, where they had one of the best schools in the world for the blind. I was five or six at the time. I didn't mind leaving Dabney House, but I hated having to leave my mother and sister behind. You see, my father was a mean old man who only cared about himself. He usually stayed drunk, and he was a mean drunk. Mother was quiet because she knew what would happen if she wasn't. We all feared him. He could be a tyrant one minute, but when he wanted something, he treated us with such kindness that we could almost forget that wasn't his true nature. Mother was a cripple—did Ted tell you that?"

Sophie and Toots looked like the air had been knocked out of them. "No, he didn't. Was she born that way?" Sophie had to know.

"No, Mother was a beautiful woman when she was young. She had the silkiest hair I've ever touched. She used to let me brush it when we were alone. Mother was the one who taught me how to read in Braille. To this day, I have a great passion for the written word, but that isn't what you came all this way to hear, is it?"

Sophie didn't answer.

"Mother had a terrible fall one night. It was the evening of her first anniversary."

Sophie looked like she had been poleaxed. *That's the connection*, she thought. *Florence came to me on the evening of my and Goebel's first anniversary. Now things are starting to make some sort of sense.*

"She fell down the stairs in the main hall. From what she told me, she thought she would die. Her doctors said she would never walk again. She was a proud woman, and couldn't imagine spending her life in a wheelchair, dependent upon my father for her every need. When her bones healed, she forced herself to walk. Every day, she would walk up and down the stairs. At the top she always looked down, and cried. One day she let me walk with her. I remember she held my hand so tight I thought it would break, but she was just trying to protect me. That day, I asked Mother why she always cried when she stood at the top of the staircase. She said it didn't matter anymore, but I begged and pleaded with her to tell me. This part I remember very clearly, like she told me about it yesterday.

"They had a dinner party with friends, to celebrate their first anniversary. I can't remember their names, but Mother said she was eager for them to leave. But my father drank all through dinner, and things started to get unpleasant, so Mother went upstairs to prepare for bed. She had a surprise for my father. She wanted to tell him as soon as their guests left, but he was already in a drunken rage when they left. Mother never even got a chance to tell them goodbye.

"Apparently my parents had words. They fought. Then, when my father had had enough, he pushed Mother down the staircase. Her legs and arms were broken, but she fought, and she lived. I asked her why didn't she just die. Of course, I was a little girl at the time, and I didn't understand death. Mother explained to me that her special surprise was me. She was pregnant with me when my father tossed her down the stairs." A single tear fell from Margaret's eye. "I'm sure that fall caused my blindness."

"I am so sorry, Margaret," Sophie said. Using the pad of her thumb, she wiped the tear from the old woman's cheek.

The dreams, the visions, Ida's possession made complete sense to her now. Florence's husband, Theodore Dabney, the man whose name she called out as she was toppling down the stairs, pushed her, and she was pregnant with her daughter, who was born blind.

Her house needed a cleansing. For the first time in days, Sophie felt confident that she could remove the evil from Dabney House.

Margaret had worn herself out telling her story. Sophie, Toots, Mavis, and Ida left when they saw she'd fallen asleep in her wheelchair, but before she left, Sophie placed the silver baby bracelet in her hand.

Chapter Ten

"I can't believe you did all of this in twenty-four hours, you sweet man." Sophie toured her kitchen. The cabinet doors had been replaced with replicas of the originals. The pantry was still lacking a few of the custom-built shelves, but there was no sign of the destruction she'd seen day before yesterday. The kitchen floor sparkled like liquid gold. Goebel had been able to buff the scratches from the floor, saving them from having to replace it, too. Margaret Dabney had walked across these floors, and Sophie intended to treat them with kid gloves from now to eternity.

"This is perfect, Goebel. I don't know how you managed to accomplish this in such a short time, but you did, and I'm so glad."

When she had left Pine Shadows yesterday, Sophie called Goebel to give him the short version of Aunt Maggie's story. They had discussed what she would have to do to rid their home of Theodore Dabney's evil spirit.

And now it was time.

She put several bunches of sage in a bag, along with three bottles of holy water that had recently been blessed by Pope Francis. She wore her rosary around her neck for protection. Daniel and Ida were on their way. Sophie felt that Ida needed to be here during this purification.

"Is there anything else you need?" Goebel asked.

Sophie smiled, the first genuine smile she'd actually felt in several days. "I have more than I'll ever need, but to answer your question, I've plenty of cleansing supplies."

"It's good to have you back, Soph. I don't like it when you're unhappy." Goebel wrapped his arms around her, kissed the top of her head, then patted her on the ass.

She pulled away from him, laughing, "So that's why you're so happy to see me. Always have sex on the brain, huh?"

"That's one reason, but not the main reason. I'm just happy to be alive and to have you as my woman."

A loud knock on the front door startled them both. "Ida's here."

"I'll let her in. Tell Daniel hello, and he can come back another time. Why don't you go with him? I think it's best if it's just me and Ida today."

"Okay, but you keep your cell phone in your pocket and call me if you feel frightened or uncomfortable in any way."

"I will," Sophie assured him.

"Promise?"

"Cross my heart promise." Sophie drew an imaginary X over her heart.

"I feel like I should say 'break a leg' or something, but that wouldn't be good, huh?"

"No. Florence Dabney wouldn't approve at all," Sophie said to her husband's back as he left to answer the front door.

"Sophia, where are you?" Ida called out from the living room a few moments later.

"In the kitchen."

"Well, it certainly looks better than the last time I was here. Now how long is this going to take? I have several meetings with my chemists. We're making a new formula for our concealer."

"That's wonderful. Maybe Toots can toss her Maybelline."

Goebel came back to the kitchen. "Daniel and I are going to the Sweetest Things, save you a trip. I know Toots wants to send Margaret a box of Jamie's pralines. Do you have that address?"

"Call Toots, she has it. Now, go on before Jamie sells out."

Goebel left with Daniel, leaving Sophie and Ida by themselves with whatever spirits still occupied the house in which Theodore Dabney had almost killed his wife and unborn child.

"Are you sure you're up to this, Ida? It can wait if you're not ready." Sophie didn't want to wait a minute longer than necessary. She wanted the spirit of Theodore Dabney gone from her house for good.

"I'm more than ready. I haven't whacked out yet, though I have to admit I've been fearing I would, and that I'd do it in front of Daniel. I would just die if that happened. Daniel is a young man. He could have a number of women if he chose to, but he chose me. I want to make sure he continues to be pleased with his choice."

"You're back to your old slut ways, I see. Daniel isn't young, Ida. He's in his late fifties, for heaven's sake. And for the record, you look much younger than he does. It's unlike you to sell yourself short. You're rich, beautiful, and smart. Daniel would be a total idiot to walk away from you."

Ida smiled at her. "You really do love me, don't you?"

Sophie looked at Ida, and together they bubbled over with laughter. In the nearly sixty years they had known each other, this was a first for them.

"Are you ready to get this show on the road?"

"More than you'll ever know."

"Follow me."

Sophie scooped up her supplies and headed upstairs.

"I want to start in the séance room first, since that's where I first felt a presence." Taking a bundle of sage from her supply bag, she lit the end with a match and aimed the white smoke away from her. She went from corner to corner, top to bottom, spreading the smoke in every nook and cranny. "You will leave my home in peace. There is no need for you to stay behind. Your daughter knows what you did to her mother, your wife, and to her. She says that she forgives you, but only if you cross over to the other side." Sophie waved the sage around the room a second time.

Next, they went to the attic. Sophie was shocked when she saw that the trunks were gone. The attic had been completely cleaned out. Goebel again. She loved that man. He hadn't wasted one minute while she was in Charlotte. She lit another bundle of sage, sending the white puffs throughout the attic. "Theodore Dabney, you have to cross over to the light. Your daughter forgives you, so move on." She fanned the smoke throughout the attic a second time. When she finished, she headed downstairs to the kitchen. This time she lit two bundles of sage, waving them up and down the length of the walls, across the windows, inside the cabinets, any open space that she felt had been touched by the evil soul of Theodore Dabney.

Next was the pantry. With the two remaining bundles, she ran them up and down the walls as she'd done in the kitchen. She opened the doors, allowing the purifying smoke to spread throughout the space. When she was finished with the sage, she started over again, only this time she took the vials of holy water.

First, she sprinkled the water in her séance room. Again, she found herself in the attic, then back to the kitchen. Sophie felt she needed to do something special to let the woman who she now knew was Margaret's mother know that she had gotten the message intended for her. She said a prayer, then stood at the top of the staircase. One step at a time, she stopped to sprinkle the holy water. When she reached the last step, she looked back up at the staircase. A beautiful bright ball of light danced up and down, and side to side, then it flew down the stairs, swirled in front of her and Ida, then shot back up the stairs like a rocket. The glistening ball stilled, then slowly diminished, right in front of their very eyes.

A lightness that she hadn't seen or felt before permeated the house. Sophie had Ida follow her to each room. When nothing happened, Sophie knew that Theodore Dabney had crossed over to the bright light. He'd been a miserable, mean man who knew he was responsible for crippling his wife and blinding his daughter. He'd been hanging around in search of a way to ask for forgiveness.

Sophie watched Ida just to make sure this was as real as she believed it was. Gone were the dark half-moons beneath her eyes. Her face sparkled, her eyes glistened like two diamonds.

Yes, Sophie could safely say her work here was complete.

Chapter Eleven

"I don't have to give you a reason, George. I've changed my mind. I am not selling. No, no, and no. I have two grandchildren who may have inherited their mother's reporter instincts. They might need a job. What kind of grandmother would I be if I snatched the opportunity away from them before they even had a chance to decide if it's what they want to do professionally? So, there you have my answer. No, I will not be selling the *Informer* anytime soon." Toots hung up the phone.

"Are you sure you want to keep it?" Phil asked her.

"Yes, I'm sure. Josh is doing a fantastic job running the rag, so as long as I own the place, I get first dibs on the papers. Did I ever tell you how I used to hoard the papers, then read them from cover to cover every Friday night while I soaked in my Jacuzzi tub?"

Phil held Frankie in his lap. "I think you forgot to mention that story."

Toots laughed. "I'm not that woman now. Though I still like to read the tabloids, I don't have time to devote an entire evening to them. I have grandchildren, and Abby, and Chris. The Canine Café. The Sweetest Things, and Jamie. I have friends that I love more than you can imagine. I'm so blessed. What more could I possibly need?"

Since Sophie had given her house and Ida the all-clear sign, they were all giddy for one reason or another. Bernice and Robert were so excited over their upcoming marriage that Toots accused them of acting like virgins. They all laughed, even Robert, who'd mellowed out just a tiny bit.

"I know something you don't have, Toots," Phil said. He held little Frankie in his lap, rubbing the top of his head. This pooch had played an important role in bringing them together, and Phil thought it only fair that he was here with them to share his news with Toots.

"You do? What would that be? I have so much, Phil, really. I want for nothing." Toots's words were sincere; she meant everything she said.

Phil stood up, taking Frankie off his lap and adjusting the pooch in his arms so that he was comfortable. "You don't have one of these." He lifted Frankie high in the air.

"But I thought you said Frankie belonged to both of us. You're taking him to New York with you, aren't you?" Toots's eyes pooled with tears. Just when life was nearly perfect, he had to ruin it.

"Toots, what are you talking about?" Phil asked.

"Frankie. You're holding him in the air like he's a prize, which we both know that he is, but I thought we were sort of sharing him. Co-owners."

Phil burst out laughing. "Come here. I want you to pet Frankie one more time."

Toots's heart sped up. "What do you mean 'one more time'?"

Hating Phil right now more than he could possibly imagine, Toots still loved Frankie, and if this was the last time she was going to get to love on him, then she was going to take full advantage of the situation. "Let me hold him."

Phil gently passed the little weenie dog to her. Frankie growled. Toots rubbed him between the ears, then turned him over to tickle his soft little belly. "What is this?" A small white square was taped to his belly. "What's wrong with you, Phil?" Toots carefully removed the white square from Frankie's belly. He growled again.

"Here, boy," Phil said, handing the little pooch a handful of treats.

"Open it, Toots."

"This?" She held out the small white square.

"Yes, that."

Toots used her fingernail as a letter opener. Surely this isn't what she thought. She looked up at Phil, who wore a grin the size of Earth. "Aren't you going to say anything?"

She needed a minute to reroute her thoughts. This path hadn't been opened for a long, long time. Suddenly, she felt like she'd been wrapped up in a silken cocoon of euphoria. "I'm stunned. I had no idea."

"Seriously?"

"Seriously."

"So now that you have an idea?"

Toots chuckled. "Well, that's for me to know and for you to find out."

"Woof!" Frankie's bark was so unexpectedly loud, they both jumped.

"It's beautiful, Phil, but I don't know . . ."

He placed a finger over her lips. "You don't have to answer me now. We've got plenty of time."

"I hate to remind you but we're both over seventy. I'm not sure that constitutes plenty of time. Of course, you being a doctor, and me being a smoker, it's only logical that you would have more time than I do."

"If you say so," Phil teased. "So, Toots, what do you think? Can you wear that diamond ring on your left hand?"

She took such a deep breath she got light-headed. "You realize I've walked down that aisle more than a time or two, right?"

"And that's supposed to matter because . . . ?"

"Eight times, Phil. E-I-G-H-T." She spelled the number out for him.

"That was in your past. I'm interested in your future."

Toots wanted a cigarette so badly she would have smoked a Camel unfiltered if she had one. "What about your book? What about the book-launch party, the second book, then the movie? You'll have to relocate to New York or California."

"You're not making sense. I canceled the book-launch party. You want to know why?"

She nodded.

"They asked me what I wanted, and I told them I'd rather they donate the money to the Animal Specialty Hospital in Naples. They saved Frankie's life, and you saved mine."

"You're truly serious?"

"More so than I've ever been in my life."

"Okay then, well, I'll have to . . . Bernice and Robert. Shit. Forget that." Toots was so tongue-tied she made absolutely no sense at all.

"Will you marry me, Teresa Amelia Loudenberry?"

Chapter Twelve

Toots had awakened at 5:00 A.M. every single day of the week for as long as she could remember, but today, on her wedding day, she woke up at three o'clock. She had so much to do, she was afraid that she wouldn't manage to get everything finished in time for the wedding in less than ten hours.

She went downstairs and made a pot of her special coffee. While she waited for it to brew, she stepped outside to smoke her first cigarette of the day. She no longer enjoyed them as much as she once had. Now that she had those two precious grandchildren to consider, she desperately wanted to be around for a long, long time. She wanted very much to watch them grow into fine adults, just like their parents had.

Abby was a terrific mother, and Chris was an excellent father. Garland would be so proud of him. He would've adored the twins had he lived. But today was a day for new beginnings, so she didn't want to dwell on anything that wasn't in the here and now.

It had been three weeks since Phil proposed to her. Three weeks of pure, happy, goofy bliss. At first, she hadn't wanted to tell anyone. Adamant that she would never marry again, she feared being judged by those who claimed to love her.

She had been so very wrong. Not only had they not judged her, they were thrilled and happy and excited and fun-loving. Abby and Chris adored Phil, and he adored them. Phil had been there when Abby had been kidnapped and recovered. They'd instantly formed a bond that day.

All the special people in her life were gathering here today to celebrate her and Phil's promise to share their lives. Toots smiled. But she and Phil weren't walking down the aisle alone. No sirree.

When Bernice and Robert heard her news, they decided a double wedding was in order. Robert reminded them just how much money they could save by splitting the cost between them. Toots assured him money was no object, but they'd agreed to share some of the expenses. When Daniel and Ida found out that Toots and Phil were tying the knot, they shared some good news of their own. Ida held out a hand, revealing a three-carat diamond. Daniel had proposed to Ida the night after he returned from his conference. And if that weren't enough, Mavis and Wade had been secretly engaged for the past three months. They explained that they had been waiting for the right time to share their news.

So, here Toots was, over seventy but happier than she'd ever been. John Simpson was the love of her young life. Garland Clay had been the love of her middle years. Phil Becker was the love of her mature life. She had to pinch herself to make sure she wasn't dreaming. Life was good. And it would get even better this afternoon when she and Phil, along with Bernice and Robert, and Mavis and Wade, Ida and Daniel, all walked down the aisle together. Four couples, four best friends finding love once again.

Tears of happiness sprang from her eyes. Joyful, beyond her wildest dreams. She didn't remember being this happy. Ever.

Toots filled a mug with coffee and took it outside. She sat down on the top step and listened to the early morning sounds. Birds chirped brightly, frogs croaked a tune that only they understood. A slight breeze scented the warm air with gardenia and night-blooming jasmine. Toots breathed in the aromatic steam from her mug of coffee. If only she could, she would bottle this moment in time so she could capture these feelings again. But since that wasn't possible, she closed her eyes and imprinted the scene on her mind, the smells, the complete serenity. A perfect beginning of her brand-new life.

She could not wait any longer. She had to talk to someone. She went inside and dialed Sophie's cell phone.

"Happy wedding day," Sophie said when she picked up the phone. "Are you shaking in your shoes yet?"

"Not at all. I'm so happy, my insides are tingling. And not the kind of tingling you're thinking either."

"You have such a dirty mind, you know that?"

"I learned it from you."

They laughed and agreed that it was true.

"Sophie, do you think I've lost my mind? I swore I would never marry again after burying that cheapskate Leland. And here I am doing it all over again."

"Don't be so hard on yourself, Toots. You have nothing to be ashamed of. Remember, your husbands all died. It's not like you divorced them."

"So that makes it a little better, you think?" Toots asked.

"Absolutely."

"Okay. I guess I needed to hear that again," she said.

"You're not having doubts, are you?"

Toots chuckled. "No, I haven't had the first doubt, not even an inkling of one."

"Then you have your answer. Phil is a good man, and he adores you. Plus, he's about to be a little bit famous. Now think of the fun you two will have."

"Thanks, Sophie, that's just what I wanted to hear. Did I ever tell you how special you are to me?" Toots's eyes pooled.

"Oh shit, don't start that ball-bagging crap! Yes, you've told me a million times how much you love me, and I've dittoed it every time. Now go upstairs, wash your face, and take a little nap. The hoopla begins at noon on the dot."

Epilogue

Later the same day...

The early afternoon sun sparkled like a giant ball of yellow fire. The sky was a clear, robin's-egg blue. The temperatures hovered just below seventy. A perfect day for an outdoor wedding.

They had all agreed to have the weddings take place in Toots's garden. She had hired a team of gardeners to trim, shape, and sculpt the shrubbery. The giant angel oak, dripping Spanish moss, reminded her of an old wedding veil that still remembered its very own special day. The sweet scent of the bubble-gum trees added an extra dose of sugary sweetness to the gardens. Camellias, gardenias, and magnolias added just the right amount of floral scent. Not too heavy, but just enough.

Chairs with big white ribbons tied to the backs were lined up in neat rows. At the end of each aisle, a garnish of fresh flowers from Toots's garden was tied to the backs of the chairs. A white silk runner spread out on the grass led to the pulpit, where the Reverend William Wainwright would perform his first quadruple marriage.

Upstairs, in Toots's master bedroom, Abby and her godmothers took turns in front of the mirror. When they all decided to get married together, Ida came up with the idea of matching dresses, in material but not design. No, they each knew what complimented their figures and at their age, they were sticking with what they knew. Creamy silk, lots of tiny white pearls, and smatterings of delicate lace. Four creations made in less than two weeks, courtesy of Mavis and her team of seamstresses. The dresses were totally unique, one of a kind.

After they each had a turn admiring themselves, Abby insisted that she should touch up their makeup, even though Ida's team of professional makeup artists had just left them. They were downstairs in the formal dining room getting a head start on the festivities. Goebel acted as bartender since he was the only man of a certain age not making a trip down the aisle today.

They had invited a few of their close friends but wanted to keep the ceremony as low-key as possible. Toots had hired members of the Charleston Symphony to play the harp, the flute, and the guitar. She didn't want loud rock; she wanted calm and slow.

Jamie had made four separate wedding cakes, each a different flavor. Toots had chosen red velvet, as this was her and Phil's favorite dessert. Ida and Daniel picked carrot cake with cream cheese frosting because they thought having a vegetable in their cake would promote good health. Bernice and Robert opted for good old-fashioned red devil's food, and Mavis and Wade wanted an angel food cake. Jamie had delivered four masterpieces this morning.

And, lastly, they all agreed that Jonathan and Amy should take part in the wedding, but Abby feared if she let them loose, they would just plop down and play in the dirt. Toots had a bright red wagon FedExed for them. They would ride in the wagon, with Coco and Frankie, and Chester would pull them down the aisle.

Soft notes from a flute wafted up to her room, her two-minute warning. Toots took a deep breath, and said, "It's time."

Sophie, dressed in a pale green knee-length dress, ushered the four brides down the stairs. They had all agreed that they didn't want the men to see them until they met at the altar, so Abby devised a plan to reroute them to the side of the house so the men could walk down the white silk aisle to meet them at the altar.

With Sophie in the lead, Toots, Ida, Bernice, and Mavis slow-stepped to the altar to the Platters' "Only You." Their eyes shone bright with unshed tears of happiness as, one by one, they walked to the pulpit to stand by their husbands-to-be.

Chester held the wagon's handle firmly in his mouth as he carefully pulled the precious cargo down the white silk aisle. There were many oohs and ahhs from their guests when they saw Jonathan and Amy and the two pooches inside the wagon. Amy said "Hi, hi, hi," and moved her little fingers up and down in a wave. Jonathan smiled and kissed Frankie right on the muzzle. More laughter, then Abby and Chris stood next to the wagon, just in case.

The music stopped, and the ceremony began.

"Dearly beloveds," the reverend began, "this is my first time marrying four couples at once." The guests laughed again, and so did the reverend. "Now, dearly beloveds, we are gathered here on this beautiful summer day to join Teresa Loudenberry and Philip Becker, Ida McGullicutty and Daniel Townsend, Mavis Hanover and Wade Martin, and Bernice Townsend and Robert Martin in holy matrimony."

The reverend went through the traditional vows, stopping to address each of them as he asked them to repeat after him. "Let's do this together, shall we?"

"Do you, Teresa Loudenberry, take Philip Becker, and do you, Ida McGullicutty, take Daniel Townsend, and do you, Mavis Hanover, take Wade Martin, and do you, Bernice Townsend, take Robert Martin to be your lawfully wedded husbands?"

"I do," Toots said as she gazed into Phil's eyes.

"So do I," Ida said, with a huge smile on her face.

"And I do as well," Mavis said, her voice pure bliss.

"I'll say yes, I do," Bernice added.

The reverend turned to the men, and they went through the process again. More subdued laughter from the guests.

"By the power invested in me by the State of South Carolina, I now pronounce all four couples husband and wife. Now kiss your brides!"

A cheer from the guests as the couples kissed, but there was still one more small ceremony to perform.

Toots, Ida, Mavis, and Sophie, who had remained at the altar throughout the ceremony, each held a hand out and took turns placing their hands on top of each other's. When they were done, the four women threw their hands high in the air, and shouted, "When you're good, you're good!"

Dabney House Peach Jam

Ingredients

8 to 10 pounds fresh peaches
8 pounds sugar

Directions

Bring water to a boil. Put peaches in the boiling water for one minute
or less, just long enough to loosen the skins. Take them out with a
slotted spoon and place them in cold water. Peel and slice peaches,
discarding the pits. Put peaches into a large, wide, open, heavy-bottomed
pot and add the sugar. Bring to a boil. Continue to boil mixture, stirring
frequently. Mixture will thicken in approximately 45 minutes to an
hour. As mixture thickens, stir more frequently to ensure that it does
not stick to the bottom of the pot. To test whether the jam is ready,
place a cold metal spoon in the mixture and tilt. The jam should form
a single stream.

Let cool. Pour jam in glass jars with lids. Refrigerate and use within
two weeks.

Dabney House Chicken Salad

Ingredients
4 cups diced or shredded chicken, cooked (about 2 pounds)*
juice and zest of one lemon
1 cup pecans, toasted and coarsely chopped
2 to 3 celery ribs, cut into small pieces
1 small Granny Smith apple, finely chopped
3 cups halved seedless red grapes
½ to ¾ cup light or regular mayonnaise
1 tablespoon Dijon-style mustard
coarse salt and freshly ground black pepper

*To cook the chicken, broil, bake, or barbecue until the center of the chicken is no longer pink and reaches a temperature of 165° F. on your meat thermometer. A store-bought rotisserie chicken is excellent for this recipe.

Preparation
Place the diced chicken in a large bowl. Add the lemon juice and lemon zest and toss to combine. Add the pecans, celery, chopped green apple, grapes, mayonnaise, Dijon mustard, salt, and pepper; toss all the ingredients together until thoroughly combined.

To allow the flavors to blend properly, cover and place prepared chicken salad in the refrigerator for about two hours before serving.

Makes 4 to 6 servings.

White Chicken Stew

1 pound chicken breasts, baked and cut in chunks
2–3 potatoes, peeled and sliced
1 pkg. frozen peas and carrots
1 can cream of chicken soup
1 can cream of celery soup
½ cup milk (more if you want it thinner)
¼ cup ranch dressing
½ cup sour cream
2 tablespoons dried minced onion
½ tablespoon Parisienne Herbs or 1/2 teaspoon poultry seasoning
1 teaspoon kosher salt
fresh ground pepper to taste

Put chicken, veggies, and potatoes in slow cooker.
Mix soups, dressing, milk, sour cream, and all seasonings together.
Pour over chicken mixture in slow cooker and mix together.

Cook on low until heated through and veggies are done.

Because this recipe is so comforting and filling, rarely is there room for dessert, but I have a sweet tooth so I serve lime Jell-O mixed with mandarin oranges. I hate to admit this, but I top it off with a mountain of Reddi-Wip. My bad. But . . . it is soooo good. Perfect ending to a great meal.